'Full of suspense, twists and turns but just when you think you've guessed the twist there will be another one waiting...'

@WHATJANEYREADS

'What a great read this was! Fast-paced, cleverly plotted and incredibly addictive. Hooked from start to finish, this is my new favourite book by McDine.'

LIFE'S A BOOK BLOG

'The plot really kept me engaged. I couldn't read fast enough towards the end as the tension mounts.'

@AMANDASBOOKCASE

THE PROMISE YOU MADE

A J MCDINE

Cherry Tree
Publishing

CHAPTER ONE

I should have realised the baby rabbit was an omen.

I was up a ladder with my hands in the leaf-clogged gutter when a muffled yowling announced the arrival of Dinah with a present for me clamped between her determined little jaws. Feeling my way down, rung by rung, I reached the back door as Dinah's grey tail disappeared through the cat flap.

'Bloody cat.' I shouldered open the door. 'Where are you?'

I found her guarding her quarry in the front room. She growled softly as I approached with the dustpan and brush. A cotton-wool tail trembled under her paws.

I banged the brush against the dustpan. Dinah dropped the rabbit and darted across the room. 'Come on, little one,' I crooned, crouching down. 'I'll make sure that nasty cat doesn't hurt you.' The rabbit didn't move, so I nudged it with the end of the brush. 'You're safe now.'

An urge to feel the soft fur against my skin caught me unawares. 'There, there,' I soothed. 'Pretty little thing.'

But as I edged closer to scoop the tiny rabbit up and nestle it against my chest, my breath caught in my throat. A hideous bulbous eye stared at me, the fur around it wet with milky discharge. I recoiled, knocking over the walnut wine table behind me. The baby rabbit shuffled around, the whiskers on its ulcerated face quivering at the sudden sound. It lurched towards the gap between the sofa and the floor. 'Oh no you don't,' I said, coaxing it into the dustpan with a flick of the brush.

The fetid smell of rotting flesh agitated the contents of my stomach like aspirin in a glass of water and I gagged.

Come on, Rose. You've seen worse.

I cleared my throat and, with my eyes averted and holding the pan at arm's length, retraced my steps along the hall to the kitchen.

Outside the back door, I paused. Myxomatosis was slowly eating the rabbit's small body away. If I let it go, it would suffer a long and agonising death. Instead, I carried it up the sloping garden to the log store, tipping it onto the beech chopping block I used for splitting kindling. I picked up my axe, holding the yellow handle with a sturdy golfer's grip. Breathing in, I swung it over my right shoulder, letting the weight of it stretch my triceps, my eyes trained on the rabbit's scabby neck. With one fluid strike, the poor creature had been dispatched. Pulling on my gardening gloves, I picked the head up in one hand and the body in the other and lobbed both into the woods for the foxes.

I clumped back down the hill, my boots sliding on the muddy ground and rain running in rivulets down the back of my neck. I was halfway to the house when I felt the sodden ground shift under my feet. I teetered for a second, then tumbled forwards, landing in a heap in a hole in the ground, my right ankle buckling beneath me. Another bloody sinkhole. It had been such a wet autumn on the chalky North Downs they'd been popping up all over the place. Just last week, one had opened up in the fast lane of the M2 between Sittingbourne and Faversham. A gaping mouth in the tarmac that caused traffic chaos and had taken several days to fill.

'What next?' I muttered, pulling myself to my feet and rotating my foot gingerly. Nothing broken, mercifully.

First the rabbit, then the sinkhole. I wasn't superstitious and had no truck with people who believed bad things happened in threes. The poor sops were only looking for patterns to find order in disorder. Nevertheless, I took extra care as I hobbled back to the house, my ankle throbbing, and instead of climbing back up the ladder, I went inside and made a cup of tea. The guttering could wait.

I sought refuge in the small room my mother had pretentiously christened the library. It was my father's favourite bolthole and, even though he'd been dead fourteen years, a faint smell of tobacco still clung to the walls. If I closed my eyes and concentrated hard enough, I could picture him, sitting with his feet up, a pipe in one hand and a book in the other.

I trailed my hand along the shelves, looking for my childhood copy of *Watership Down*. After the part I'd reluctantly played in the baby rabbit's demise it suddenly seemed imperative that I spend the evening losing myself in the world of Hazel, Fiver, Bigwig and even General Woundwort. Finding the dog-eared copy between an English O-level study guide and a Penguin Classics edition of *The Friend of Madame Maigret*, I pulled it out, dusted it off and settled down to read.

Outside, the rain continued to fall, and the sky slowly darkened. At seven o'clock, I closed the book and went in search of sustenance. When I returned to the library, Dinah dignified me with her presence, curling into a ball on my lap, and I was grateful for her warmth as night closed in and a chill crept into my bones.

I had just reached the chapter where Bigwig and Kehaar set off to rescue the does from Efrafa when there was a bang on the door. I glanced at Dinah in surprise. We didn't get many visitors, especially at nine o'clock on a wet and windy Saturday night.

'Who on earth can that be?' I asked her. She stared at me with narrowed eyes. 'Well, it can't be Amazon, because I haven't ordered anything, and the local elections aren't until May. Sod it,' I said, picking up my book and finding my place. 'If it's that important they can come back tomorrow.'

Another rap on the door sent Dinah scurrying off my lap and out of the room. I climbed stiffly out of the armchair and tramped down the hallway, pulling my cardigan tightly around me.

My mystery caller pounded on the door again. 'All right, all right, I'm coming,' I said, making sure the security chain was in place before I turned the lock and opened the door a couple of inches.

Any notion I'd had of giving my visitor short shrift melted away when I saw a slim figure on the doorstep. Her right arm was raised, and her hand was curled in a fist, as if she was about to pummel down the heavy oak door. She was wearing a big black overcoat, the type we used to call donkey jackets back in the day, and her long dark-blonde hair was drenched and as straggly as seaweed. I couldn't tear my gaze away from her face. My heart beat furiously and goosebumps multiplied like a virus on my skin. As they would, wouldn't they, if you found yourself staring into the face of a ghost?

The girl turned her pale face towards mine.

'Rose?' she said. 'Rose Barton?'

I licked my lips. 'Who's asking?'

She peered through the gap between the door and the jamb. 'Don't you recognise me?'

I recognised someone, but it wasn't her.

My grip on the safety chain tightened. 'I said, who's asking?'

'It's me. Eloise. Juliet's daughter. Your goddaughter.' She shivered.

'What are you doing here?'

'I came to see you.'

'No one comes to see me.'

'Can I come in? Please?'

I stepped back. 'It's very late. Why don't you come back in the morning?'

She frowned, and all at once she reminded me of someone else entirely. 'You promised to help me,' she said. 'At Mum's funeral, remember? You said…' she gulped, almost choking on her words, 'you said if I ever needed help, that I should come to you.'

'Did I? It's such a long time ago.'

'Ten years,' the girl, Eloise, said. 'I was only eleven, but I've never forgotten. We were standing by Mum's grave. You said if there was ever anything you could do for me, I only had to ask.'

I watched, mesmerised, as she wrestled with the buttons of her jacket. Her eyes on mine, she pulled it open to reveal a ripped white cotton top covered in blood. Splashes of the stuff darkened the base of her neck and her jutting collarbone. I lowered my gaze.

'It's time, Rose,' she said. 'Now's the time I need your help.'

CHAPTER TWO

Focus on the practicalities, I told myself as I ushered the girl inside. Her teeth were chattering, and she was shaking like a leaf.

'Second door on the left. There's a fire. Sit down and I'll make you a hot drink.'

In the kitchen, I flicked the kettle on, then leaned against the worktop and attempted to compose myself.

Juliet's daughter was here, in my house, covered in blood and asking for my help. What on earth had happened? My chest fluttered at the endless possibilities. A car crash, a mugging... or worse? My mother always said I had an over-active imagination. But no, I was getting ahead of myself.

Eloise was hunched on the edge of the armchair nearest the fire, still in the donkey jacket, when I returned. Trying my best to ignore the pervading smell of wet sheep, I set a mug of soup on the hearth.

'Why don't we get you out of that wet coat?' I said. 'You'll never warm up, otherwise.'

She nodded and pulled herself unsteadily to her feet. As she swayed, I wondered if she was drunk, but I couldn't smell alcohol on her breath. More likely, she was suffering from mild hypothermia, in which case I needed to raise her core temperature. I helped her out of the jacket, wrapped a throw around her shoulders, and guided her back into the chair.

'For you,' I said, handing her my old Winnie-the-Pooh hot water bottle.

She stared at it, a glimmer of a smile on her face. 'You don't look like a Winnie-the-Pooh sort of person,' she said.

'Appearances can be deceptive.' I hung her coat on the back of a chair. 'Drink the soup. It'll warm you up.'

She picked up the mug and wrapped her hands around it but didn't take a sip.

'It's all right. I haven't laced it with arsenic or anything.'

She blinked and, too late, I realised how batty I must sound. But I wasn't used to visitors. In fact, I couldn't remember the last time anyone other than me or Dinah had stepped foot inside the house.

I desperately wanted to ask why she was here, but the question lodged in my throat. Instead, I said, 'Did you walk from the village?'

'No, I drove.' She trembled, her whole body juddering so violently, cream of asparagus soup slopped over the brim and onto the hearth rug. She clapped a hand over her mouth.

'Oh my God, I'm so sorry.'

'It's fine. I'll get a cloth. It's seen worse.'

When I returned, Eloise was staring into the dying embers of the fire.

'I should get going,' she said quietly.

'But you've only just arrived.'

'Coming here was a mistake.'

'Don't be silly. It's a lovely surprise,' I said, even though we both knew it wasn't. 'Where are you living these days? Still in Marylebone?'

'I haven't lived there since Mum died.' As she sipped her soup, the throw slipped from her shoulders, revealing a gash just above her collarbone. I'd pretended I hadn't seen the blood, but I couldn't ignore that.

'You're hurt!' I cried.

She shook her head. 'It's nothing.'

'Let me look at it.'

I took her shrug as permission and knelt down to inspect the wound. It was a clean cut, about an inch long, as if someone had scored her with a knife.

'I'll fetch a bowl of water and we'll get it cleaned and dressed,' I said, hurrying into the kitchen.

I washed and dried my hands and gathered some sterile dressings, a pod of saline solution and gauze from my first aid kit under the sink. As I filled a mixing bowl with tepid water, a clatter at the back door made me jump. It was only Dinah. She shook off the raindrops, padded over to her empty bowl and miaowed pitifully.

'In a minute,' I said. 'Can't you see I'm busy?'

She followed me back down the hallway and into the front room. 'Come and meet our visitor,' I said.

Eloise sprang up from her chair. 'I thought you lived alone.'

'Dinah's my cat,' I said. 'Dinah, my goddaughter, Eloise.' The word sounded unfamiliar but not unwelcome, and I felt a jolt of something unexpected. If I had to stick a label on it, I'd say it was pleasure. 'I say she's my cat. But every cat owner will tell you, they own us, not the other way around. I am merely here to serve her needs.' It was the longest sentence I'd uttered since I phoned up the council to complain they'd missed my brown bin.

Dinah lingered in the doorway like a teenage girl at her first dance, her owlish eyes fixed on Eloise. Eloise slowly lowered herself to her knees, extended a hand and made a kissing noise with her lips.

The cat strutted over, sniffed Eloise's hand and, apparently deciding our guest was friend not foe, started purring loudly.

'She doesn't normally like strangers,' I said.

Eloise smiled as she looked at me. 'But I'm not a stranger, am I?'

'You are to Dinah.'

'It's a cool name for a cat.'

'It's not very original. I have Lewis Carroll to thank.'

'Who?'

'You know, *Alice in Wonderland*? Dinah was Alice's cat.'

'Never read it.'

'You've never read *Alice in Wonderland*? But it's one of the classics.'

Eloise shrugged again. 'I didn't have that kind of childhood.'

'We need to rectify that at once. I'll lend you my copy.'

While Eloise petted Dinah, I rinsed her wound with water, tipped the saline solution onto a square of gauze and dabbed it until I was satisfied it was clean, before patting the area dry.

'There,' I said, sticking a sterile dressing over the top. 'That should be fine. But you should keep an eye on it and if it shows any signs of infection, take yourself to minor injuries and get it seen to by the professionals.'

'But you trained as a doctor, didn't you? I remember Mum saying.'

I almost dropped the bowl of water. How much had Juliet told her? 'Only for three years,' I said. 'My mother had a stroke, and I was needed here.' It was more or less the truth. 'But never mind that. Tell me, Eloise,' I said gently. 'What the hell happened to you?'

CHAPTER THREE

Eloise sat back in the armchair and patted her knee. At once, Dinah jumped onto her lap.

'She's a lovely colour,' my goddaughter said. 'Is she one of those British Blues?'

'No, she's a common or garden moggy from the local rescue centre.'

'Her colouring's so unusual.'

'She's a dilute tortoiseshell. A mutation in her melanophilin gene diluted her pigments, fading the black pigment to a bluey-grey, and the red pigmentation, which would be orange in a true tortoiseshell, to apricot.'

'A mutation?'

I nodded. She was side-stepping my question, but there was no point pushing her if she wasn't ready to talk. 'The mutation's recessive,' I said. 'So, both her parents must have carried the mutated gene for it to show in her coat.'

'So, it's her defect that makes her so beautiful,' Eloise

said softly, stroking Dinah under her chin. Her purrs increased in volume.

'More a genetic blip than a defect,' I said. 'They're called dilute calico cats in America, I believe. Quite unusual. Anyway, that's enough about Dinah. Her ego's already big enough as it is. Tell me why you came.'

Eloise bit her lip. 'I didn't know where else to turn. I don't have anyone, you see. Not now Theo's...' A sob caught at the back of her throat.

'Theo?'

'My boyfriend,' she said, taking the handkerchief I offered her. 'Well, he was.' She shook her head and blew her nose.

Everything was starting to make sense. Eloise had had a bust up with her beau and didn't have anywhere else to go. I pictured her flinging clothes into a suitcase, hefting it down the stairs and storming from the house in a flood of tears, Theo watching silently from the hallway.

And the cut I'd so carefully washed and dressed? Had he lashed out in a fit of anger? My blood ran cold at the thought.

'You can stay here until it all blows over,' I found myself saying.

Eloise turned her red-rimmed eyes to me. 'I can?'

'I'll make up a bed.'

'I'll help,' she said, her hands on the arms of the chair. She'd stopped shivering, but her face was still waxy-pale.

'I won't hear of it. You stay by the fire with Dinah. I won't be long.'

As I left the room, she gave me a wan smile. 'Thank you, Rose,' she said in a quiet voice.

I bobbed my head. 'You're very welcome.'

I dithered at the top of the stairs, unsure which direction to turn. There was my mother's room, still looking like a shabby side room in a poorly funded NHS hospital, with its hospital bed, mobile commode, walking frame and grab rails, and an underlying smell of piss. On the wall, my mother's extensive collection of stuffed birds. Kingfishers, jays, woodpeckers, yellow hammers and chaffinches, each frozen in time in their glass-fronted cases. She'd collected them for as long as I could remember, scouring boot fairs and antique markets for new pieces. According to her, Queen Victoria had amassed a vast array of stuffed birds over her lifetime and there was no shame in preserving our feathered friends for posterity, but I'd always found her fascination with dead creatures disturbing. There was no way Eloise could sleep in there.

Across the landing was my father's room. Apart from a monthly hoover and polish, I hadn't touched a thing in there since the day he died. I opened the door and scanned the room. What would Eloise make of the heavy mahogany furniture, the masculine striped wallpaper, the folded pyjamas on the bed, and the ivory shaving set on the dressing table? Was it even legal to own ivory these days? I made a mental note to check. It wouldn't do to be seen breaking the law. The room was as I'd left it - immaculate and fragrant with beeswax polish - but it was no place for a young woman in emotional turmoil.

My bedroom wasn't an option, so that left the box room at the back of the house. It was tiny - just about big enough for a narrow put-you-up bed, a chest of drawers and a Victorian balloon dining chair. But it had done the job when my mother's carers stayed over, and it was better than the sofa.

I opened the window an inch to air the room and found sheets, pillows and a couple of blankets in the tallboy on the landing. Bed made, I headed back downstairs. Eloise was examining the collection of photographs on the sideboard.

'Is this you?' she said, holding up a thin wooden frame.

It was a school photo, taken in the summer of 1982. I was wearing a blue and white gingham dress and a glum expression. My hair was cut in an unflattering pudding-basin style - if style was indeed the right word. An army of freckles marched across my nose and forehead and I had an angry-looking pimple on my chin. I was coming to the end of the first year at my girls' grammar school and already I was persona non grata. A social outcast. The class pariah. Billy No-Mates. Call it what you will. A rose by any other name....

'Yes. That's me.'

She smiled. 'Your hair was such a pretty colour.'

My cheeks flared red. 'Your mum thought so, too. Everyone else called me carrot top. Or worse.' Once, in the fourth year, the class bully and two of her sidekicks dragged me into a toilet cubicle, lifted my skirt and pulled down my pants just to see if I had a ginger minge. I didn't tell Eloise that.

'Well, I think it was beautiful.'

'I'm more strawberry blonde these days,' I said, self-consciously patting my greying locks.

'What's this one?' Eloise asked, fingering an ornate silver frame.

Even after five years, I felt a little swell of pride deep in my chest. 'It's me with my MBE.'

'Your what?'

'MBE. Member of the Order of the British Empire. Prince Charles gave it to me for services to charity.'

Eloise seemed underwhelmed.

'Ed Sheeran got one the same day.' Now I had her attention. 'Actually, he made headlines because he touched Prince Charles's arm as they shook hands, which is not the done thing at all. Straight to the Tower and off with his head, I say!'

Eloise looked bemused.

'Breach of royal protocol, you see.'

She nodded her understanding and peered at the photo, as if she was expecting to see Ed Sheeran loitering in the background with his guitar. 'Which charity?'

'Charities,' I corrected her. 'I've given my time to so many over the years. The RSPCA, Asthma UK, The Stroke Foundation. At the moment, I volunteer for Sisterline. We provide a listening ear to women in emotional distress. Our phones are manned three hundred and sixty-five days a year, and we've just launched a new texting service which is proving very popular.'

'Popular?'

'Sorry, poor choice of words. What I'm trying to say is that it's been in great demand. We've helped a lot of women.'

Women like you, Eloise, I thought, as I tried not to stare at the red stain that was already seeping through the dressing on her collarbone. What kind of mess was she caught up in?

We were both silent for a moment, then Eloise replaced the frame carefully on the sideboard. 'Please could I use your bathroom?'

'You could, but *may* you?' The words spilled out of my mouth before I could stop them. 'Sorry,' I said again, clocking her raised eyebrow. 'It's something my mother used to say. The difference between can and may. Anyway, it's not important. Of course you can use the bathroom. Up the stairs, third door on the right.'

I busied myself throwing another log on the fire and straightening cushions until Eloise reappeared. She'd washed off the smears of blood and colour was returning to her cheeks.

'I can lend you one of my nightdresses for tonight, if you like?' I said. 'We can pop into Canterbury in the morning to pick you up some things.'

'It's OK. I brought an overnight bag.'

Outside, the wind whistled, and the rain battered the windows and Eloise shivered as if a ghost had tiptoed across her grave.

'Do you want to talk about it?' I said.

She frowned. 'What?'

'Your fight with Theo. I'm a good listener. And you know what they say about a trouble shared. Bottling things up is not good for anyone.' She was silent, so I tried another tack. 'Your cut,' I said, touching my own collarbone. 'Did Theo do it?'

She closed her eyes and gave the faintest of nods.

I leaned forwards and took her hand in mine. 'You poor girl. Have you reported him?'

She shook her head.

'You must, Eloise! The cut's inches from your throat. He could have killed you!'

'But he didn't.'

'This time, maybe,' I muttered. 'Has he ever hurt you before?'

'He was very... protective of me.' She looked at me with a haunted expression. 'But only because he loved me.'

I snorted in a most unladylike fashion. I knew all about men like Theo, thanks to a brief spell as a trustee for a women's refuge. Men who controlled their partners' finances and dictated who they saw, who manipulated and lied and cheated and bullied. I'd seen first-hand the mental toll their emotional abuse left on the women they claimed to love.

'It's true, he really did,' Eloise insisted. 'He wanted to keep me safe. At least that's what I thought. But yes, you're right. I saw him for what he was today.'

I squeezed her hand. 'And what was that?'

'He's a bully.'

'Where is he now?'

She took my other hand, so our fingers were entwined. 'That's why I'm here.'

Touched she'd come to me in her hour of need, I gave her a reassuring smile. 'I promised I would help you, and I will. I am nothing if not a woman of my words.'

'The thing is…' Eloise fiddled with a strand of her hair, winding it round and round her finger. 'Theo's in the car.'

The smile slid from my face. 'You brought him here? But I thought you said he'd attacked you?'

'I mean he's in the boot.'

My chest tightened. 'The boot? What are you talking about?'

'I killed him, Rose. I killed Theo,' she said, breathlessly. 'I panicked and I didn't know what to do. But you promised you'd help me.'

'Yes, but —'

'Please, Rose, I need your help to get rid of his body.'

CHAPTER FOUR

The earth tilted on its axis, and I stared at my goddaughter in disbelief.

'*What?*'

'I didn't mean to hurt him. It was self-defence.' Eloise pulled her hand from mine and fingered the dressing over her collarbone. 'He said he was going to kill me.' She was trembling violently now. A long-buried memory from med school surfaced and my face cleared.

'Your mind's playing tricks on you,' I said.

'What?'

'I think you might be hypothermic. Early signs include confusion and memory loss.'

Hope flared behind her eyes.

'I expect Theo's sat on the sofa with a beer in his hand watching football right now,' I told her.

'Do you think so? But it seems so real.' She thought for a moment, then leapt to her feet. 'Can we, sorry, *may* we check?'

I glanced at the window. Rain was still coming down in buckets. I shook my head. 'You'll catch your death. It'll wait until morning.'

'Please, Rose?' she implored. 'I won't sleep a wink until I know you're right.'

I sighed. 'All right, all right, but you must promise me you'll wear a raincoat and hat.'

She was across the room, as nimble as a sprite, before I'd hauled myself out of the armchair. In the hallway, I handed her my knee-length waterproof coat and wellies and shrugged on my father's old Barbour.

As Eloise pulled a rain hat on her head and gave me a tentative smile, a memory assuaged me, and my stomach flipped.

Glastonbury, June 1989.

It was my first and last experience of a music festival, and my memories of it were hazy, blurred by pints of cloudy scrumpy and suspiciously fat roll-ups. Juliet had talked me into going. She'd said it was a rite of passage. And I'd agreed, because I would have done anything Juliet asked.

It had been hot that year, almost eighty degrees, and as we'd headed across the parched festival ground to watch the Pixies' set, she'd dragged me to a stall and picked a denim hat with daisies embroidered on the sides from a pile on the table. She tucked my hair behind my ears and, placing the hat on my head, took a step back and regarded me, one hand under her chin.

'It suits you,' she said at last. 'And it'll stop you from getting heatstroke. You should buy it.'

'I'll buy you one, too,' I said. 'That way we'll always be able to find each other.'

She pulled a hat on and twirled on the spot. 'How do I look?'

'Yeah, not bad,' I said, because Juliet didn't like it when I got all heavy.

We made our way to the Pyramid stage, but it turned out the Pixies weren't my kettle of fish, although Juliet seemed to like them, swaying to the music with her eyes closed as if she was in a trance.

'Are you OK?' said a voice, and I looked up, startled to see Eloise, not Juliet, standing next to me.

'Sorry, miles away.' I picked up my torch and glanced at her. She gave another nervous half-smile and I squeezed her shoulder.

'It'll be all right,' I said.

'And if it isn't?'

My breath caught at the raw vulnerability in her voice.

'If it isn't, we'll fix it.'

I tramped across the sodden garden to the top of the drive and waved the torch around. The beam picked out the coal bunker, the wheelie bins and my elderly Land Rover, but no car.

'Where did you park?' I shouted to Eloise over the wind.

'In a layby next to a water pumping station about a mile away.' She pointed towards the village.

'No wonder you were soaked to the skin. Why didn't you drive to the house?'

'I didn't want to link you to my car because of the... because of Theo.'

Bless. She really thought she'd killed him.

'We'll cut through the woods. It's quicker,' I said. She nodded and followed me through the gate in the back fence. 'This way.' I plunged into the trees where it was darker, and the wind whistling through the branches sounded like the crazed whispers of a dozen gossipmongers spreading their poison. As a child, I'd been terrified of the woods, convinced they were home to all manner of ghastly creatures. Later they became my sanctuary and now, in my middle age, we lived comfortably alongside each other like an old married couple.

'People with severe hypothermia often take off their clothes,' I said as I puffed and panted my way up the steep track to the ridge. 'It's called paradoxical undressing. It's when the body's blood vessels contract to prevent loss of heat from the extremities. They think they're burning up, even though they're actually dying from the cold.' I stopped to catch my breath. 'Do you see where I'm going with this?'

'You think I've imagined everything,' Eloise said.

I smiled, even though I knew she couldn't see it. 'I do.'

We trudged down a flinty track before turning onto a bridleway that led to the road and the pumping station. Every so often a branch whipped my face, or a tree stump sent me stumbling forwards. Beside me, Eloise was as graceful as a deer, just like her mother.

Finally, we reached the gate onto the lane. The yellow beam of the torch lit mud-splattered black metal. I followed the line of the vehicle from bumper to bumper.

Eloise must have pressed the key fob as there was a bleep and the hazard lights flashed orange in the darkness. She grabbed my arm.

'Wait!' she said. 'A car's coming.'

I turned off the torch and scuttled back into the shadows as the sound of an engine grew louder and headlights appeared at the top of the hill. Eloise shrank back and, after a moment's deliberation, I put a comforting arm around her shoulder.

The car reached the bottom of the valley, but instead of accelerating up the hill, it slowed and pulled into the layby alongside Eloise's car. It was a small red hatchback, the kind favoured by boy racers. The driver killed the headlights. The passenger door clicked open and a lanky frame in a hoodie and jogging bottoms let himself out.

'Fuck,' Eloise hissed, drawing away from me.

The youth glanced up and down the road. Then, apparently happy the coast was clear, he sidled over to the driver's side of Eloise's car, cupped his face against the window and peered inside.

'Anything?' the driver demanded.

'There's a sat nav and a wallet. And a coupla bags on the back seat.'

'Nice. We'll have them alloys, too. Reckon they're worth at least fifty quid.'

The first youth grunted his agreement and pulled on

the door handle. When he realised the car wasn't locked, he crowed in triumph. 'This is gonna be a piece of piss.'

'Wait, bro. You don't reckon it's one of them police traps, do you?'

'Nah, mate. You worry too much.' He turned his attention back to the car. Eloise bent down, her hands laced behind her head, and groaned softly.

I had to do something. Before I could talk myself out of it, I switched the torch back on, stepped out of the trees, and cleared my throat.

'You two look lost. Can I help?' I said pleasantly, pointing the torch in the hooded youth's face. Shielding his eyes, he jumped back in surprise, colliding with the hatchback's wing mirror and cursing loudly.

'Have you broken down? I can help you with a bump start if you like.' I had no more idea how to bump start a car than how to build a rocket and fly to the moon, but they weren't to know.

'Nah, miss, we're good. We was just checking everything was OK here, weren't we, Jaden?' the youth said, slipping his hand in his pocket.

In the hatchback, the driver nodded vigorously.

'If you say so,' I said. 'Only we've been having problems with car thefts in the village. The local Neighbourhood Watch co-ordinator sent out an email only yesterday, asking us to report any suspicious behaviour. We're supposed to dial 999 if we see a crime in progress,' I added with a disarming smile.

The youth in the hoody felt behind him for the door

handle, yanked it open and jumped inside. Jaden floored the accelerator, and the hatchback sped off up the hill in a fog of exhaust fumes. Only once the taillights had disappeared did Eloise leave the cover of the trees to join me.

'Jesus, Rose, what were you thinking? They could have had a knife.'

'They were two gormless boys looking for easy pickings. They wouldn't have hurt me.'

Eloise shook her head, opened the passenger door, and looked inside.

'Anything missing?' I asked.

'No,' she said. 'It's just as I remembered it. Which means…' She rubbed her temple with the heel of her hand.

'Open the boot,' I said, pointing to the keys.

She gave a tiny nod but didn't move. I held out my hand, and she dropped the fob into my palm. It felt as smooth as a pebble and I ran my thumb over the top and pressed a button experimentally. The boot clicked open.

'Here goes,' I said, smiling at my goddaughter as I lifted the door, held the torch aloft and shone it into the boot's cave-like interior.

At first, all I could make out was a jumble of clothes, as though Eloise had shoved the entire contents of her wardrobe into the back of the car. She stood behind me, so close her breath warmed my neck. I felt a flutter of something deep in my belly - Fear? Anticipation? Déjà vu?

The beam of light fell on the face of a man, his waxen cheek squashed up against a wheel arch. His legs were bent at the knee and his arms were flung out at right angles to his body as if he was reaching out to us. I dropped the torch in the puddle by my feet. As darkness wrapped itself around us, Eloise screamed.

CHAPTER FIVE

It only took a moment for me to pull myself together. It wasn't as if it was my first brush with the dead. As a first-year medical student, I'd honed my anatomy skills on a cadaver my seminar group nicknamed Beryl, a buxom woman with heavy jowls and dimpled thighs. All we were told was that she'd died of lung cancer aged forty-nine. A heavy smoker, we'd assumed, although there were no tell-tale yellow stains on her fingers. With the pungent, pickle-like smell of formaldehyde in my nostrils, I'd sliced Beryl open and picked my way through her ravaged vital organs without a flicker of revulsion. At the end of the year, our seminar group attended her funeral, as was the tradition at our medical school. It was only then that we learned Beryl was in fact Lynda and had worked as a singer in working men's clubs across the north of England for decades. She'd never smoked a cigarette in her life. It was breathing in other people's smoke that had killed her.

I reached down and felt Theo's neck for a pulse. His

skin was as cold as marble. And prickly, as though he hadn't shaved for a couple of days. Feeling nothing, I pushed my index and middle finger deeper into his carotid artery.

I pulled back as if I'd been stung.

'Rose?' Eloise's voice quavered, her fear palpable. What had Theo done to her to instil such terror? I slammed the boot shut, then turned to her, my arms open wide. She collapsed against me, her whole body shaking, and I held her close until her sobs subsided.

'It's all right,' I whispered. 'Everything's going to be all right.'

'I knew I'd killed him,' she wailed. 'What are we going to do?'

It was obvious what we should do. We should call the police and tell them what happened. And then what? Before we knew it, patrol cars and forensic teams would screech down the lane towards us, sirens wailing and blue lights pulsing. Inscrutable detectives would fire questions at Eloise, warning her she was under caution and anything she said might harm her defence, blah blah blah. I'd have to watch helplessly as they arrested my goddaughter and carted her off in the back of a police van.

That was the right path to take. But what of the honourable path? I'd made a promise a decade ago, a promise to help Eloise if she ever needed it, and by Christ, she needed it now.

'We'll get him home and decide,' I said, fishing the car keys out of my pocket. 'I'll drive.'

Minutes later, I pulled up in the driveway at home alongside the Land Rover and switched off the engine.

'You can't leave the car here,' Eloise said, her voice rising in panic. 'What if someone sees it?'

'I told you, no one ever comes here. It'll be safe until we decide what to do.'

She cradled her head in her hands and rocked back and forth in the passenger seat. 'Oh God, what have I done?'

'It was self-defence, you said so yourself.'

'What are we going to do with him?' Her breaths were coming in shallow puffs, hard and fast. 'We should hide his body. Yes, that's it. Somewhere no one'll ever find it.' She looked at me wildly. 'There must be somewhere around here. Is there a well? Or a lake? Or maybe we should burn him and then there wouldn't be a body to find. Because I can't go to prison, Rose,' she screeched. 'It would kill me.'

'No one's going to prison.'

'Oh God, I can't believe it. I *killed* him, Rose. I killed Theo.' The veins in her neck were bulging and her nostrils were flared.

'Eloise, listen to me. You need to calm down.'

'I'll bury him myself if I have to,' she said, unclipping her seatbelt and reaching for the door handle.

'No!' I said sharply.

'Please help me, Rose,' she said, her voice disintegrating. 'You promised you would.'

I touched her arm. 'I am helping you. But we need to think this through before we do anything rash. We can't afford to make any mistakes. First, I need you to tell me exactly what happened tonight. Not here,' I said quickly, glancing over my shoulder. 'In the house.'

Eloise closed her eyes briefly, then nodded. Out of habit, I locked the doors, although if Jaden and his shifty friend came back and stole the car and its contents, they'd be doing us a favour.

Eloise stumbled towards the house, her eyes fixed on the light by the back door. I took my time, wondering what the hell we were going to do with the lifeless figure in the boot of my goddaughter's car. Christ, what a mess.

We shrugged off our dripping coats, then I threw another couple of logs on the fire and poured us two hefty measures of brandy.

'I'm sorry,' I said, handing her a glass. 'I genuinely thought you must have imagined everything.'

'Because you don't think I'm capable of killing someone?'

'Everyone's capable of killing someone if they're pushed hard enough.'

'You really believe that?' she said, her eyes searching mine.

'I do.' I took a sip of brandy and winced as the alcohol hit the back of my throat. 'Tell me about Theo. Where did you meet?'

She shook her head. 'I've killed my boyfriend and you want to know how I *met* him?'

'Humour me, please.'

She shrugged. 'At work. Theo is - *was* - a chef. I was temping at the country house hotel where he worked.'

'In the kitchen?' I realised I knew nothing about Eloise. Where she lived, how she spent her spare time and whether she'd been to university. I'd cut all ties the day we buried her mother, and the decision did not reflect well on me.

'On reception,' Eloise said. 'It paid the rent, you know?'

'Of course. When was this?'

'Easter.' She swirled the brandy around her glass. It glowed amber in the firelight. 'Everyone was talking about the new chef and how hot he was. The other girls on reception kept finding excuses to go into the kitchen so they could check him out.'

'Not you?'

'God no. Not my style at all. I bumped into him in the car park. The girls were right. He was hot. And such a charmer.' She smiled at the memory. 'He turned up for our first date with the biggest bouquet of red roses you've ever seen.'

I arched an eyebrow.

Eloise met my eye. 'I couldn't believe my luck. That this gorgeous man was interested in *me*. Because he fell head over heels in love with me, Rose. I know it's probably hard for you to believe, but he did.'

'And why shouldn't he? You're beautiful, clever and brave. Of course he fell in love with you.'

'On our second date, he told me how striking our kids

would be. On our fourth date, he suggested we live together. Two months after we met, I gave notice on my flat and moved in with him. It was as if we were caught up in this amazing whirlwind. And then…' She took a gulp of brandy, then set the glass down. 'And then he changed.'

'How?'

'He started kicking off if I met the girls for a drink after work. He wanted to know where I was when we weren't together. Once, I caught him looking at my phone. He said he'd heard it ring but when I checked, the call log was empty.' Eloise bit her lip. 'I should have seen him for what he was, but now and then he'd buy me flowers, or cook me an amazing meal, and I'd forgive him. He took me for a fool.'

'Don't be too hard on yourself,' I said. 'I heard so many stories like yours when I volunteered at a women's refuge. Sweeping you off your feet with romantic gestures and asking you to move in with him after a matter of weeks is textbook behaviour for your average psychopath.'

'*Psychopath?*' she said, her eyes widening.

I took her hand. 'Once he'd successfully won you over, he became paranoid, possessive and controlling, am I right? He was a walking cliché. But you mustn't blame yourself. Sometimes you don't see what's right in front of your nose.'

Eloise stared into the fire, her shoulders hunched. 'I guess,' she mumbled.

'When he threatened to kill you last night, was that the first time he'd been violent towards you?'

'No.' Her voice was flat. 'One of the other receptionists

suggested a drink at the pub to celebrate my birthday a while back. I didn't want to go, but she wouldn't take no for an answer. Theo was working and assumed I'd gone straight home. When he found out I'd gone to the pub without him, he hit the roof.' She touched her cheekbone and gave a hollow laugh. 'His idea of a birthday present was a black eye.'

'Did you take a picture?'

'No, why?'

'It might help, you know, when you talk to the police.'

She stiffened. 'The police? But I thought you were going to help me?'

I took a deep breath. 'We need to call them, Eloise. It's the right thing to do. It was self-defence. They won't charge you when they hear what he put you through. And I'll be by your side every step of the way.'

'That's not helping me, that's throwing me under a fucking bus!' Eloise jumped to her feet and began pacing the room, her arms wrapped around her slender body.

'We have no choice,' I said desperately. 'Anything else is madness.'

She stopped pacing, dropped to her knees in front of me, and took my hand. 'Have you never made a mistake, Rose?'

I was silent.

'I regret what I did with all my heart,' she said. 'And if I could turn back the clock I would in a heartbeat. But I can't change the past.'

'No one can,' I whispered. 'But they can make amends.'

'How?' she pleaded. 'How can I make amends?'

'I wasn't talking about you.' I massaged my temple. Maybe helping Eloise would lay my own demons to rest. It had to be worth a shot, didn't it? I reached a decision. 'All right, I'll help you, Eloise. I'll keep my promise.'

CHAPTER SIX

Was it weird that I sometimes imagined what it would be like to be a fly on the wall at my own funeral? What would the vicar have to say about my life? That here was a woman who'd worked tirelessly for good causes? A woman who prided herself on giving something back? A community champion. A force for good. A woman whose whole raison d'être was to help others?

'Rose Barton was one of those rare things - a truly selfless person who always put others first,' the vicar might say. 'And the world will be a poorer place without her.'

Was I a truly good person, or was I trying to be good? And did it even matter, because the end result was, surely, the same? Helping people made me feel needed. So, was it so bad that I felt a tingle of anticipation as I poured us each another brandy and took control?

'I need to know exactly what happened between you and Theo tonight,' I said. 'We have to make sure we've covered our tracks.'

Eloise cradled her glass and cleared her throat. 'I told him I was moving out. He went berserk.'

'Details, Eloise.'

She described how Theo had yelled at her for dropping his favourite mug when she was unloading the dishwasher that morning. Then she'd burned his toast. He'd sprayed her face with spittle as he'd screamed at her, telling her she was a worthless, bloodsucking leech. It had been the final straw.

'I couldn't go on,' she said. 'I packed my bags while he was at work and planned to be gone before he came home.'

But Theo, perhaps sensing something was amiss, had returned early to find Eloise writing a note to him at the kitchen table.

'He went ballistic, screaming and shouting. Saying it wasn't my choice to leave and that, if anything, he should be throwing me out because I was pathetic and useless and,' her voice caught on a sob, 'that the world would be a better place without me in it.'

'Could anyone have heard him?' I asked.

'His flat's above a carpet shop. There are offices on either side. It was seven o'clock in the evening. Everyone had gone home for the day.'

'OK. So, he loses the plot. What happened next?'

Eloise swallowed. 'He started shoving me, telling me he wished he'd never met me.' She shivered. 'Then he stopped yelling, and I thought, maybe he's got it all off his chest and he'll let me go. But when I went to pick up my handbag, he lunged at me with a kitchen knife. His eyes,

Rose. They were… they were completely blank.' She buried her face in her hands.

'That's when he cut you?'

She touched her collarbone. 'I ducked out of the way, so it was only a nick. Then I ran into the hallway. I'm not sure exactly what happened next. It's all a blur. But somehow, he tripped and fell face first onto the floor. I grabbed the first thing to hand. My kettlebell was right there, next to the shoe rack. I wasn't thinking. I just picked it up and swung it as hard as I could. I never meant to kill him, I swear.'

'Kettlebell?'

'It's a weight I use for strength training. Theo stopped me going to the gym because he was worried I might meet someone else,' Eloise said with a small shake of her head.

'And you only hit him once?'

She nodded. 'I gathered my things and was about to leave but, I don't know, something seemed wrong. He was so still.' She looked up at me. 'I tried to find a pulse, but there was nothing. I thought about calling the police or an ambulance, but I panicked. I knew the police would never have believed it was self-defence. They'd have taken one look at my record and thrown the book at me.'

I felt a tug of surprise. 'What record?'

She glanced at the ceiling, then lowered her gaze. 'I went off the rails a bit when I was younger. Nothing too heavy,' she said quickly. 'Possession and a bit of shop-lifting, that's all. I fell in with the wrong crowd. But the police wouldn't see it like that.'

Whether or not she was right was of little consequence. The line had been crossed and there was no going back.

'How the hell did you manage to get him from your flat into the boot of your car?'

'It wasn't easy. I dragged him out of the fire door and onto the fire escape and parked my car at the bottom.'

I gasped. 'Are you sure no one saw you?'

'It was pitch black and raining. I'm pretty certain.'

'And then you drove straight here?'

'After I went back for the kettlebell and Theo's phone. I thought if I texted his work and pretended he'd gone home to Paris because of a family crisis or something, they wouldn't report him missing over here.'

'Paris?'

'Didn't I say?' Eloise ran a hand across her face. 'Theo's French.'

The fact that Theo was from another country added a whole new perspective to his disappearance. Eloise explained that his wealthy parents owned a small chain of high-end restaurants in France and had virtually disowned him when he dropped out of university to bum around Europe, working in kitchens to fund his travels. By the time he'd started work as a sous chef in an upmarket country house hotel near Rochester, he hadn't spoken to them for years.

'So, it's unlikely they'll report him missing?'

She nodded. 'And if his boss thinks he's gone back to France, he won't, either.'

I pulled a face. It all seemed too easy. 'What about friends?'

Eloise shrugged. 'He didn't really have any.'

'What about your friends? Won't they wonder where you are?'

'Theo didn't like me seeing anyone. That's why I came here. You're all I've got.' She leaned forwards, her elbows on her knees and her face eager. 'And even if someone reported him missing, the police would never connect him to you. No one knows you're my godmother.'

I was silent as I digested the facts. I felt nothing for Theo but contempt. Frankly, men like him had it coming. When would they learn that women were not chattels to do with as they pleased? Hadn't the #MeToo movement penetrated their thick skulls? It was time women took a stand. Men like Theo made me sick. I didn't feel a shred of sympathy for him.

'If we buried his body here, on your land, no one would ever find him,' Eloise said.

I held up a hand. 'Just slow down a minute. There's something you need to know.'

She carried on talking as if I hadn't spoken. 'No, Rose, the sooner we get rid of him the better.' She jumped to her feet. 'I feel terrible about what's happened, but maybe it was meant to be. Like, I've stopped him from hurting me, but I've also stopped him from hurting anyone else. Other women will live because he died, do you see?'

'Eloise,' I said, taking a deep breath. 'Please, just listen to me for a minute.'

She sank back onto the sofa. 'Now he's gone I won't have to worry about saying the wrong thing, or wearing the wrong clothes, or cooking the wrong tea. I won't have to live in fear any more. Say you'll help me, Rose. Please.'

'I -'

'Would you have done it for her?' she asked. 'For my mum?'

I'd have died for her. 'Of course.'

'Then do it for me. Please, Rose. You're all I have. We'll be Thelma and Louise, watching each other's backs. Always.'

And if I'd been wavering, that clinched it.

CHAPTER SEVEN

SEPTEMBER 1990

'Eat your hearts out, Thelma and Louise!' Juliet yelled, as the opaline green Austin Metro juddered down the slip road and onto the motorway. Seeing a motorbike roaring up behind us, Juliet yanked the steering wheel to the left, and I ducked as a yucca plant rolled off the boxes on the back seat, almost decapitating me.

'You don't need to drive off a cliff to kill us,' I said breathlessly. 'Just a few junctions along the M25 should do it.'

Juliet hooted with laughter and pressed her foot on the accelerator. The Metro's engine whined as the dial on the speedometer edged towards seventy miles an hour. The car had been a twenty-first birthday present from her mum and dad. They'd wrapped it in a red ribbon and parked it on the driveway of their Surbiton home, so it was there when she came down for breakfast. Juliet, like me, was an only child of older parents. It was one of the many things we had in common. Only she was cosseted, indulged. Me, not so much.

I rescued the yucca from the footwell and squeezed the plant pot between my feet. The plant's sharp sword-like leaves scratched my bare legs as the Metro rattled along in the inside lane. Juliet had christened it, as students were wont to do, and as I gingerly gripped Kevin's thick, woody stem between my knees, she looked sidelong at me, a smile playing on her lips.

'It's about time you tried a bit of cock, isn't it?'

'Juliet!' I cried, heat racing up my neck and colouring my cheeks, although I should have been used to her by now. She had a filthy mind for someone so outwardly demure. A paradox I still found hard to get my head around.

'Oh, come on, Rose. Don't be so stuffy. We're about to start our third year at university and you haven't had a single boyfriend. And it's no good saying you want to concentrate on your degree, because it won't wash.'

'I *need* to concentrate on my degree,' I said. And it was true. I'd been top of the top set at my girls' grammar school, but I'd had a nasty shock when I discovered I was fair to middling on a good day at med school. Being surrounded by people who were far cleverer than I could ever hope to be was dispiriting for someone so easily intimidated as I was.

Juliet would be the first to admit she wasn't naturally

academic. She never appeared to do any work, yet she still managed to breeze through her exams and assessments, whereas I had to burn the candle to scrape a pass. It hardly seemed fair, but I couldn't begrudge her for it. Not Juliet.

'Life's passing you by. You'll be in your fifties before you know it, living on your own in the middle of the woods with a cat for company, you mark my words,' she warned. 'You need to find yourself a man before it's too late.'

'I don't have the time or the inclination,' I said, crossing my arms and staring out of the window. But I couldn't stay cross with her for long. 'Hey, d'you realise we met each other two years ago almost to the day?'

She tapped her fingers on the steering wheel. 'Yeah, I suppose we did.'

'What was your first impression of me?' I asked, unable to stop myself.

'You reminded me of Henry.'

'Henry?' I asked, wondering what I had in common with the family labrador.

'Because you were so bloody eager to please.' She checked her mirror and pulled out to overtake a horsebox.

'Charming,' I said, even though she was right.

'Question is, what was your first impression of me?' she said, pulling back into the slow lane.

I thought you were the most beautiful thing I'd ever seen. You were so shiny, so polished, I wanted to reach out and stroke your cheek just to check you were real. That public school drawl, the way you oozed confidence, your ability to make friends as easily as breathing, both fascinated and flustered me. I was mesmerised. I still am.

'I liked your denim jacket,' I said at last.

Juliet laughed again. 'Oh Rose, you crack me up.'

'Why?' I said. 'What did I say?'

But Juliet didn't answer. Instead, she chuckled to herself, her eyes on the road ahead.

Two years may have passed, but I remembered the day I met Juliet with such clarity it could have been yesterday. Waking up at five o'clock, my stomach writhing with nerves and excitement. Forgoing breakfast in favour of a mug of black coffee, not because of my nerves, but because I wanted to be thin and beautiful, like the girls in the university prospectus that I'd pored over for months.

Reading medicine had been my dream for as long as I could remember, and now the day had arrived. At university, I could reinvent myself, shed my boring, pasty skin like a snake. Say goodbye to timid, frumpy Rose and embrace a cool, confident new me. All my new friends, for there would be many, would regard me as kooky, not weird. I would be part of the gang. Accepted for who I was. I wouldn't have to watch my life from the sidelines ever again.

My father had slipped me some money on the quiet to buy myself some clothes for university a fortnight before the start of term.

'Best not tell your mother,' he said, as he popped an

envelope on my dressing table with a smile and a wink. I'd opened it with fumbling fingers, my eyes wide as I'd counted out the ten-pound notes. There were, to my amazement, twenty of them. Two hundred pounds! I'd never seen so much money in my life. I had to count the notes twice, just to be sure. God only knew how he'd saved it. My mother handled the family finances with the rigid control of a communist dictator. He wasn't allowed near them.

I found him in his armchair in the library and kissed the top of his head.

'Thank you so much, Daddy.'

'My pleasure, darling girl. We couldn't have you turning up for medical school looking like the poor relation now, could we?' His tone was jovial, but there was a sadness behind his eyes that his smile couldn't mask. I knew it upset him that his job as a clerk at the Post Office barely paid enough to meet the bills. My mother getting a part-time job was out of the question, of course. Instead, she marched me along to every jumble sale within a five-mile radius, holding dead people's moth-eaten garments against me as if she was a personal shopper in Harrods, to my acute embarrassment. Second Hand Rose was just one of my many monikers at school.

So, with the two hundred pounds in my sticky fist, I'd caught the bus into Canterbury and ventured into the shops my mother normally marched me past, a firm hand on my shoulder. Dorothy Perkins, Snob, Next, Topshop. Even their names seemed synonymous with style and sophistication. I wasn't to know that the truly cool kids were shopping in Benetton and French Connection.

As I trailed around the shops, my eyes agog and my father's money burning a hole in my pocket, I wished more than anything that I had a friend to go shopping with. But I was an outcast at school and fraternising with the village children was expressly forbidden because they were, according to my mother, "common". The only person I could even loosely call a friend was a glum lump of a girl called Sonia Merryweather, who, like me, was doing all three sciences for A-level. But our friendship was confined to the classroom. Outside school, my best friend was our black cat, Smokey, and I could hardly take him shopping.

In Snob, a pretty shop assistant with an impressive cloud of permed auburn hair a few shades darker than mine, took pity on me, bringing armfuls of clothes into the changing room for me to try on.

'Green is your friend,' she said, handing me a cotton top the colour of emeralds. 'But blue is good, too, especially navy and cobalt, because it highlights fair skin.'

I had no idea what cobalt was, but I nodded anyway.

'We redheads look amazing in purple as long as we choose a shade with blue undertones and steer well clear of lavender.' She ferreted through the clothes and pulled out a bright purple cable-knit jumper. 'Try that on with the jeans,' she ordered, and I did as I was told, savouring the casual way in which she'd included me. *We redheads*. The possibility that I had anything in common with this luminous-skinned beauty made me fizz with happiness.

'Pastels will wash you out and avoid yellow and orange like the plague,' she continued, looping a chunky black necklace around my neck.

'I will,' I whispered fervently. 'How much if I have all this?'

An hour and almost two hundred pounds later, I strutted out of the shop, my arms weighed down with four heaving carrier bags. I had just enough left for some makeup in Superdrug. Emboldened now, I asked a friendly looking woman stacking shelves to help me choose an eyeliner, eyeshadow, mascara and lip gloss.

By the time I caught the last bus home, tired but jubilant, the transformation was complete. I pulled up the collar of my new denim jacket. Wiping away the condensation on the bus window, I blew my reflection a kiss and whispered, 'Rest in Peace, Second Hand Rose.'

The euphoria lasted until I let myself in the back door later that afternoon. I'd already had the foresight to hide my new clothes in the log store, planning to smuggle them into my bedroom when my mother was at bridge club. But she looked up from her tapestry the second I walked in and barked, 'What's that muck on your face?'

'Just a bit of makeup.'

'Makeup?' she snorted. 'You're far too young to be wearing makeup. You think you look pretty?' She jumped up, pinched my chin between her finger and thumb and studied me, her mouth turned down at the corners. Finally loosening her grip, she pushed me away. 'Well, you don't. You look like a good for nothing tart.'

And with that, my happiness leached away like rainwater down a storm drain, leaving a swell of bubbling resentment in its place.

'Where did you get the money to pay for it all?' she asked. 'I hope you didn't steal it.'

It was my turn to laugh. 'Of course I didn't steal it! The woman in Superdrug let me use the samples, if you must know. She took pity on me because I look like a refugee.' I plucked at my baggy sweater.

Her eyes narrowed. 'Don't answer me back. And show some gratitude for the clothes on your back. There are children in Africa who have to make do with rags.'

'Give me a break,' I muttered, turning to go.

'What did you say, young lady?'

Old Rose would have backed down and apologised. Anything to keep the peace, ever her father's daughter. But New Rose had had enough.

'I said, give me a break, you poisonous old cow.' My gaze swept over the drab 1960s kitchen with its tired Formica units and chipped floor tiles, lurid yellow and brown curtains and matching wall tiles. 'God, I can't wait to leave this dump.'

'I beg your pardon,' she spluttered, her face slowly turning red with rage.

'You heard,' I said coolly. 'I'll come back in the holidays, but only because I have to. When I've qualified as a doctor you won't see me for dust.'

CHAPTER EIGHT

'All right,' I said at long last. 'But there's one proviso. And it's non-negotiable.'

Eloise clasped her hands together. 'Anything.'

'You leave Theo to me. I'll take care of him.'

'But -'

'I mean it, Eloise. Seeing him - his body - will only upset you. Promise you'll let me deal with him?'

She nodded. 'OK, I promise. And thank you. You don't know how much this means to me.'

I waved her words away with a sweep of my hand. 'Run yourself a bath, then go to bed. Everything will look much brighter in the morning.' It was something my father used to say, although in my experience it was rarely the case.

'Where will you...?' Eloise began.

'I think it's best you don't know, don't you?'

She nodded again and was halfway across the room when she stopped, came back and pecked me on the cheek. Her lips felt cool and soft on my skin. 'Night night, Auntie Rose.'

I touched the cheek she'd kissed and smiled. 'Good-night, Eloise.'

Once she'd disappeared upstairs, I pulled on my coat and wellies, picked up the torch and her car keys and ventured outside. It was still raining, a fine drizzle that stuck my hair to my head and dribbled down my neck. I followed the beam of the torch to the small shed behind my father's allotment. A handful of straggly redcurrant bushes and a gnarly apple tree were all that remained of his once-pristine vegetable patch. As anything I ever planted inevitably shrivelled up and died, I'd let nature take its course. Within another couple of years, the entire area would vanish under a tangle of brambles.

I unlocked the shed door and ferreted around for the things I would need - gardening gloves, shears, secateurs, a shovel, a can of WD-40 and a length of rope - flinging them into the wheelbarrow that was propped up outside. Heading back into the shed, I swept piles of plastic plant pots off the metal trunk in the far corner, heaved the lid open and grabbed my father's air rifle and a tin of pellets. I loaded the gun and laid it carefully next to the shovel.

I pushed the wheelbarrow up the slope to the woods at the top of the garden. As I passed the sinkhole, I stopped and waved the torch over it. Water was already pooling at the bottom. The sight of it triggered a memory of Eloise's christening. A huddle of people standing around a font. The vicar, a thin man with a nasal twang. Juliet's parents, already well into their seventies, wearing proud smiles and their Sunday best. Juliet, regal in an elegant silk shift dress and matching jacket. My fellow godparent, a hapless man called Greg or Gavin or some such, who was knocked off his bike by a courier a week later and died instantly. And at the centre of things, a red-faced baby called Eloise, named not after the 12th-century French scholar and philosopher Héloïse, but after her mother's favourite song by The Damned.

'Will you pray for her, draw her by your example into the community of faith and walk with her in the way of Christ?' the vicar intoned.

I was a committed atheist, but I'd pushed my principles, such as they were, to one side, and murmured, 'With the help of God I will.'

'Will you care for her, and help her to take her place within the life and worship of Christ's Church?'

'With the help of God, I will.'

Empty promises before a God I didn't believe in. Yet, twenty-one years later, here I was, standing on the side of a sinkhole about to put my life on the line for that red-faced baby. I caught myself wondering how it would all end.

I pushed the wheelbarrow through the undergrowth, wincing as hazel branches whipped my face and hands, aiming for the ridge Eloise and I had followed earlier. But this time when I reached it, I turned deeper into the woods towards an old pillbox at the northernmost tip.

The squat, concrete building had been part of a network of defences thrown up in 1940 to defend Britain against the anticipated Nazi invasion. Never needed, it had slowly disappeared under a mass of brambles and bracken and when my parents bought the cottage as newlyweds in the late 1950s, they had no idea it was there. My father discovered it by chance when he was clearing a fallen tree some years later and had fitted a sturdy wooden door so he could use it as a log store until a small colony of pipistrelles made it their home. He built another log store nearer the house and left the pipistrelles in peace.

Years passed, and the pillbox was smothered by scrub once more. When I was about twelve, curious to see inside the little concrete building, I took a pair of shears to the undergrowth and cut a path to the narrow door. I slid back the bolts and pulled my hood firmly over my head as I stepped inside, worried the bats might dive-bomb me and entangle themselves in my hair. But they were asleep, tucked into tiny crevices, and had no interest in me. I retraced my steps, my nostrils filled with the faint scent of ammonia, bat droppings crumbling to dust beneath my wellies. My curiosity satisfied, I'd never been back.

Until now.

The pillbox was further from the house than I remembered, and I was wondering if I'd already passed it when the beam of my torch fell on a slab of rough concrete swathed in brambles. Balancing the torch on the wheelbarrow, I pulled on my gardening gloves, picked up the shears and began attacking the brambles as if my life depended on it. Twenty minutes later, sweat had joined the dribble of rain down the back of my neck, but the path to the pillbox was clear. I grabbed the torch and picked my way to the door.

It was no surprise that the two bolts had rusted stuck since my last visit almost forty years before. I gave them both a liberal spray of WD-40, hammered them open with the end of the shears and stepped inside and waved the torch around.

The pillbox was about ten feet square and just under six feet high. The tang of ammonia was still there. So were the bats, hanging like dried leaves from narrow cracks in the concrete. I checked the two window slits through which soldiers would have stuck their machine guns if the Germans had made it across the Channel. They were wide enough to stick an arm through but narrow enough to suit my purpose. Which was just as well, as the pillbox was my only option.

With one last glance around the compact space, I tossed the can of WD-40 into the wheelbarrow and headed back through the woods. As I neared the house, my heart rate quickened. I'd promised Eloise I'd take care of Theo.

And that's exactly what I intended to do.

CHAPTER NINE

When I'd felt the flicker of a pulse in Theo's neck, I thought I must have imagined it. He was supposed to be dead. Eloise had killed him. She was certain of it. Holding my breath, I'd increased the pressure. And there it was. Faint and slow, but steady. Almost indiscernible and yet utterly indisputable.

Theo had a pulse.

He was alive.

Eloise hadn't killed him, she'd only knocked him out. A single blow in self-defence. Surely there wasn't a court in the country that would ever send her to prison for that.

Relief made me giddy, and I'd gripped the side of the car for support.

Theo was alive.

Alive!

I was about to blurt the news to Eloise when the words died on my lips. Theo had attacked her twice and had been emotionally abusing her for months. She was terrified of him. His death had brought her peace. The end of a terrifying ordeal that had broken her spirit and almost cost her life.

He said he was going to kill me.

How could I break the news that the man who'd attacked her was still alive?

I couldn't do it.

Instead, I'd slammed the boot shut and promised her everything would be all right.

And it would be. Because it had to be. And it was up to me to make sure it was.

The house was in darkness, but I needed to be sure Eloise was asleep. I slipped inside, crept up the stairs and listened outside her door until I was satisfied I could hear her rhythmic breathing.

I hurried back outside, locking the door behind me, and jogged over to the wheelbarrow. I felt about in the darkness for the length of rope and my father's gun, banking on the fact that a city boy from Paris wouldn't know the difference between a shotgun and an air rifle. I blipped the key fob and as the boot clicked open, I turned on my torch and shone it inside.

When two panic-stricken eyes stared back at me, it took every ounce of my self-control not to recoil in shock. Instead, I played the torch along the length of Theo's body, from his face to his feet and back again. He was still lying on his side with his knees tucked into his chest and his head bent against the wheel arch.

I took a step closer and waved the rifle in his face.

'Get out,' I hissed.

'Where is Eloise?' he whispered in a heavy French accent.

I tutted under my breath. I was hardly going to tell him. 'Get out,' I said again, prodding him in the chest with the muzzle of the rifle.

He scrambled out of the boot, clutching his head. His eyes darted about.

'Is she here?' he said.

I ignored him.

'Who are you?'

I pointed the rifle at his right kneecap. 'Shut up or I'll shoot.'

His eyes widened, and he held up both hands in surrender. 'What do you want?'

'Walk,' I instructed, waving the rifle towards the woods. 'And don't try any funny business.'

'What?'

'You heard me. Start walking.'

'Are you mad? I do not even know who you are,' he said.

'You don't need to know. All you need to understand is that if you don't do what I tell you, I'm going to put a bullet in your leg. Now walk!'

Theo jumped when I shouted and began stumbling up the garden, his hands clasping his head. A trickle of dried blood stained the back of his neck like a claret-coloured birthmark. I followed him, the muzzle of the gun pressing into the small of his back.

He was still wearing his chef's whites over blue and white checked trousers. He was shorter than I imagined and had narrow shoulders and a lean frame. From the picture Eloise had painted, I'd expected him to be broad and brutish. But bullies came in all shapes and sizes.

We made our way slowly up the garden, passing so close to the sinkhole that it would have taken just one sharp shove for Theo to disappear down it. So easy to finish the job Eloise had started. I was going to have to fill in the bloody hole anyway. He might as well be in it. The world would be a better place without men like Theo.

But, tempting as it was, I couldn't quite bring myself to kill him. Not yet, anyway. I needed more time to decide what I was going to do with the man who had ruined my goddaughter's life.

'Turn right,' I instructed as we reached the trees.

'Where are you taking me?' he whimpered.

'Somewhere no one will find you.'

'But why? I don't understand. What have I done?'

'Stop talking,' I said, jabbing him with the rifle.

Yelping, he blundered into the trees.

When we reached the pillbox, Theo stopped in his tracks and looked around.

'What is this place?'

I nudged him with the rifle, but he was rooted to the spot.

'Move it!' I barked.

When he still didn't budge, I felt a flutter of fear in the pit of my belly. I'd had the upper hand so far because Theo's head injury had left him disorientated, but he was still much younger and stronger than me. If he turned on me here, in the middle of the woods, I didn't stand a chance.

My hands tightened on the gun as he turned towards me. If he attacked, I was ready. It took a moment to register the fear in his eyes and when I did, I tutted to myself. Like all bullies, he'd crumpled the minute someone stood up to him. He was the worst kind of coward.

'Get in,' I growled, waving the rifle towards the door of the pillbox. Theo shuffled through the door, defeated.

He was silent as I tied his wrists and ankles with the rope I'd brought. Then, I inspected the cut on the back of his head. It could have done with a couple of stitches, but at least it had stopped bleeding.

'Why am I here?' he asked so quietly I had to bend down to hear him.

'Why d'you think?'

'Whatever you want, you can have it. My family, they have money. They will pay for my release.'

He thinks he's been kidnapped, I realised. Which could only work to my advantage. He'd assume I had accomplices, which would make him more compliant. Much more likely to sit tight and wait while his family back in France stumped up the ransom money.

'We're making contact,' I confirmed. I gave him a gentle shove, and he sat down on the dusty floor with a thump. 'You'll stay here until we have our money. We'll have men guarding the door. They'll all be armed, so don't try to be a hero.'

He nodded, as if this made perfect sense. Wondering just how rich his parents were, I closed the door, slammed the two bolts into their keepers and set off for home.

It took eighteen barrow-loads of loamy soil, dug from my father's vegetable patch, to plug the sinkhole. I topped it off with some turf, carefully peeled from a small piece of lawn behind the oil tank. No doubt the soil would settle and leave a shallow depression in the ground, but that could be sorted in time.

For now, I would let Eloise continue to believe she'd killed Theo, and I'd buried his body. That way, she would feel safe.

The chances of someone stumbling upon him in the pillbox were remote - the woods were private property and the nearest footpath was a couple of miles away. And it wasn't as if anyone was going to come looking for him. Eloise was right. No one knew she or Theo were here. As long as everyone assumed he'd hightailed it back to France, we were in the clear. I knew I couldn't leave him in the pillbox forever, but I had plenty of time to figure out what I was going to do with him.

My back aching and my arms heavy, I clumped back to the house. I yearned to soak my weary bones in a bath, but when I felt the tank, it was stone cold. I had a quick flannel wash instead, scrubbing at my dirt-stained hands until every last speck of mud had disappeared down the plughole. As I crossed the landing to my bedroom, Eloise called my name.

'You're awake,' I said, sticking my head around the door.

'Is it done?'

I nodded. 'You don't need to worry about Theo ever again.'

She pressed her palms to her eyes, then lifted her head and gave me a watery smile. 'Thank you.'

'I'm glad I could help.'

'There is one more thing,' she said in a small voice.

'Name it.'

'Can I stay for a while? I don't have anywhere else to go.'

'What about work?'

'That's the thing about temping. I can phone the agency and tell them I'm not available for the next couple of weeks. That's if it's all right for me to stay that long?'

Suddenly my aching bones felt as light as air. 'Of course it is, darling girl,' I said. 'I can't think of anything I'd like more.'

CHAPTER TEN

It was still dark when I woke. I pulled on yesterday's clothes and tiptoed downstairs. In the kitchen, I filled an old plastic bottle with water, cut a corner of cheese from the block of cheddar in the fridge and fished out the remnants of a white sliced loaf from the bread bin. As an afterthought, I crept back upstairs and pulled a couple of blankets from the tallboy. Dinah watched with narrowed eyes as I threw the blankets, water, cheese and bread into a shopping bag and left the house.

Theo was lying on his side when I peered through one of the window slits of the pillbox twenty minutes later. I coughed, and he gave a start, his head jerking in my direction. I opened the door and threw the shopping bag on the floor.

'Food and water,' I said, nodding at the bag.

'How can I eat like this?' he croaked, glancing over his shoulder at his hands tied behind his back.

I'd turned to the internet the previous night for advice

on tying people up and had been left speechless at the search results. The lengths to which some couples went to spice up their love lives was astonishing. But I had found a couple of useful tips.

'Turn around,' I instructed Theo. I undid the rope, then retied it with his wrists in front of his chest. I then lashed the rope circling his wrists to the one around his ankles so he could eat and drink but couldn't get far.

'Merci,' he breathed, closing his eyes and rubbing his hands together. 'My parents, have you spoken to them?'

I gave a non-committal shrug. I was halfway to the door when he said, 'Eloise, did she put you up to this?'

I clenched my jaw. How dare he blame Eloise when she was the victim in all this? I was about to march back and give him a piece of my mind when I thought better of it. Instead, I stalked out of the pillbox and slammed the door shut with as much force as I could muster.

When I returned to the house, Eloise was at the kitchen table eating cornflakes.

'I found them in the cupboard,' she said, tapping the bowl with her spoon. 'Hope that's OK?'

'Of course it is.' I smiled, then touched her shoulder. 'Did you sleep?'

'Better than I thought I would.' She looked at me curiously. 'Do you always go for walks before breakfast?'

'Now and again.' I shrugged off my coat and hung it on the back of a chair. 'It clears my head. Listen, I was thinking. We need to get rid of your car. It's going to be covered in Theo's DNA.'

She swallowed a mouthful of cornflakes. 'Of course, but how?'

The internet had provided me with an answer to this, too. My plan was to drive the car to a remote spot, douse it with petrol, and set it alight. But even the most intense fire wouldn't destroy the chassis number, which meant that any self-respecting police officer could identify Eloise as the car's owner. She listened carefully as I explained this.

'That's OK. I'll say it was stolen from the car park at the country park where I go running.'

And just like that the plan was agreed. We'd destroy the car and, as far as Eloise was concerned, her nightmare was over.

My nightmare, on the other hand, had only just begun. I couldn't leave Theo tied up in the pillbox forever. At some point, I needed to decide what the hell I was going to do with him.

Usually I had an answer for everything. Not this time.

By six o'clock it was pitch black outside. I pulled on my coat and asked Eloise for her car keys.

She frowned. 'You can't use them.'

'Why ever not?'

'Because the car's supposed to have been stolen while I was out running,' she said. 'We'll have to hotwire it.'

It was my turn to frown. 'How on earth are we supposed to do that?'

Eloise shrugged. 'Google it?'

So, for the second time in twenty-four hours I found myself carrying out some dubious searches on the internet. After I'd played Eloise a couple of YouTube videos she jumped to her feet.

'Let's give it a go,' she said. 'It looks pretty straightforward with an old car like mine.'

I found flat-head and Phillips screwdrivers, a roll of insulating tape, some wire cutters, and a pair of my father's leather driving gloves. Eloise pulled on the gloves and took the tools.

'There's a can of petrol in the back of the Land Rover,' I said. 'I'll fetch it.'

She was waiting outside the back door when I returned a couple of minutes later with the petrol can and a box of matches.

'Ready for a bit of breaking and entering?' she said.

The thought was strangely exhilarating. That was the problem when you spent your life trying to be good. Every now and then, the urge to break the rules was too strong to resist.

I found myself thinking about Thelma and Louise as we tramped over to Eloise's car. The film had come out the summer Juliet graduated. I had another two years at university ahead of me, and that was before I'd even thought about the two-year post-graduate foundation course, let alone the minimum three years' specialist training after that. As Juliet started applying for jobs in London art galleries and looking for flats to rent in trendy-sounding places like Primrose Hill and Little Venice, I'd questioned my choice of career.

We saw the film at the local Odeon one sticky July night. As I'd sat in the darkened auditorium, Juliet's bare shoulder almost feverishly hot against mine, I'd felt as though we were watching ourselves. The parallels between Juliet and Geena Davis's ditzy, too trusting Thelma, were striking. And I felt an unmistakable kinship with Susan Sarandon's streetwise, tough talking Louise, whose love for her friend was such that she was prepared to kill to keep her safe from predatory men.

Overcome with emotion, I stopped, my hand on my chest.

'Are you OK?' Eloise asked in alarm.

'I was thinking about the time your mother and I went to see Thelma and Louise. It was one of her favourite films. Mine, too. We had a lot in common like that.'

'You still miss her, don't you?'

'I do.' I smiled into the night. 'Did she ever tell you we were planning our own road trip the summer she graduated? Only she met your father and, well, the plans changed.'

The fact she'd chosen to spend her final summer with a cocky lifeguard with an ego considerably larger than his intellect rather than me, her best friend, still stung thirty years later.

'You were around when they first met?' she asked, a little breathlessly. 'At the lido?'

In an instant, I was back at the pool, with the smell of chlorine in the air and the shouts and squeals of over-excited children as they splashed about while their mothers gossiped poolside. 'I was,' I said.

'Tell me about it.'

'I expect you already know your dad had a part-time job as a lifeguard while he was studying at uni?'

She nodded.

'I doubt their paths would have ever crossed if we hadn't spent all our spare time at the lido working on our tans. Well, to be factually correct, your mother worked on her tan and I worked on my freckles.'

Eloise didn't laugh. Instead, she gazed at me with a hunger in her eyes.

'All the girls had a bit of a thing for him,' I said, remembering. Danny Reeves was tall, blond and broad-shouldered. He wore tight swimming trunks and aviator glasses. Testosterone oozed out of every pore. The term alpha male might as well have been invented for him. Whistle in hand, he strode up and down the side of the pool with the swagger of a cockerel, bawling kids out for bombing or diving, not caring if he reduced them to tears.

'You, too?'

It took a minute for me to realise what Eloise was asking. I laughed. 'Oh no. Danny wasn't my type at all.'

'But he was Mum's type?' she pressed.

'He must have been.'

'Was it love at first sight?'

'I don't know about that.' Keen to change the subject, I handed Eloise the carrier bag. 'Shall I hold the torch while you do the honours?'

She nodded, pulled out the flat-head screwdriver,

rammed it into the ignition, and turned it clockwise. 'The guy on YouTube said this sometimes does the trick,' she said. And then, when nothing happened, added, 'But not today. Can you pass me the Phillips screwdriver please, Rose?'

Her face was the picture of concentration as she carefully removed the screws in the grey plastic panels on the top and bottom of the steering column.

'It's a good job it's an old heap,' she said, as she took the flat-head screwdriver and prised off the panels, exposing an array of wires underneath. 'The YouTube man said new cars are almost impossible to hotwire.'

She peered at the complicated jumble of red, brown and yellow wires. 'Wirecutters, please.'

I fished them out of the bag and handed them to her, like a theatre nurse handing a pair of dissecting forceps to a surgeon.

'Be careful,' I warned, a dart of anxiety quickening my heart rate.

'You worry too much,' she said, bending her head closer to the wires. I had no idea what she did next, but within seconds, the car's engine rumbled into life. She pressed the accelerator a couple of times, then jumped out.

'She's all yours,' she said with a little bow. 'Unless you want me to come with you?'

'No, go back to the house. I'll deal with this.' I climbed stiffly in, pressed my foot on the clutch and, once Eloise had set off towards the house, slipped the car into first gear. I eased my foot up, feeling for the bite point, because stalling wasn't an option.

I'd thought long and hard about the best place to set fire to the car. I needed somewhere remote where no one would see the flames yet close enough that I could walk home. I'd settled on a small area of coppiced sweet chestnut about a mile away. The woodland was part of a private country estate peppered with *Keep Out* signs to discourage dog walkers. It was a dank, foggy night, which suited my needs perfectly. And if, by morning, the fog cleared and someone spotted a plume of smoke curling up through the trees, they'd assume it was a woodsman's bonfire.

Tractor tyres had gouged deep furrows into the loamy soil. With only the car's sidelights to guide me, it was almost impossible to avoid them, and the car threw me violently from side to side as it lurched towards the clearing.

'This'll do,' I said to the empty car, yanking up the handbrake. I was about to reach for the keys in the ignition when I remembered there weren't any. Leaving the engine idling, I picked up the petrol can and matches from the passenger seat and let myself out.

I felt another flutter of nerves. Using an accelerant to start a fire wasn't just irresponsible, it was downright foolhardy. What if I spilled petrol on my clothes and set myself alight? Fire would race up my polyester trousers with the speed of an electrical current, and within seconds, I would be writhing on the ground in agony. No one would hear my screams, not out here. What if I just left the car without setting it alight? The police would assume joyriders had ditched it. A conscientious officer might have the steering wheel and doors swept for fingerprints, but I doubted it. The local PCSO was always lamenting how short-staffed they were. They'd certainly have no reason to scour the boot for forensic evidence.

But I'd promised Eloise I'd burn it, so burn it I would. It was worth the risk to make her feel safe. I doused the car liberally with petrol, but the first match fell from my fumbling fingers onto the ground before I could strike it. After a couple of strikes, the second match lit and I threw it towards the car, but it fizzled out mid-air. 'Third time lucky,' I muttered to myself, pulling another match from the box. I took a deep breath and, cupping the tiny flame in the palm of my hand, dropped it and sprinted out of the clearing, a whooshing sound ringing in my ears.

When I reached the trees, I stopped and turned back to inspect my handiwork. The windscreen and bonnet were already ablaze, and flames were curling towards the back of the car. As I caught my breath, there was a crack as loud as a gunshot and I clutched my chest in terror, fearing that any minute a gamekeeper would come crashing through the undergrowth towards me, a shotgun in his hand. But it was only the windscreen cracking in the heat.

Slowing my breathing, I watched the fire until I was satisfied the whole car was engulfed in flames. I turned for home, grateful for the cool air on my burning cheeks.

CHAPTER ELEVEN

SEPTEMBER 1988

My mother feigned a migraine the day I was due to leave for university, and that suited me just fine. I didn't want her negativity colouring the first day of the rest of my life. I couldn't bear the thought of her picking fault with my tiny room in halls, turning her nose up at my new flatmates and criticising my choice of university.

'You'd think she'd be proud that her only child was doing medicine,' I grumbled as my father drove at a steady sixty miles an hour along the motorway towards the campus.

'She is proud. She just finds it hard to show it sometimes,' he said, his voice mild.

'Sometimes?' I gave a bark of laughter. 'She has a heart of stone. In fact, I bet if you opened her up and looked inside, there would be a cavity where her heart should be,' I said, warming to my theme.

'She's a product of her upbringing,' my father said, glancing at me. 'We all are.'

'I hope not.' I shuddered. 'I'd rather die than end up like her.'

'Rose,' he said reprovingly. 'You don't mean that.'

I did, but I hated the world-weariness in his voice, so I changed the subject and, before I knew it, we were turning off the motorway and following signs for the university and my new life.

My father was helping me unpack my stuff when there was a knock on the door. Not a timid tap-tap, but a confident rat-a-tat-tat. A knock that meant business.

I dumped the armful of sweaters I'd pulled out of my suitcase, but before I was halfway across the room, the door burst open and a girl breezed in. Tall and slim, with a shaggy blonde perm, a faded denim jacket and thin gold hoop earrings, she looked as if she'd walked straight out of the pages of *Just Seventeen*.

'I'm Juliet,' she announced. 'I'm your next-door neighbour!'

'Rose,' I said with a shy smile.

Juliet glanced around the room. 'God, they're like prison cells, aren't they? I wanted a room with an en suite but I had to go through clearing because I didn't get my grades, so it was all rather last minute.'

She had the easy confidence and plummy accent that screamed public school. Old Rose would have felt intimidated, but New Rose wasn't about to be tethered by her hang-ups.

'Me too!' I said. My father's head jerked up. I shot him a pleading look and a flicker of understanding passed across his face. 'What are you reading?'

'History of Art,' Juliet said with a dismissive shrug. 'I couldn't think what else to do. What about you?'

'Medicine,' I said, unable to keep the pride out of my voice. 'It's the only thing I've ever wanted to do.'

'Wow, a brainbox,' Juliet said. 'I couldn't even pass my eleven plus. God knows how I've ended up here.' She tipped her head back and laughed. A golden locket shimmered in the dip between her clavicles. Her suprasternal notch. An ugly name for something so beautiful.

'Jules!' a woman called from the corridor. 'D'you want to show me where you want your posters?'

Juliet sighed. 'Coming,' she called. She paused in the doorway. 'D'you fancy coming over to mine once the parents have gone? I pinched a bottle of Blue Nun from home. We can celebrate the start of our university life.'

I smiled again. 'Thank you, Juliet,' I said, liking the way her name tripped off my tongue as if we'd known each other all our lives. 'That would be cool.'

'God, they've lumped us in with all the mingers and weirdos,' Juliet said, reaching for the wine bottle on her desk. There was a picture of a nun on the front of the dark blue bottle. Dressed in a royal blue habit and white wimple and carrying a basket of grapes, she reminded me of Julie Andrews in *The Sound of Music*.

'The eponymous nun,' I said, dipping my head towards the bottle as Juliet splashed wine into a glass and handed it to me.

'You've lost me,' she said, taking a slug from her own glass. Her hazel eyes, I noticed, were slightly glazed, and it occurred to me she had sampled some of the eponymous nun's wares before my arrival.

'Seriously though,' she said, jerking a thumb towards the far wall. 'The bloke next to me has long greasy hair and is wearing a Black Sabbath T-shirt and filthy jeans. And I mean *filthy*.' She pulled a face. 'The girl opposite doesn't speak a word of English, and the two on either side of her are complete saddos.'

I'd said hello to a couple of girls as I'd arranged tins of baked beans, spaghetti hoops and peaches into my allotted cupboard in the shared kitchen and they'd looked completely normal to me, but I pulled a face, too, and said, 'God, yes, I know exactly what you mean.'

She stuck out her bottom lip. 'My best friend went to Warwick. It's where I was going, too, until I screwed up my A-levels.' She took another long draught from her glass. 'And now I'm stuck here, less than an hour from home. My parents are threatening to visit every bloody weekend, can you believe it?'

I took a tentative sip of the Blue Nun. It was lukewarm and fruity. Hiding a grimace, I took another. Better. It was obviously an acquired taste. 'The whole point about going to university is to be independent. To cut the apron strings,' I said with fervour.

'Exactly!' She pointed at me with her glass. Wine sloshed against the sides. 'You get it, Rose. You totally get it. My parents are...' she paused, searching for the right word. 'They're *suffocating*.'

'I couldn't wait to leave home, either,' I said, my tongue already loosened by the wine. 'My mother's a grade A bitch. I wouldn't piss on her if she was on fire.'

Juliet frowned, then burst out laughing. 'You're so funny, Rose.' She clinked her glass against mine and smiled. 'Thank God I found you.'

Juliet took to university life like she was born to it. History of Art seemed to involve few lectures and lots of leafing through the kind of books posh people had weighing down their coffee tables and waffling about ancient paintings and sculptures.

I'd known that by choosing medicine I'd be working harder than most, but that first term, the sheer tsunami of work caught me unawares. My days were packed with lectures and tutorials. There were essays to write, practicals to prepare for and lecture notes to digest. I had to work late into the night to stand a chance of keeping on top of my studies. While Juliet partied till the small hours, I sat hunched over my desk, working until my hand cramped and my vision blurred.

I worked extra hard during the week because Saturdays were our day. We'd catch a bus into town and have bacon sandwiches and coffee in a cafe before hitting the shops. I never had any money, and I certainly didn't have time for a job, but Juliet's parents gave her a generous allowance and she enjoyed spending it. I found the fact that she asked me - me! - for sartorial advice both flattering and amusing. Luckily, she was one of those people who looked good in rags, otherwise she might have realised my skills as a personal shopper were sketchy at best.

We spent Saturday afternoons back at our halls, readying ourselves for a big night out, and before we hit the town, we always played a game of Scrabble while sinking a bottle of Lambrusco or cider or Bacardi or whatever the drink of the day happened to be.

This was my favourite time of the week, not because I invariably won at Scrabble, but because I had Juliet all to myself.

CHAPTER TWELVE

Funny, isn't it, how the simplest, most pedestrian of acts can become so significant, so symbolic? Like making a pot of tea for two. Filling the kettle, warming the teapot, allowing the teabags to infuse for exactly long enough. Reaching for a pair of mugs that clink together pleasingly. Pouring the tea, adding a dash of milk. A final stir. Actions as automatic as breathing. The last time I'd made a pot of tea for two, I had no idea that my father was already growing cold in his bed above me, after suffering a massive heart attack in his sleep.

After I'd kissed his forehead, straightened his sheets and called the doctor, I'd washed up the teapot and stowed it at the back of the cupboard. I had no use for it any more. Every single morning since, I'd thrown a teabag into a mug of milk and hot water and stirred it half-heartedly a couple of times before fishing it out with a teaspoon. Making tea was no longer a soothing ritual, a gesture of kindness, but a necessary task to provide a hit of caffeine to start my day.

But that morning, as I dug out the teapot and two mugs, a rush of emotion almost knocked me for six and I had to clutch the sink and take a few calming breaths.

From her bed by the radiator, Dinah watched me, the end of her rabbit-grey tail flicking scornfully.

'Rich coming from you,' I told her, reaching in the cupboard above the cooker for my vitamins. I gave the bottle a shake and made a mental note to pop into the health centre for a repeat prescription. 'You'd have welded yourself to her bed if I hadn't shut you in here last night.'

Dinah yawned, stretched and stalked over to the back door, disappearing through the cat flap with another dismissive swish of her tail. I was pouring milk into a jug when the pips sounded. I darted to the radio and turned up the volume.

'This is the eight o'clock news,' said the Radio Kent presenter. 'And these are the headlines: A Sevenoaks man has been given a life sentence after admitting the murder of his former partner. Police are appealing for witnesses after twenty manhole covers were stolen from a single Folkestone road. And birdwatchers are flocking to a Kent nature reserve following reports of a rare warbler in the area…'

I exhaled. There was no mention of a man being reported missing from his Rochester home. Eloise was right. Theo's work colleagues would assume he'd returned to France. There was nothing to worry about.

Reassured, I carried the tea upstairs and knocked on Eloise's door.

The springs of the put-you-up bed creaked, and the door opened. 'Tea. How thoughtful,' Eloise said, taking the tray.

'I wasn't sure how you liked it, so I brought the pot.' I drifted over to the window. The rain clouds had retreated, and the sky was the same washed-out blue as the forget-me-nots that self-seeded themselves in the garden every spring, pervasive little blighters. My gaze strayed to the woods, and I wondered if Theo had managed to sleep trussed up like a turkey on the dusty floor of the pillbox. At what point would he realise there was no one outside guarding the door? And when he did, would he have the strength to kick it down and escape? What then?

'Rose, did you hear me?' Eloise said, dragging me back to the room.

'Sorry, I really must book a hearing test. What did you say?'

'I was asking what you're doing today.'

'I have an interview I can't miss.'

'For a job?'

I nodded. 'The charity where I volunteer is looking for a new chief executive.'

'The suicidal charity?'

I bit back a smile. It was exactly the kind of thing Juliet would have said. 'Yes, Sisterline. I'm sure I don't stand a chance, but the chair of trustees told me I ought to apply, so…'

'You totally should. I bet it's yours for the taking.'

'You're very kind, but we'll see. You should come with me and have a wander around town. There are lots of nice coffee shops.'

'Thanks, but I think I'll stay here, if that's all right?' She ran a hand over her forehead. 'I'm still feeling a bit under the weather.'

My thoughts flitted back to Theo. What if he forced his way out of the pillbox and came looking for Eloise? No, I mustn't catastrophise. Everything would be fine.

'Of course. I'm sure Dinah will keep you company. Oh, you're reading *Alice in Wonderland,*' I said, spying my childhood copy open on the chest of drawers.

'I remembered you said I should, so when I couldn't sleep last night, I went downstairs and found it. I hope that's OK?'

'It goes without saying. Though I'll find you a bookmark, so the spine doesn't get broken. I'll be back by twelve. What do you fancy for lunch?'

'Mum always made me chicken soup when I was feeling poorly.'

I smiled. 'Chicken soup it is.'

I'd been lying when I told Eloise I didn't stand a chance of getting the chief executive's job at Sisterline. I was pretty sure I was a shoo-in.

It was almost thirteen years since I'd stumbled across an article in the local paper appealing for volunteers for a fledging support line specifically for women.

Sisterline was the pet project of a flamboyant woman called Edwina Armstrong, a provocatively misogynist-hating *Guardian* columnist who moved to Faversham from her Blackheath home in her late fifties, seeking a slower pace of life. When her youngest and favourite sister jumped from the Clifton Suspension Bridge after an acrimonious divorce, Edwina - or Eddie, as she preferred to be known - handed in her notice at *The Guardian* and formed the charity.

'If I can stop one woman with suicidal thoughts and feelings from taking that final, irreversible step, then I will have achieved my goal,' she'd been quoted as saying, and I didn't mind admitting it had touched a nerve.

I'd joined the first cohort of volunteers answering Eddie's call for help. She'd been looking for open minded, empathetic, supportive, discreet, accepting and honest people and I'd been confident I was all of those things and more. But when I started taking calls, I discovered that although discretion and honesty came easily, some of the other qualities were another matter.

I had to bite my tongue when a nineteen-year-old with two children and an online bingo habit called in to lament her lack of funds because she'd gambled away her benefits. Refraining from passing comment when women phoned to say their husbands had thrown them out after discovering an affair was almost impossible. And the urge to tell the sad cases who hadn't befallen any drama or tragedy but were still "struggling to cope" to get a grip was overwhelming.

So I had a quiet word with Eddie and asked if my skills

would be put to better use looking after the charity's admin, finances and fundraising, and she'd bitten my hand off. No one wanted a backroom job. They all craved the glory that came with talking a caller down from her literal or metaphorical cliff.

For over twelve years, I'd virtually run the organisation single-handedly, so when the well-meaning but ineffective chief executive took early retirement, the job had my name on it.

I was so focussed on the upcoming interview that I only gave a cursory glance left and right as I turned onto the A2. The long blast of a horn from behind took me by surprise. I checked my rear-view mirror. A dazzlingly white Subaru SUV was inches from my back bumper and the driver - male, overweight - was gesticulating madly at me, both hands off the steering wheel.

Lifting my chin, I looked him square in the eye and mouthed, 'Irresponsible'. In response, he slammed a hand on the horn a second time, causing an elderly woman walking her Dachshund to stop and stare.

I drove sedately through the residential streets towards the car park in the centre of town with SUV Man still tail-gating me. I tapped the brakes as I neared the zebra crossing just before the railway bridge, keen to send him a message that his bullying behaviour would not intimidate me. I was so busy staring into the rear-view mirror to see his reaction that I didn't see the old man on his mobility scooter until his front tyres were on the crossing. I stepped on the brakes just in time, glad I'd only been crawling along. The old boy touched his cap in thanks as he trundled past. Behind me, SUV Man's face contorted, and he waved his fist at me.

I waited a few seconds before I thrust the Land Rover's gearstick into first and set off again. When I reached the car park, the Subaru was still sitting on my bumper and I was wondering if I'd been a little foolhardy. It was apparent the man had anger management issues. What if he was a complete psycho with a knife in his glove compartment?

I found a space and turned off the ignition. The Subaru pulled up behind me. Playing for time, I ferreted around in my bag for an old lipstick, flipped down the sun visor and pretended to apply it while watching the man jump from the driver's seat, slam the door shut and march towards me.

CHAPTER THIRTEEN

SEPTEMBER 1990

Saturdays were our day until Juliet met that charmless fucker Danny Reeves a week into the first term of our third year. After that, Saturdays mainly involved me hanging around like a fifth wheel while they shamelessly mauled each other.

For the life of me, I couldn't see what she saw in him. Juliet was a product of her middle-class upbringing and her prestigious public school. Indulged by her parents, she'd led a charmed life. She was beautiful, confident, articulate, self-assured. Danny was a working-class hero from a Hackney tower block. He was loud and brash. His swagger barely concealed the deep-rooted chippiness beneath his muscle-bound shoulders. Julia joked he was her bit of rough, but couldn't she see she deserved so much better? He was so obviously a player he might as well have had the word tattooed on his forehead.

The one time I'd tried to warn her against him, she'd narrowed her eyes and said, 'Anyone would think you were jealous. Are you jealous, Rose?'

I was, of course. But not in the way she thought. And so, I watched and waited, hoping her obsession with him was a phase, that she'd tire of him eventually, and when she did, I would be ready to pick up the pieces.

Danny was a third-year sports science student who had a part-time job as a lifeguard at the local lido, although he spent more time eyeing up the local talent and topping up his tan than he ever spent saving lives. They'd been seeing each other for a couple of months when Juliet spotted a flyer for the student union's Christmas piss-up. By then Juliet and I were sharing a house on the outskirts of town with three girls from her History of Art course. She burst into my tiny room overlooking the handkerchief-sized back garden and waved the flyer in my face.

'Look, a Snow Ball!' she said, as excited as a five-year-old on Christmas morning. 'With snow machines and a Santa's grotto.'

I took the flyer and raised an eyebrow. 'And a reindeer rodeo and free Santa hats. Wow.'

'I've bought four tickets,' she said.

'Four?'

'Danny has a mate…'

I groaned. 'Not another blind date. I've told you, I'm not interested.'

'No, really, Johnno's lovely. Very studious. And he has

a wicked sense of humour. You two are going to get on like a house on fire.'

'Johnno?' I rolled my eyes. The name conjured a beer-swilling rugger bugger, not someone with whom I might have a half-decent conversation.

'Johnno,' Juliet repeated. 'You can borrow my green dress. It really suits you. And I'll do your hair and makeup if you like. *Please,* Rose.'

'You've got Danny. Why are you so desperate for me to come?'

'So I have someone to talk to if he gets a better offer.' Seeing the look on my face, she held up a hand. 'I'm joking, obviously.' Her gaze flickered to the door. 'Danny wants you and Johnno to hit it off, so you'll spend less time hanging around with us.'

Her words were like arrows to my heart. 'You don't want me around?'

'That's not what I said. But it would be nice to spend time as a couple, yes. And I keep telling you it's about time you had some fun. So, will you come?' She clasped her hands under her chin as if she was praying.

It was a rhetorical question because we both knew I could never say no to Juliet.

'All right then,' I muttered ungraciously. 'I'll come.'

The student union's Snow Ball was as tawdry as I'd feared. The bouncers wore Santa suits and scantily clad girls dressed as Christmas elves shimmied up and down the queue handing out cheap felt Santa hats. Inside, the so-called snow machine pumped out foam while the DJ, a silicone-enhanced "celebrity" from a local radio station, pumped out dance music. The air was dense with cigarette smoke and the floor was slick with spilt beer.

We'd arranged to meet Danny and Johnno inside and, spying them by the bar, Juliet grabbed my arm and dragged me over. The man standing next to Danny was unremarkable looking with light brown hair, heavy glasses and girlishly narrow shoulders. As we approached, Danny gave him a nudge, spilling the pint he was holding down his striped shirt. He swept away the beer ineffectually, then held out a hand.

'You must be Rose,' he hollered over the music. 'I'm John. Nice to meet you.'

I let him buy me a Jack Daniels and Coke and followed the three of them to a booth with an uninterrupted view of the stage. My mouth twitched with disapproval as Danny picked up a reserved sign on the table and flung it into a corner. He really was insufferable. I sat primly, my knees together and my drink clasped in my lap, while John shouted in my ear.

'Danny says you're a medic. I'm doing computer science. Bit of a nerd, I'm afraid.' His girlish shoulders rose and fell in a self-conscious shrug.

'How do you know Danny?' I yelled back.

'I lived next to him in halls.' He gave the glimmer of a smile. 'He only ever calls when he wants something.'

'Why doesn't that surprise me?'

We watched Danny give Juliet's knee a squeeze, then

weave through the clubbers to the female DJ. He leaned towards her, cupped a hand to her ear, and whispered something. In response, she threw her head back in laughter, her bare throat exposed. Next to me, Juliet stiffened.

'He doesn't mean any harm,' John bellowed.

'That's what the British Establishment used to say about the Third Reich, and look what happened there,' I countered.

He laughed. 'Touché.'

'So, let me guess what Danny wanted this time,' I said. 'He wanted you to get off with me, so I back off and give him and Juliet a bit of space.'

He took a sip of his beer and regarded me. 'You're pretty direct, aren't you, Rose?'

'What's the point pussyfooting about? But his plan won't work, you know. I'm not interested. Never will be, I'm afraid. It's nothing personal.'

He frowned, then his eyes widened in understanding. 'Doesn't mean we can't still enjoy ourselves,' he said eventually, tipping his pint towards me.

I smiled properly for the first time that evening as I clinked glasses with him. 'D'you know what? You're right.'

'More booze?' he asked, glancing at Juliet, who was watching Danny flirt with the DJ with a look of miserable resignation on her face. 'To numb the pain?'

I drained my glass and handed it to him. 'Why the hell not?'

When alcohol enters the bloodstream, it can reach the brain in five minutes, stimulating the release of dopamine and serotonin, the so-called feel-good hormones. Inhibitions fall away and the drinker feels happy and confident. Blood vessels widen, leading to flushed skin and a feeling of warmth. Everything has a rosy glow.

That's how I felt after four more Jack Daniels. I was the life and soul of the party, pulling Juliet and John onto the dance floor. For a straight man, John was a surprisingly good dancer, whereas Juliet, who usually loved to dance, was as wooden as a marionette, her eyes continually roving for Danny, who'd disappeared muttering something about scoring some Es and hadn't been seen since. The celebrity DJ had also sloped off, leaving a spotty youth manning the decks.

Good, I thought fuzzily as I bopped around like a ball bearing in a pinball machine. Perhaps Juliet would realise Danny was a grade A shit, and she was better off without him.

'Why is Danny such an arsehole?' I shouted to John. But he only smiled and nodded and went in search of more drinks.

An hour and another three Jack Daniels later, I had lost one shoe and both my dancing partners. I made my way unsteadily to the bar, ordered a bottle of wine and two glasses and stumbled over to our seats. Juliet was alone, and I sat heavily beside her.

'Blue Nun,' I said, thrusting the bottle into her hands. 'For old times' sake.'

'That's very sweet, but I'm going to head home.'

'But it's only eleven!'

'I'm really tired.'

'Tired my arse. You dragged me here even though I didn't want to come. The least you can do is stay.'

'But I can't find Danny. What if something's happened to him?'

I stared at her. 'Like what?'

'I don't know, like he's taken a dodgy E or something. It's not like him to just disappear.'

'How can you say that?' I said belligerently. 'You've only known him five minutes. You don't know what he's like.'

Her fingers worried at the delicate gold chain around her neck, and I found myself softening. I reached out and took her hand in mine. 'Don't worry. He's a big boy. He can look after himself.'

She was silent for a moment, then sighed. 'You're right.'

'So, will you have a glass of Blue Nun with me?'

'Go on then,' she said. 'Just the one.'

One became two, and two became three, and before long we were on our second bottle, both as drunk as skunks.

'Did you know that alcohol causes your blood vessels to widen when it enters your bloodstream?' I asked Juliet. Her pupils were pinpricks as she struggled to focus on my face. 'Then it depresses your central nervous system, messing with your brain's communication pathways. That's what makes you slur and fall over.'

'I haven't fallen over,' she said indignantly.

'Not yet,' I said, refilling her glass. 'Alcohol suppresses the hormone vasopressin, which means the kidneys release more water, making you pee more.'

'Speaking of which,' she said, struggling to her feet. She held out a hand. 'Coming, Doctor Rose?'

We stumbled around the edge of the dance floor arm in arm, heading for the loos. I stared at my face in the mirror above the sink. It was like looking into the face of a stranger. A stranger with dishevelled red hair, flushed skin and glittering eyes framed by the charcoal-black eyeshadow Juliet had applied before we'd left our digs.

'Looking hot, chick,' she said, blowing me a kiss before she cannoned into a cubicle. As she peed, I ran my fingers through my tangles, sniffed an armpit and blew into my palm to check my breath.

'Shit,' Juliet said in a muffled voice. 'Do you have a tampon?'

'In my bag,' I said. 'I'll get it. Won't be a sec.'

I pushed my way back through the scrum to our table and grabbed my bag. As I turned to go, I felt a heavy hand on my shoulder, and I spun around.

'Rose,' John said, peering myopically at me. 'I have drunk enough to sink a battleship, and I'm going home. It was nice to meet you.'

'Do you know where Danny is?' I asked.

He opened his mouth, then closed it again.

'John,' I repeated. 'Where's Danny?'

He tugged on an earlobe as his gaze slid to the spotty youth on the decks. 'He's, er, otherwise engaged.'

'Otherwise engaged with who?'

He shook his head. 'No one.'

'John!' I said sternly. 'Just bloody tell me. Who is Danny otherwise engaged with?'

He sighed. 'The DJ. Not that one,' he said hurriedly as I glanced at the stage. 'The blonde one. I went outside for a fag and saw them getting into a taxi. They were all over each other.'

'What about Juliet?' I cried, outraged.

He grabbed my shoulder again. 'You're not going to tell her?'

'Of course I am,' I said, shaking my head. 'She has a right to know.'

Sobering up, I pushed him away and ran towards the toilets. 'It's me,' I said, pushing the door open. I held a tampon under the cubicle door.

'Thanks,' Juliet said, snatching it up. Moments later, the door swung inwards and she lurched over to the sink. Her face had turned white with a greenish tinge. 'I feel like shit,' she said. Her eyes widened, and she clamped her hand over her mouth.

'Are you going to puke?'

She nodded, and I steered her back into the cubicle and held her hair while she decorated the toilet bowl with the contents of her stomach.

'Urghh,' she groaned, retching and coughing. 'That bloody eponymous nun.'

Touched beyond words that she remembered, I stroked her back until the coughing stopped and she sat back on her haunches.

'Come and wash your face. It'll make you feel better.' I

ran the tap, and she bent over the sink and gargled before splashing her face with cold water. I handed her a stick of chewing gum.

'Thank you,' she said in a small voice.

I rubbed her arm. It bristled with goosebumps. 'Shall we go home?' I said.

'But what about Danny?'

'He's left already.'

She gripped the edge of the sink. 'How d'you know?'

'John told me.'

'John's wrong. He wouldn't have gone without me.'

I wavered for a moment, then reached a decision. I would derive no pleasure from telling her, but she had to know. 'He went home with that blonde DJ. John saw them leaving in a taxi together.'

She reared away from me. 'You're lying!'

'I'm not, I promise. Ask the kid she left on stage if you don't believe me.'

'All right, I will.' She pushed past me to the door and I scurried after her, watching from the edge of the dance floor as she climbed onto the stage and tapped the spotty-faced kid on the shoulder. He lifted a headphone and listened, then nodded and pointed towards the doors. I didn't need to be able to lipread to know what he'd told her because the slump in her shoulders said it all. I went to our seats, gathered our bags and coats, and met her at the bottom of the steps to the stage.

'Come on,' I said, holding out her coat. 'Let's get you home.'

Back at our student digs, I made us both a mug of cocoa and shepherded Juliet into the tiny front room. I lit the gas fire and joined her on the sofa. We sat in silence for a while, sipping our drinks in the half-darkness, then Juliet sighed.

'I'm done with men. They're all bastards.'

I felt a flutter deep in my belly. 'You've just been unlucky.'

'The thing is, I really thought Danny was The One.'

'Danny?' I couldn't keep the surprise out of my voice.

'I know you've never liked him, but there was this chemistry between us.' She gave a self-conscious laugh. 'I know it's a cliché, but it felt right, you know? That we were meant to be together. That we fitted, two halves of a pair. How wrong can you be?' She placed her mug on the floor, rested her head on my shoulder and stared into the fire.

I shifted my weight towards her and tucked my legs under me. 'Don't be too hard on yourself. Agreed, he's a prick. But there are decent blokes out there.' I thought for a bit. 'John seemed nice.'

'I told you, I'm not interested.'

I'd longed to hear those words since the day Juliet walked into my room in halls looking like a *Just Seventeen* model. Holding my breath, I picked up her hand and began tracing circles on the inside of her wrist with my index finger, round and round.

'Mm, that's nice,' she said sleepily, her head heavy on

my shoulder. 'You were right about him,' she added. 'You're always right, Rosie. What would I do without you?'

Pleasure flooded my body and I bent my head until my lips brushed her hair. Something told me it was now or never.

'Juliet?' I murmured.

'Mmm?'

I stroked her cheek then turned her chin towards mine and kissed her lightly on the lips. They were soft, yielding. My heart banging in my chest, I closed my eyes and kissed her again. But something was wrong. She was shaking her head, pulling back, pushing me away. For a second our eyes locked, and I saw a flare of revulsion, then she turned away.

'I thought you...' I began, my voice barely above a whisper.

'No, Rose. God, no. No! Whatever made you think I would...?' She jumped to her feet and crossed the room, as if she couldn't bear to be near me.

'You said you were done with men. I thought you meant... I thought there was a chance of you and me... of us,' I finished lamely.

'No,' she said, still shaking her head as she half-ran out of the room. 'Never.'

I knew it was futile to go after her. So, I crumpled to the ground, tears coursing down my cheeks as I realised with equal measures of shame and sorrow that I'd ruined everything.

CHAPTER FOURTEEN

The hairs on the back of my neck prickled and something my mother used to say came back to me.

'You think you're clever, Rose, but remember, no one likes a smart-arse. One day it'll be your downfall, you mark my words.'

'Silly old bat,' I muttered as I pretended to busy myself putting the top back on the lipstick, taking my keys out of the ignition and gathering my bag. I sneaked another look in the mirror. There was no sign of SUV Man and I tipped my head back and closed my eyes for a moment, relief washing over me. He was probably half-way to the nearest pub or betting shop already. He looked the type.

But as I reached for the door handle, I gasped as a face peered through the window. SUV Man was so close I could see the veins in his temples bulging and flecks of spittle at the corners of his mouth. He banged the window with his fist and yelled, 'Oi, I want a word with you!'

Reluctantly, I wound down the window. 'Yes?' I said.

'What do you think you're playing at, you stupid cow?'

'I'm sorry, I don't understand what you mean.'

'Cutting me up on the A2 then driving like a fucking pensioner all the way through town to wind me up.'

'Haven't you seen the signs? It's twenty miles an hour now.'

He rested a hand on the sill and leaned in until his face was so close, I could smell his breath. Coffee with a trace of stale alcohol. I shrank back in the seat and fought the urge to gag.

'And braking,' he hissed. 'Trying to teach me a lesson, were you, you silly bitch?' He balled his hand into a fist and stared at it, then scowled at me. 'I want an apology.'

I chose my words carefully. 'I'm sorry if you feel my driving wasn't up to scratch,' I said primly. 'Now if you don't mind, I have an appointment and I'm running late, so if you'll excuse me...' I looked pointedly at the door.

His nostrils flared. 'That's not a fucking apology, that's a...'

'Hello, Rose, everything all right?' said a cheery voice, and SUV Man stepped back, his fist unclenching and his expression shifting from hostile to inoffensive so quickly I wondered if I'd imagined his outburst. Dorothy, Sisterline's chair of trustees, was clambering out of her car a handful of spaces away.

'Not really -' I began, but SUV Man cut across me.

'I thought one of the lady's tyres was flat,' he said. 'I was advising her to get the pressure checked. That one,' he said, aiming a kick at the Land Rover's offside rear wheel. The entire vehicle shook. He lumbered back to his car without a backward glance.

'Goodness am I glad to see you,' I said to Dorothy under my breath. 'He wasn't concerned about my tyres at all, he was giving me an earful because I was sticking to the speed limit. What a nasty piece of work.'

'And there I was, worrying I was going to be late for your interview. Looks like I was in the right place at the right time after all.'

As we walked towards the parking machine, she said, 'I can't help thinking I've seen him before.'

'SUV Man?'

'Yes.' She shook her head as if trying to dislodge a memory, then frowned. 'Getting old is not to be recommended, Rose. Ah, well, I'm sure it'll come to me.'

Tickets bought, we returned to our cars. The Subaru had disappeared from the space behind mine, but I couldn't escape the feeling I was being watched. I scanned the car park, my gaze finally falling on its dazzlingly white bonnet squeezed between a van and a Ford Galaxy. Even from this distance, I could see a bulky mass in the driver's seat. SUV Man, watching me.

Sisterline was based in an anonymous-looking red-bricked building a two-minute walk from the car park. Even though there was nothing outside the building to give even a hint of what went on inside, the fact it was home to a women's phone line was common knowledge in the town and now and then we'd arrive for work to find the remains of an egg oozing down the brickwork, or the planters either side of the door kicked over, their contents spilling onto the tarmac. Whether these acts of vandalism were the work of disgruntled callers, aggrieved relatives or random miscreants, we never knew.

Eddie brushed aside my apologies for being late and ushered me and Dorothy into her office.

'Lovely,' she said, as one of the volunteers bustled in and set a tray on the coffee table. 'Shall I be mother?' While she busied herself with milk and sugar, I tried to put both Theo and the man in the SUV out of my mind and focus on the interview ahead. Finally, Eddie took a seat beside Dorothy.

'I'm sure this is merely a formality, but we have to be seen to be following due process, especially as you're not the only person from within the organisation to apply for the role,' she said.

'Oh, I'd assumed I was the only internal candidate.'

She smiled but wouldn't be drawn. 'Tell me, Rose, why are you applying for this post?'

As I described my vision for the future, I felt myself relax. Sisterline was good at what it did, but it was a small charity with limited resources and sometimes women's calls went unanswered. Eddie's lack of ambition had always frustrated me. If I was steering the ship, I'd put far more emphasis on income generation. I'd want Sisterline to be as well known as the Samaritans.

'According to your CV, you've volunteered for many charities over the years. Why be the chief executive of

Sisterline when there are so many other good causes out there?' Eddie asked.

I stared at my hands, which were clasped in my lap. 'I once lost a very dear friend because she thought her life was no longer worth living.' I held Eddie's gaze. 'I'm convinced that if she'd picked up the phone and called me, I could have persuaded her that her life was very precious indeed.'

'Yet you prefer working in the office to manning the phones?'

I shrugged. 'I know my strengths.'

'And there's nothing wrong with that,' Eddie said, looking at her notes. 'One of the responsibilities of the chief executive is to handle complaints. If you were made aware that someone had complained on social media about the service they received from us, how would you handle it?'

Occasionally callers or their families claimed we'd failed to respond appropriately to a call or text, and they tended to voice their dissatisfaction on social media before raising it with us. But such was the way of the world. Eddie was currently dealing with someone who'd posted a series of cryptic but inflammatory tweets claiming we had blood on our hands and tagging everyone from the local MP to the police.

'I would reply to the post saying we were sorry to hear she'd had a negative experience and ask her to fill in a complaints questionnaire,' I said. 'Once we'd received that, I would speak to the volunteer involved to check their version of events. If necessary, I would make a formal apology on Sisterline's behalf, and if any learning was required, I would make sure that was in place, so it didn't happen again.'

Eddie nodded.

'I see from your CV that you trained for three years at medical school, but you left before finishing. Why is that?' Dorothy asked.

'My mother suffered a stroke at the end of my third year. I went home to look after her.'

My selflessness was met with sympathetic smiles from both women. My mother had suffered a stroke, true, but it wasn't the real reason I quit med school. But giving up my dreams of becoming a doctor to care for my poor, afflicted mother suited my narrative. I was Rose Barton, doer of good deeds and all-round thoroughly decent person. The kind who sacrificed her life for others without batting an eyelid.

An image of Theo's huddled form forced its way into my mind, but I pushed it away and arranged my features into a suitably self-effacing smile. 'It was an honour to care for her,' I said.

Dorothy pulled a handkerchief from her sleeve and dabbed an eye. Eddie jotted something in her notepad, and I fidgeted in my seat, hoping they hadn't noticed the dull flush creeping up my neck.

CHAPTER FIFTEEN

Eddie shook my hand firmly at the end of the interview, assessing me over her half-moon glasses. 'Thank you, Rose. You'll be hearing from us shortly. We have a couple of interviews left to do, so for obvious reasons I can't make you a concrete offer at this stage, but let's just say the interview went very well from our perspective.'

My heart beat a little faster, and I realised just how much I wanted the job. 'Thank you. I'd stay and tackle the invoices, but my goddaughter is staying with me at the moment.'

'How lovely,' Dorothy gushed. 'Are you very close?'

I thought about it for a second. 'We are,' I said with a smile.

As I made my way back to the car park, I went over the interview in my mind, examining my answers, wondering where I could have made improvements. But Eddie was right. It had gone well. I'd put across my plans for the charity without criticising the current management's lack of ambition. I'd given it my best shot. Now all I could do was wait.

There was no sign of the white Subaru in the car park and I walked over to the reassuringly solid bulk of the Land Rover with a happy heart. The interview had been a success and, for the first time in more years than I could remember, I had someone to tell when I got home. Because a snarky cat who tolerated me because I fed her didn't count. I found my keys at the bottom of my handbag, opened the driver's door, and jumped in.

The Land Rover started first time, an unusual occurrence that added to my feeling of serendipity, and I slid the gearstick into first, released the handbrake and set off for home. But as soon as I inched out of the parking space, I could tell something was wrong. The steering wheel juddered in my grip, and behind me, a loud clunking noise set my teeth on edge. Leaving the ignition running, I climbed out and inspected the source of the noise. The offside rear wheel, the wheel SUV Man had aimed his kick at, was flat as a pancake.

'You've got to be kidding me,' I muttered, crouching down to take a closer look. Deep gashes crisscrossed the rubber like a crazed game of noughts and crosses. I ran my fingers over them, shocked I'd stirred such rage.

Eloise listened in disbelief as I described my encounter with the Subaru driver.

'You're lucky he didn't attack you,' she said, shaking her head.

I stared at her. 'You think he might have?'

She shrugged. 'You read about arseholes like him all the time. Just as well you stopped in a busy car park. If it had happened on a quiet country road…' She paused, then frowned. 'He didn't follow you home, did he?'

'I don't think so.' Truth was, my mind had been on other things after an hour-long wait for the AA man who then informed me helpfully that my spare tyre was also "buggered".

'Is that the technical term?' had been my tart reply, but he'd just laughed and offered to tow me home.

'I was in the cab with the recovery man. But I'm sure I would have seen him if he had.'

'Hm. But you ought to be careful, Rose. People like that hold a grudge.'

I could feel my earlier buoyancy sinking like a badly made raft on a team building away day, and a familiar weight settled on my chest, squeezing the air from my lungs. I pulled out a chair from the kitchen table and sat down heavily.

'Are you all right?' Eloise asked.

'I'm just feeling a little faint. I don't suppose you could pass me a glass of water and my vitamins? They're in the cupboard above the cooker.'

'Of course.' Eloise picked up a glass from the draining board, filled it, and reached into the cupboard. 'Multivitamins for the over 50s,' she read from the brightly coloured label. 'Vitamin D, calcium, Vitamin B12 and Omega-3.

You know, you don't need to take these if you're eating properly.'

'You're probably right,' I said, reaching out a hand for the bottle. I undid the childproof cap with trembling fingers, tipped one of the little orange pills into my palm, and knocked it back with a slug of water. 'That's better.'

'I'll heat the soup,' Eloise said. 'Would you like a cheese and pickle sandwich with it?'

'That would be lovely, thank you, darling.' The endearment slipped out before I could filter it, and I watched carefully for a reaction, but if Eloise noticed she obviously didn't mind because she started humming to herself as she pulled a loaf from the bread bin and reached in the fridge for the butter. Seeing her cut thick slices of cheddar reminded me I hadn't given Theo anything to eat all day. Reluctantly, I pulled myself to my feet.

'Can you wrap a bit of clingfilm over mine? And don't worry about the soup. I just remembered I need to feed Mary's fish.'

'Mary?'

'The old dear who lives up the lane. She's gone to stay with her sister for a few days. I promised I'd feed her precious coy while she's away.' I grabbed my coat. 'Won't be long.'

Checking Eloise wasn't watching, I picked up the carrier bag from the passenger seat of the Land Rover and the bucket from the footwell and made my way down the drive and along the lane for a couple of hundred yards before turning into the woods. As I drew closer to the pillbox, my heart rate quickened. What if Theo had kicked the door down and escaped? What if he was hiding in the woods, watching and waiting for the right moment to pounce? I paused every few minutes to listen for a tell-tale crackle of a twig or rustle of a branch, but the only sound I could hear was the thump-thump-thump of my own racing heart.

My anxiety eased when I reached the pillbox, and the door was still bolted shut. I set the bucket down, slid the bolts across, and ducked through the doorway.

Theo was still curled up in the far corner, his eyes closed and his body so still that for a moment my stomach swooped in fear at the thought he might be dead. But then I saw the gentle rise and fall of his chest and my panic subsided.

He must have sensed my presence because he looked blearily in my direction. His eyes widened a fraction when he saw me, and he jolted to a sitting position.

'Who are you?' he said in alarm.

'You don't remember?'

He looked around, his gaze taking in the thick concrete walls and the dusty floor, the meagre light from the two window slits and the open door behind me. He licked his lips as his gaze returned to me. His pupils were huge.

'What is this place?' he croaked. 'Why am I here?'

It was possible he was still punch drunk from the blow to the head, but he could also be bluffing. I pulled a bottle of water from the carrier bag and offered it to him. He took it and stared at it as if he'd never seen one before.

'Let me,' I said, taking it back and unscrewing the lid. I held the bottle to his lips, and he drank deeply.

'Thank you,' he said eventually, wiping his chin on his shoulder.

'There's food in the bag. And I've brought you a bucket,' I added.

His eyes clouded in confusion. 'A bucket?'

'For you to… In case you need to… Well, it's there if you need it.' I stood and dusted off my trousers.

'Where are you going?' he cried.

'We're still trying to contact your parents.'

'My parents?' He shook his head as if he was trying to clear the fog inside it, then groaned. 'I cannot remember anything.'

My patience was waning.

'You don't need to remember anything. Just stay put and do as you're told. There are men outside watching. I'll be back tomorrow.'

'Please, madam…' he began, but the four walls of the pillbox were closing in on me and I needed to get out. I closed and bolted the door, pushing all thoughts of Theo from my head as I tramped back through the woods to the house.

'How were the fish?' Eloise asked, handing me my sandwich.

I pulled off the clingfilm and bit into the bread, even though my appetite had deserted me.

'Mm, lovely,' I said, smiling my thanks. 'Not very communicative, but otherwise fine.'

'And you have to feed them every day?'

I nodded. 'Until Mary's back.'

'How long's that?'

Until I decide what the hell I'm going to do with Theo. 'A few days,' I said vaguely. 'Shall I light the fire?'

We sat in companionable silence, Eloise's head buried in *Alice in Wonderland,* me with *The Times* crossword on my lap. When the black and white squares drifted out of focus, I set the paper and my reading glasses on the coffee table and, my head cocooned in a warm fuzz, drifted off to sleep until a knock at the front door woke me with a start.

CHAPTER SIXTEEN

In the blink of an eye I was transported back to the night Eloise turned up on the doorstep, bloody and desperate, the body of her lover in the boot of her car. I glanced around the room, but she wasn't there. The copy of *Alice in Wonderland* was on the side table beside her empty chair, a leather bookmark just visible three-quarters of the way through the book. Perhaps she'd tired of reading and gone out for some fresh air while I dozed. I hoped to hell she hadn't ventured anywhere near the pillbox.

There was another knock, and as I hurried along the hall, I was filled with an irrational fear that I would find Theo standing on the doorstep, his fingers wrapped around the handle of a hunting knife and his eyes as black as pebbles.

'Who is it?' I called in a shaky voice.

'PCSO Steve Sutton, Kent Police,' a deep voice boomed.

My fear escalated. What if someone had chanced upon the pillbox and found Theo tied up inside? What if his confusion had all been an act, and he'd managed to escape and raise the alarm? Had I bolted the door properly? I cast my mind back but, to my horror, I couldn't actually remember sliding the bolts home. I gripped the newel post and sucked air into my lungs.

Then the rational side of my brain took over. If the police had received a report of a kidnapping, they'd have turned up in force. They certainly wouldn't have sent a solitary police community support officer who didn't have the power to make an arrest. Exhaling slowly, I pasted a smile on my face and opened the door.

I recognised the hirsute man flashing an identity card in my face. I'd seen him and his impressive beard from a distance at various village events over the years. Last year he'd dressed as Long John Silver for the school's summer fete and bravely spent an afternoon with his head in the stocks while feral village children threw wet sponges at him.

'Mrs Barton, isn't it?' He smiled. 'There's nothing to worry about. I'm just carrying out some inquiries into a car found burnt out in the woods off Badger's Hill Lane.'

Relief flooded through me, and I widened my eyes. 'That's just down the road. Any idea who it belongs to?'

'We're not sure yet, the registration plates have burnt to a crisp. Looks like an old Audi.' He pulled a notebook and pen out of his top pocket. 'I don't suppose you heard or saw anything suspicious?'

'Last night?'

He nodded. 'No one saw the car on fire, but a couple of horse riders spotted what was left of it just after eleven this morning.'

I tutted. 'It's lucky the whole wood didn't go up in smoke.'

'Absolutely. I don't like this kind of thing happening on my patch.'

'I'm afraid I'm not going to be much help. I didn't see or hear anything.'

'Ah, well, it was worth a try. Does Mrs George still live up the road?'

'Mary?' I glanced over my shoulder to check Eloise hadn't appeared, then nodded. 'She does, but you won't get anything out of her. She's as deaf as a post.'

He flipped his notebook shut and was putting it in his pocket when I had a thought. I would never be the prime suspect for setting a stolen car on fire. As I'd reached my fiftieth birthday, I'd realised with a jolt that middle-aged women were so invisible to the rest of society we could get away with virtually anything. That being said, a little smoke and mirrors wouldn't hurt.

'I did see something you might be interested in, but it was the night before last.'

The PCSO's eyebrows shot up. 'Oh yes?'

'I sometimes like to take an evening stroll. Just to help me sleep, you know. Anyway, I was walking past the pumping station at the bottom of Kettle Hill Road when I saw two boys in a car.'

'Boys? You mean children?'

'Sorry, youths,' I said. 'When you're my age, everything is relative, Steve. Can I call you Steve?'

He nodded.

'Well, Steve, these youths were in a small red car. Maybe a Fiesta or a Corsa? They looked like trouble. You know the type. Hoodies and tracksuit bottoms.' I tutted again. 'Is it just me, or do the youth of today seem totally incapable of buying a decent pair of slacks?'

'They were out of the car?'

Too late, I realised my mistake. I didn't want PCSO Sutton to know that the two boys had been about to break into Eloise's car.

'One of them was relieving himself against a tree,' I improvised. 'With total disregard to anyone else, I might add.' I replayed the encounter in my mind. 'He shouted something to the driver. Called him Jaden.'

'Jaden,' PCSO Sutton said, jotting the name in his notebook. 'He shouldn't be too hard to track down. Thank you, Mrs Barton. You've been very helpful.'

'It's Miss Barton,' I said. 'But I'm glad I could be of assistance. And if that's all, I have something on the hob I should attend to.'

I had barely closed the front door when Eloise appeared at the bottom of the stairs. She was playing with a length of her hair, twisting it round and round her finger.

'Who was that?' she said.

'Just the local PCSO.'

'What did he want?'

'He was asking about your car.'

A flicker of fear crossed her features and she folded her arms across her chest.

'It's all right,' I soothed. 'We knew someone would come across it sooner or later. No one saw the actual fire.'

She frowned. 'You said he asked about my car. How does he know it's mine?'

'Sorry, I meant he was asking about *the* car. They haven't identified it yet. He was asking if I saw anything suspicious last night.'

Eloise's arms dropped to her sides, and she walked slowly along the hallway towards me, her fingertips trailing along the wall. 'What did you tell him?'

'That I hadn't seen anything, of course.' I smiled. 'You don't need to worry, Eloise. I've taken care of everything. You can forget all about Theo.'

Her pale face tightened. 'Don't say that bastard's name!'

I blinked. 'I'm sorry, I…'

She shook her head and held out a hand. The sight of her nails, bitten to the quick, made me want to gather her in my arms and never let her go.

'No, I'm sorry,' she muttered. 'It's just that I see his face every time I close my eyes.' Her voice broke and a single tear trickled down her cheek. 'I hear his voice when it's quiet, telling me I'm a useless fucking bitch. He haunts my dreams, and he invades my every waking thought.' She brushed the tear away with the back of her hand. 'I can't bear to hear his name.'

'Then we won't mention him ever again.'

She nodded, apparently satisfied. A grief counsellor

would have advised Eloise to talk about her ordeal, because sweeping everything under the carpet was like papering over a damp wall. The mould always found its way to the surface in the end. But I was happy to go along with her plea. Not just for her well-being, but because it suited me, too.

Eloise seemed strangely shaken after her outburst, so I suggested a quiet evening in with a bottle of wine and the Scrabble board.

'It sounds perfect, but you'll have to teach me. I've never played it before.'

'Everyone's played Scrabble,' I said, askance.

'In your world, maybe,' she said, sweeping a hand around the room. 'Not mine. My foster families just watched the telly, and at the children's home it was *Call of Duty* on the X-Box or nothing.'

'Well, I shall consider it one of my duties as a godparent to teach you,' I said, setting out the board and giving the letters a good shake inside their dark green bag.

Eloise listened intently as I outlined the rules and grinned when she picked her seven letters.

'You are so going to take a beating,' she said.

'We'll see.' I rearranged my letters a few times, wondering if it was possible to make a word with six vowels and a K. 'Your mum and I used to play Scrabble when we were in halls together. Things got quite competitive at times.'

'Tell me about her,' Eloise said, a look of longing on her face. 'I want to know what she smelt like, how she sounded. Do I have her eyes? Her hair? Her mannerisms? What did she want from her life? A husband and family or a high-flying career? Was she really as beautiful as I remember? Was she loved?'

A hard mass was forming at the back of my throat as Eloise spoke, the words tumbling out of her like water from a fountain. I swallowed the mass down and forced myself to smile. 'So many questions! Perhaps I'd better start with the last.' I closed my eyes, picturing Juliet's face. Those leonine eyes. Her flawless skin. 'Yes, Eloise. She was loved.'

CHAPTER SEVENTEEN

'What can I say about your mum?' I said, raising an eyebrow as Eloise spelled out "monster" for an impressive twenty-four points. 'I know it's a cliché, but she was the kind of person who lit up a room the minute she walked into it. She was the girl everyone wanted to be friends with.'

Eloise took seven more letters out of the bag, her eyes never leaving my face.

'It was 1988, the year fashion forgot, but somehow your mum even made a shaggy perm look cool. I have some photos somewhere, if you'd like to see them?'

Her eyes shone. 'I'd love to.'

'I'll see if I can find them. But no peeking at my hand while I'm gone.'

She grinned and held her hand in a Girl Guide salute. 'Promise.'

I found the box of photos in the drawer under my bed where I'd stuffed it the day we buried Juliet. Over the years there had been times when her face threatened to fade from my memory, and I'd been tempted to retrieve the box, dive in and spend a couple of hours wallowing in self-pity. But I never had. What was the point? It wouldn't bring her back. Nothing would.

Before I retraced my steps downstairs, I opened the box and picked up the top photograph. I needed to know that I could control my emotions. It wouldn't be fair to fall to pieces in front of Eloise. I may have lost my best friend, but she'd lost her mother.

In the photo, Juliet and I were standing side by side at the bar in the student union. I was wearing the emerald-green cotton top I'd bought in Snob and had taken time with my makeup and hair. Juliet was slightly blurry, as if she'd moved the moment the photo was being taken. But it gave the impression she was ethereal. Other-worldly.

Looking at our younger selves with the clinical impartiality that can only come with a thirty-year interval, I could see that Juliet was beautiful. But she had the anodyne girl-band good looks that were universal and, dare I say it, a bit vanilla. Whereas I, with my serious green eyes and red hair that framed my face like a hoop of fire, had been unconventionally pretty. If only I'd known it then. Instead, I'd spent my late teens and early twenties thinking I was a carrot-topped freak.

I touched Juliet's face with the tip of my index finger, like a child might dip a toe into the sea, then closed my eyes and waited for waves of desolation to wash over me anew.

Standing at Juliet's graveside, grief had paralysed me.

For one mad second, I almost threw myself on top of her coffin, because being buried alive with her seemed preferable to living without her.

But life moved on. Although I felt a certain wistfulness, the anguish had faded. And as I gazed at Juliet's face, so similar to her daughter's they could almost be sisters, another emotion bubbled to the surface. Gratitude that Juliet had sent Eloise to me and I had someone to love again.

As I waved goodbye to Eloise and drove into Faversham on Tuesday morning for a four-hour shift at Sisterline, I felt a lightness in my heart that I hadn't felt for years. A heady cocktail of contentment, joy, and positivity that made me almost giddy. Spending time with her had been a revelation. The more I got to know my goddaughter, the more fascinating I found her, from her passionate views on global warming – "If we don't start respecting the planet like, *now*, we're all fucked" - to her binary opinions on politics – "All politicians are essentially corruptible because politics attracts the power-crazy and those who seek power can always be bought". Having spent much of my life with people who sat on the fence, terrified to express an opinion on anything in case they were labelled sexist, or ageist, or racist, or fatist, or whatever else-ist, I found her arbitrary views strangely refreshing.

The occasional twinge of guilt I felt when I thought of Theo locked in his concrete prison vanished as I watched

Eloise sparkle. Freed from his controlling grip, she was gregarious and funny. It was as if someone had flipped the switch on a printer, turning it from grey-scale to full colour. Her hazel eyes sparkled, and her laughter filled the house. She was charming company and for the first time in years, I'd felt complete. Happy. *Alive.*

The previous evening, replete after a bowl of spaghetti bolognese cooked by Eloise and fortified by half a bottle of cabernet sauvignon, I'd walked into the kitchen, reached in the cupboard for my vitamins, and chucked the entire bottle in the bin.

'What are you doing?' Eloise had asked in alarm.

'I don't need them any more,' I'd said. 'You were right. I'm getting everything I need.' And I had Eloise to thank.

Traffic was light, and I was soon pulling into the car park, relieved to see there wasn't a single sports utility vehicle in sight. I locked the Land Rover, hooked my bag over my shoulder and walked the short distance to the office. A couple of volunteers were already in their booths, their headsets in place, the murmur of their voices as soft and reassuring as the babble of a brook. I headed for the small kitchen, making the T sign as I passed the booths, then poked my head around Eddie's door. Her head was buried in her hands. I coughed discreetly, and she gave a start.

'I was going to ask if you'd like a coffee, but you look as though you could use something stronger,' I said.

'What? Oh, no, just dealing with a tricky customer.'

'Caller or relative?'

'Relative.' Eddie grimaced. 'He's threatening to go to the Charity Commission.'

'But he's supposed to complain directly to us first, isn't he?'

She sighed. 'He already has. And he's not happy with our response.'

'Which was?'

She beckoned me to come in and close the door. 'That we were truly sorry to hear about his daughter's death, but that all calls to us are confidential and we aren't at liberty to discuss her case.'

'Sounds pretty standard.'

'It is. But now the coroner's waded in and asked us to give evidence at the girl's inquest.'

I raised an eyebrow. 'Can they do that?'

'They can. And of course I'll comply. I don't actually have a choice. But I'm worried about the message it'll send to the women who use our service.'

I nodded in understanding. 'They'll think our promise to respect their privacy and maintain confidentiality at all times isn't worth the paper it's written on.'

'Exactly.' Eddie sat back in her chair. 'The irony is that we have nothing of consequence to tell them, anyway.'

'What do you mean?'

'Although his daughter called us the day she died, we classed the call as low risk.'

'Ah,' I said. If someone was low risk, we didn't consider them to pose a risk to life. 'But she was?' I asked. 'At risk, I mean?'

Eddie rubbed her face. 'Put it like this: she drove to

Graveney, parked her car by the level crossing, walked onto the tracks and straight into the path of an oncoming train. Died instantly.'

'Well, you would.' I shook my head, my heart going out not just to the girl, who at least had a choice, but to the train driver, who didn't. 'I don't remember reading about it.'

'It was back in the summer, but the phone enquiries have only just come back, apparently. According to the police, the last two calls made from her phone were to her father and Sisterline.'

'And it's easier for her father to blame us than himself,' I said. 'Who took the call to us?'

Eddie's face closed off.

'Sorry, I shouldn't have asked. None of my beeswax.'

She picked up a fountain pen, unscrewed the lid, inspected the nib, and screwed the lid back on again. 'No, you're all right. It'll be coming your way soon enough. It was Rhona. Rhona took the call.'

Rhona Richards began volunteering at Sisterline a week before I joined and, having *so* much more experience, considered herself to be my superior in every way. She was a small, dumpy woman in her late fifties, with skin like bread dough and beady currant eyes. Slouchy, too, like a filled sack of potatoes. Despite her size, she had an uncanny knack of sidling into a room and listening in to a private conversation unnoticed, especially if she thought it might be about her. Which it often was, because she was about as popular as a fart in a lift.

'Rose?' Eddie said.

'Sorry, I was miles away.'

'You won't say anything about the matter we've been discussing?'

I smiled. 'Of course not. And if there's anything I can do…'

'I'll let you know.'

I picked up Eddie's cup and made my way to the kitchen. I was halfway through the tea run when the significance of what Eddie had said hit me. *It'll be coming your way soon enough.* Did that mean the job was mine?

CHAPTER EIGHTEEN

APRIL 1991

Danny crawled back with his tail between his legs in the first week of the new term. Apparently, he'd "seen the error of his ways" and had realised Juliet "was the love of his life". My suspicions that his change of heart had more to do with the fact that the radio DJ had dumped him were confirmed when I bumped into John in the library a couple of days later.

'She kicked him out when her ex turned up on the doorstep with a bunch of roses and an engagement ring,' John said.

'Serves him right.' I gathered my books and shoved them into my bag. 'Someone should tell Juliet.'

'No, they shouldn't.'

I started to protest, but John shook his head.

'She won't thank you for it. You know what they say about shooting the messenger.'

'I'd want to know if I was in her shoes.'

'But you're not, are you?' He stared at the library ceiling, then back at me. 'Leave them be. It'll soon fizzle out, anyway. Danny has the attention span of a toddler. He'll move onto someone else and you'll have Juliet all to yourself again before you know it.'

I fixed him with a look, then said grudgingly, 'You're surprisingly emotionally mature for a computer nerd.'

He doffed an imaginary cap at me and shuffled off.

For once in my life, I did what I was told, because I knew John was right. If I told Juliet Danny was a waste of space, she'd think I was jealous. And things were already strained between us. She'd been decidedly chilly with me the morning after the Snow Ball, and whenever I'd called over the Christmas break, her parents had informed me politely but firmly that she couldn't come to the phone.

So, I watched from the sidelines as Danny smarmed his way back into her heart, waiting to pick up the pieces when things inevitably imploded.

I also had other things on my mind. My grades had been gradually slipping, and I'd been called in a couple of times by my tutor to discuss why. I couldn't bring myself to admit I was way out of my depth, and that while my fellow medics breezed through topics, I was struggling to take even the simplest principles on board and, as a result, my confidence was at an all-time low.

Lying was easier, so I told her my parents were going

through a messy divorce and if she allowed me extra time to finish my backlog of essays, I would catch up. Even as I said it, I knew I never would. Because I was in over my head. All I was doing was prolonging the agony.

I would've loved to have confided in Juliet about my grades, but with her obsession with Danny growing by the day, she barely acknowledged my existence. She stayed at his digs most nights, only coming home if he was out with his mates. When she was home, she avoided me. But I pretended everything was fine, because if I didn't, I knew I would fall to pieces.

On the first day of the summer term, I was home alone when there was a knock at the door. Glancing through the spy hole, I was surprised to see Danny lounging on the doorstep, a four pack of cider under his arm.

I opened the door and regarded him coolly. He gave me a disarming smile.

'Is Jules in?'

'No.' I went to close the door, but he stuck a foot in the way.

'When will she be back?'

'I don't know, I'm not her social secretary.'

'Can I come in and wait?'

I thought for a moment. Entertaining Juliet's meathead boyfriend until she came back from wherever she was held zero appeal. But currying favour with Danny might help thaw some of her frostiness towards me. It had to be worth a try.

'All right,' I said, stepping aside as he swaggered past me to the front room.

'Want one?' he said, holding up the cans.

'It's a bit early for me.' I looked pointedly at the seventies sunburst wall clock over the gas fireplace. It was half-eleven in the morning.

'Suit yourself,' he muttered, tugging on the ring pull and taking a deep slug. He wiped his mouth with the back of his hand, then sneezed. 'Where is she, anyway?'

'She didn't mention where she was going. The library, perhaps?'

'What, Jules?' He laughed. 'Doubt it. She's a babe, but she's no Stephen Hawking, is she? Easy on the eye, but not much up here,' he added, tapping his temple.

Indignation surged through me, but I bit back a retort. Instead, I cleared my throat and said, 'Did you have a nice Easter break?'

He took another slurp of cider. 'Ibiza was so cool, man. Jules was right. It's the fuckin' dog's bollocks.'

I couldn't stop myself. 'You and Juliet went to Ibiza for Easter?'

His gaze slid across to me and he smirked. 'You didn't know?'

'I only got back last night. We haven't caught up yet.'

'Yeah, right.'

I bristled. 'What's that supposed to mean?'

He sneezed again, spraying a fine mist of mucus across the room. 'You need to take a hint, Rose. Jules doesn't want you hanging around like a sad fuck. She's moved on.' He rubbed his eyes, then looked at me suspiciously. 'Is there a cat in here?'

'A cat? Why?'

'I'm allergic to them.'

'No cats here, but I have one at home.' Smokey had spent the previous evening on my lap as I'd flicked through *The Oxford Handbook of Clinical Medicine,* one eye on *The Darling Buds of May*. 'He's moulting at the moment.' I smiled sweetly at Danny. 'Badly.'

His answering groan turned into a cough. 'D'you have any antihistamines?'

I shook my head. 'Sorry.'

'Thought you were a bleedin' doctor?'

'I'm a third-year medical student. I won't be qualified for at least another three years,' I said primly, before sighing. 'I'll have a look in the bathroom cabinet to see if anyone else has any.'

I took my time in the bathroom, having a pee and washing and drying my hands before studying my reflection in the mirrored bathroom cabinet. I arranged my features into an imitation of Danny's cocky sneer. 'You need to take a hint, Rose,' I mimicked. 'Well, you can fuck right off, Danny Boy. You're the sad fuck, not me. And, anyway, people aren't allergic to cat hair. They're allergic to a protein called... oh, I can't remember what it's called, and anyway, it's irrelevant. They're allergic to a protein in cats' saliva and dander, so there. And if you don't know what dander is, look it up, you thick git,' I added, sticking my tongue out at my reflection.

I opened the cabinet and rifled through the contents. Tampax, aspirin, a bottle of after-sun lotion, a half-empty box of plasters and some out-of-date mouthwash, but no antihistamines. 'Bad luck, loser,' I said, closing the door and heading slowly back downstairs.

Danny was perched on the edge of the sofa, coughing. His face was pale yet beads of sweat gathered in his frown-lines. His breathing was fast and when he exhaled, he made a high-pitched whistling noise.

Well, well, this was a turn up for the books.

I dusted off my jeans and sat on the coffee table in front of him, imagining the miniscule flakes of Smokey's dried skin inflaming the tiny breathing tubes that carried air in and out of his lungs.

'I didn't know you had asthma,' I said.

'Had it since I was little,' he wheezed.

'Where's your inhaler?'

He coughed. 'Left it at home.'

'That was silly.' I thought for a bit, trying to remember something I'd read in my second year. 'Did you know three people die from asthma every day in the UK?'

'Come... on, Rose, don't be a... bitch,' he puffed. 'Help me, please?'

I narrowed my eyes. Why should I help him, the cocky prick? If it wasn't for him, everything would still be fine between me and Juliet. He had driven a wedge between us, caused a breach I wasn't sure our friendship would survive.

'Rose -' he begged, clutching his chest.

I went to stand, and he lunged at me, his eyes full of fear. He was gasping now, each breath a struggle. I pushed him and he slumped back on the sofa. My mind was whirring, running through the possibilities. What if he died? Juliet would blame me for not helping him. But if I saved his life, I would be a hero. She would love me again, if only as a friend. And that would be enough.

Reaching a decision, I stood in front of Danny with my hands on my hips.

'Sit upright,' I told him.

His eyes widened, and I tutted. 'I'm trying to help you, moron. Sit up straight, it'll make breathing easier.'

He did as he was told. Aware my jeans were covered in cat hair, I pulled them off and threw them into the hallway. Dressed in just my T-shirt and pants, I sat opposite him again.

'Take long, deep breaths,' I told him. 'Watch me.' I demonstrated, breathing in, then out again as slowly as I could. 'Try to stay calm. Panicking will only make it worse. I'm going to make you a coffee, OK?' His eyes widened again. 'The caffeine will help,' I said.

While I was in the kitchen, I heated pans of water on the gas hob, and when the kettle had boiled and I'd made Danny's coffee, I balanced a plate on the switch, so the water kept boiling. As the room filled with steam, I went to find him.

'Come in here,' I said, pulling him up from the sofa. 'It'll help clear your airways.'

He sat at the kitchen table nursing his coffee as the steam worked its magic, and before long, his breathing eased, and he stopped wheezing.

He was quiet for a while, then took my hand and said quietly, all trace of cockiness gone, 'Thank you, Rose. Thank you.'

I was about to reply when the door to the kitchen burst open, and Juliet appeared. She looked from me to Danny and back again, her mouth dropping open as she registered our clasped hands and my lack of trousers.

'What *the fuck* is going on?' she screeched.

CHAPTER NINETEEN

When I'd finished the tea round, I spent a couple of hours attacking a mountain of admin, paying and filing invoices, filling in a funding application and replying to a couple of emails from prospective volunteers. Then, curiosity got the better of me and I googled "fatal train death Faversham".

A couple of stories popped up from two local news websites, and I clicked on the first.

Tributes have been paid to a Teynham woman who was struck by a train at a level crossing near Faversham.

India Matthews died instantly when she was hit by the Ramsgate to Faversham train close to the level crossing in Graveney shortly before 10am on Friday, July 30. A post mortem examination revealed she died of multiple injuries.

Her family has described the 21-year-old, who worked as a carer in a nursing home in Sittingbourne, as a much-loved daughter and sister. In a statement they said: 'India was a caring, loving and beautiful woman who always put others before herself, and her death has left a massive hole in our lives.

'India had a cheeky sense of humour and always had a smile on her face. She lived life to the full and had so much to live for. The world is an emptier place without her in it.'

British Transport Police are not treating India's death as suspicious. A spokesman said: 'Following a report of a person being struck by a train at the level crossing in Monkshill Road, officers attended along with local emergency services. Unfortunately, a woman in her early 20s was pronounced dead at the scene.

'Officers investigating the death are appealing for anyone who saw the woman or her car - a green Nissan

> Micra – at the level crossing on Friday to come forward.'
>
> An inquest into India's death has been opened and adjourned.

Accompanying the article was the obligatory photo of a pile of cellophane-wrapped floral tributes at the scene, plus a handful of pictures of India, pilfered, no doubt, from her social media accounts. On a beach; in a bar with a bottle of beer in her hand; wearing a royal blue football top sporting the Gillingham Football Club logo. She was a plain girl with a high forehead and straight, shoulder-length brown hair. But her smile was wide, and her walnut brown eyes were kind and even though I hadn't met her and never would, I rued the loss of this slightly overweight, friendly faced girl who'd spent her days ministering to geriatrics. What could drive someone like her to walk into the path of an oncoming train, knowing there could be no other outcome than instant death?

Shaking my head, I clicked onto the second story. The headline read: `Train victim India Matthews was on phone when killed.`

> Officers investigating the death of Teynham woman India Matthews have revealed she was on her phone when she was hit by a train on a level crossing near Faversham.
>
> The news comes amid calls for safety measures at the crossing to

be improved following India's death in July.

Villagers in Graveney are urging Network Rail to carry out a full assessment of the crossing 'before any more lives are lost'.

Friends and family of 21-year-old India held a candlelit vigil at the level crossing on Friday to mark the three-month anniversary of her death.

In a comment on her Facebook page, her father Roy said, 'There's no words to describe how I feel. You broke my heart the day you left us. You were, you are, my everything. Sleep tight, baby girl.'

The inquest into India's death will be held at Archbishop's Palace, Maidstone, on Tuesday, November 23.

My eyes widened. Eddie had said the last two calls made from the dead girl's phone were to her father and Sisterline. She hadn't told me India had been on the phone when she'd died. Perhaps she didn't know. My thoughts whirled. Who had India Matthews been talking to when the Ramsgate to Faversham train bore down on her? Her father… or Rhona?

Eddie needed to see this. I hit print, pushed my chair back and jumped to my feet with the vigour of someone half my age. I was crossing the office on my way to the printer when Rhona appeared, flapping an A4 sheet in my face.

'Is this yours?' she demanded.

'Depends what it is,' I said. I put my reading glasses on and peered at the sheet. 'Train victim India Matthews was on phone when killed,' I read under my breath, then said, 'Yes, that's mine. Thanks so much for popping it over.' I went to take it, but Rhona snatched it back.

'Why have you printed this out?'

'It's just some background information for a campaign I'm putting together,' I said.

'What campaign? Eddie didn't mention anything.'

'Eddie doesn't have to run everything past you.'

Rhona smiled knowingly as she handed me the print-out. 'Not yet, she doesn't,' she said.

I replayed Rhona's words as I popped into the super-market after work. It was obvious she was the other in-house candidate for the chief executive role and she clearly thought the job was hers. Well, she was wrong on that score. Eddie had already intimated it was as good as mine. I imagined the look of shock on her doughy little face when Eddie told her I was her new boss. I grinned as I selected a bottle of shiraz for dinner. I'd been waiting years for Rhona to get her comeuppance and it seemed the time had finally come.

In fact, life would be pretty much perfect if it wasn't

for Theo, I thought, as I dropped a packet of Cornish pasties into the basket. Three days had now passed since Eloise had unwittingly saddled me with him. Three days I'd kept him locked up because I had no idea what to do with him. But I couldn't bury my head in the sand forever.

I scanned the shopping at the self-checkout on autopilot, plans forming in my mind. The way I saw it, I had two options: let him go or let him die.

I couldn't let him go. He'd be on the phone to the police the second he was free. I would be arrested for kidnap and, likely as not, jailed. And Eloise would never be safe again.

But I couldn't let him die, either. The very idea that I, Rose Barton, soon-to-be chief executive of a respected women's charity and thoroughly decent person, could be responsible for someone's death was out of the question. More than that: it was reprehensible.

Especially after the last time.

'Are you all right there, love?' said a voice, making me jump. I glanced up to see a woman in a green Morrisons fleece looking at me with concern. 'Only that one's been playing up all morning.'

'Oh, no, it's fine. I was just thinking about what to have for dinner,' I said. I waved the pasties over the till until it beeped, tapped my card on the reader and wandered out to the car, a bag of shopping in each hand.

Before long, I was pulling into the lay by, no closer to reaching a decision. Something else my father used to say came to me. 'When you don't know what to do, do nothing, and the answer will come to you.'

It was as good a plan as any.

Theo was sitting where I'd left him and if it hadn't been for the scrape marks in the dusty ground underneath each of the two window slits, I'd have assumed he hadn't moved at all. But he seemed more alert than before, and his pupils looked almost normal.

'Cornish pasties and water,' I said, dropping the carrier bag at his feet. 'Supermarket own brand, I'm afraid, but needs must.'

He made no move to pick the bag up, just gazed at me with an expression I found hard to read. I reached for the bag I'd brought him the previous day, surprised to see he'd eaten less than half of the bread and cheese and had only drunk a quarter of the bottle of water.

'I suppose you'd have preferred brie, a baguette and a bottle of Beaujolais?' I said sarcastically.

He frowned, then shook his head. 'No, you are wrong. I was making it last. I did not know when you would bring me more food.'

I felt an uncomfortable sensation in the pit of my stomach. 'I'm not planning to starve you,' I said.

'Then what are you planning to do with me?'

I didn't answer because I still didn't know.

'Why are you keeping me here?' he pressed.

Stick to the script. 'I told you. We're waiting to make contact with your family. Once we have the ransom money, we'll let you go.'

'But who are you?'

'You don't need to know.'

'Where is Eloise?'

Ignoring him, I picked up the bucket and, holding it at arm's length, carried it outside and emptied it in the bushes.

'I do not believe you,' Theo said when I returned. 'You have not kidnapped me for money. I listened all night and heard nothing but the hoot of an owl. You were lying. There are no guards at the door. There is you, and somewhere there is Eloise, pulling your strings.'

'You're wrong, we -'

'Don't deny it. I know her. She is playing one of her games. Punishing me for something she thinks I have done wrong.'

'I'm not listening to any more of your nonsense,' I said, marching out of the pillbox and bolting the door. I coughed, then said loudly, 'Oi, you two bozos. Make sure he doesn't give you any lip, you hear me?' I lowered my voice to a rasp and channelled the man in the white Subaru. 'Awright, boss. See yer later.'

I was no Kate Winslet, but if my deception put even a shred of doubt in Theo's mind, it was worth it.

'I'll bring more food tomorrow,' I called to him through the door.

Probably.

CHAPTER TWENTY

I smelt the lilies before I saw them. An intoxicatingly sweet smell that hit my nostrils the moment I pushed open the back door. A smell that was at once both honeyed and cloying. A smell so synonymous with funerals that I shuddered. Puzzled, I scanned the room, soon locating the source: a vast bouquet of deep pink stargazer lilies on the worktop by the sink. They were perfectly arranged in a glass vase I hadn't seen for years. Spying a corner of pink tissue paper and cellophane poking out of the bin, I dumped the shopping on the kitchen table and pulled it out, looking for a card. Not finding one, I called through to the front room.

'Eloise?'

She appeared moments later with Dinah cradled in her arms.

I dipped my head towards the lilies. 'Thanks so much for the flowers. They're beautiful. But you shouldn't have.'

Her forehead puckered. 'I didn't. They were on the doorstep when I came down for breakfast.'

'But if they weren't from you, who else would they be from?'

'What d'you mean?'

'There is no one else.' The words fell out of my mouth before I could edit them, so I laughed to soften their bitter edges. 'It's just that I'm not in the habit of receiving bouquets. In fact, I don't think anyone's ever bought me flowers in my life.'

Eloise tilted her head to one side. 'That's sad.'

I shrugged my shoulders. 'Life's a bitch and then you die.'

It was Eloise's turn to laugh. 'Oh Rose, you crack me up.'

A sense of déjà vu combined with the funereal scent of the lilies made my head spin. 'What did you say?'

'You crack me up. Your sense of humour is so out there.' She watched me for a moment. 'Why, did I say something wrong?'

I shook my head. 'It's what your mum used to say to me.' And it was true. I'd simply make an observation about something or other and Juliet would fall about laughing. It wasn't until years later that I'd realised that what Juliet saw as my deadpan, acerbic views on life, the universe and everything, were just me being literal. Case in point: life literally was a bitch. And then you died.

Eloise hugged Dinah tightly until the cat wriggled out of her arms and shot through the cat flap into the garden.

'I couldn't see a card,' I said, unpacking the shopping.

'There wasn't one.'

'Most strange.' I bent over the vase, inhaled deeply, then sneezed as the pollen particles tickled my nose.

'Maybe your boss at the charity sent them as congratulations for getting the job?' Eloise said.

'She hasn't told me I've got it yet.'

She arched an eyebrow. 'Perhaps you have a secret admirer.'

'I don't think so.' I found plates and knives and rinsed the grapes I'd bought under the tap. 'I expect they took the address down wrong,' I said, setting bread and stilton on the table. 'There'll be an irate wife waiting for her anniversary bouquet at the other end of the village as we speak, you mark my words.'

Eloise snorted and reached for the butter while I chewed on a corner of bread and wondered who could have sent me such a lavish bunch of flowers.

Sleep that night was elusive. I felt jittery and restless, like the time at university I'd inadvisedly taken ten Pro Plus pills at once to help me hit an essay deadline. I'd finished the essay, but the little white pills had triggered a period of insomnia that had lasted several weeks.

As I lay in bed staring at the ceiling, I pushed all thoughts of Theo to the back of my mind and instead reflected on everything I had learned about India Matthews. In the thirteen years I'd been involved with Sisterline, there'd been any number of suicides, so why did her death bother me so? She was the same age as Eloise, so perhaps it was that. Perhaps Eloise had stirred my deeply buried maternal instincts. Perhaps I had a soul after all.

What had gone so terribly wrong in India Matthews' brief life that she'd seen suicide as her only option? I knew nothing about her, of course. She could have been abused as a child, up to her eyeballs in debt or the victim of vicious online trolling for all I knew. Had Rhona offered words of comfort to her in the moments before she died, or had she said something that had pushed India over the edge?

And then, inevitably, my musings turned to Juliet. If she'd phoned me the day she died, what would I have said? And, more importantly, could I have stopped her? The previous week, in a tearful phone call, she'd described her recent mood swings and insomnia, her feelings of hopelessness and crippling panic attacks. I'd offered to drive up to see her there and then, but she'd talked me out of it, promising she'd make an appointment with her GP. And when I'd called a few days later, she'd sounded almost like her old self. The doctor had prescribed antidepressants and had referred her for cognitive behavioural therapy. She was over the worst, she assured me. She was determined to get better, for Eloise's sake.

More fool me for believing her.

The very next day, while Eloise was at school, Juliet had driven from her Marylebone home to Dover, parking in the National Trust car park at the top of the White Cliffs. A couple out walking their labradoodle later told police they'd seen a woman sitting close to the cliff edge looking out to sea. When they came back from their walk an hour later, the woman had gone. They hadn't reported the incident, even though the area was a notorious spot for suicides, because she'd looked so serene, so untroubled, they assumed she was just admiring the view.

Juliet had arranged a sleepover for Eloise that night, so it wasn't until the following afternoon when she didn't turn up for the school run that alarm bells started ringing. A couple of days later, police located Juliet's car in Dover and her body was found on the rocks below the cliffs.

I'd been in the garden a week later cutting back brambles when the phone started ringing. Reluctantly, I'd dropped the secateurs and stomped into the house.

'Yes?'

'Is that Auntie Rose?' a wobbly voice asked.

Auntie Rose? I pulled a face. An only child, I wasn't anyone's auntie. 'Who is this?'

'It's me, Eloise.'

'Eloise?'

'J-Juliet's daughter.'

'I know who you are,' I said, rather abruptly. It was the shock. 'What's the matter?'

A sniff. 'They've been talking. The social services people. They say I can't stay with Holly and her mum any more. They say I've got to have a foster mum and dad.'

'Well, that's good, isn't it?'

She made a strangled noise, then said, 'No, it's not. What if they're horrible?'

'Why would they pick horrible people to be foster parents? They'll be perfectly nice, I'm sure.'

'But I don't want to live with strangers!' Another sniff. 'I want my mum. I want things to go back to normal.'

'You're twelve, aren't you, Eloise?'

'Eleven.'

'Well, eleven's old enough to understand that things can never go back to normal. You just have to make the best of it. We all do.' I cleared my throat. 'Was there anything else?'

'Yes, actually. They, the social services people, asked if I had anyone I could live with. You know, like family and stuff.'

'Right,' I said, realising where this was heading.

'I told them I could come and live with you.'

My grip on the handset tightened. 'And what did they say?'

'I gave them your number. They're going to phone you to have a chat about it.'

'A chat?'

'That's what they said. That'll be all right, won't it? I've always wanted to live in the middle of the woods.'

'But what about your school? You wouldn't want to leave, would you?'

'I wouldn't mind. I'll be going to secondary school soon, anyway. Is that all right, then? Can I come and live with you?'

I licked my lips. 'Of course. But I don't think we should get our hopes up. Social services might not think I'm a suitable guardian. I'm not family, after all.'

Eloise sniffed again. 'You're all I have left.'

I put the conversation out of my mind until the week before Juliet's funeral, when the phone rang again. This time a woman announced cheerfully that she was Kirsty Meadows, Eloise Cavendish's social worker.

'I'm so sorry for your loss,' she began.

I swallowed the mass of tears that was permanently wedged in my throat like gauze packing in a wound.

'As you've probably guessed,' she continued, 'I'm phoning about Eloise.'

'She said you might call.'

'So, you know why I'm ringing? That Eloise has stated a preference to come and live with you, her godmother, rather than go into foster care?'

'That's what she said, yes.'

'Unfortunately, Miss Cavendish didn't name a guardian for Eloise in her will. In these situations, an application is made to the court for a guardian to be appointed. Usually that's a willing family member or friend, which is why I wanted to speak to you.'

'Oh.'

'I understand from Eloise you don't have children yourself?' she said.

'No.'

'And you live alone?'

'That's right. Spinster of this parish.'

Kirsty Meadows didn't laugh. 'If it were possible, how would you feel about becoming Eloise's legal guardian? Do you think you could take on an eleven-year-old girl?'

Here was the rub. I didn't think I could. I couldn't see

how a grieving, hormonal almost-teenager would ever slot into my ordered, solitary life. What would I do with her? I wouldn't know where to start.

'I am very busy…' I began.

'Eloise didn't mention you had a job.'

'It's not a job as such. I'm involved with several charities on a voluntary basis. Heavily involved,' I added. 'The thing is, I'm not sure I have the bandwidth to give Eloise a home.' I instantly regretted my choice of words. It sounded as though I was being asked to re-home a dog. 'What I'm trying to say is that I don't think it would be in her best interests to come and live with me.'

'Her best interests, or yours?' Kirsty Meadows' cheery demeanour had disappeared and there was a steely tone to her voice.

'Hers and mine,' I said. 'I'm just not cut out to be a parent.'

'Right.' I heard papers being shuffled. 'Perhaps I can be blunt with you, Miss Barton,' the social worker said. 'Eloise's father is dead, as are both sets of grandparents. Neither parent had any siblings. With her mother gone, Eloise has no living relatives. If you don't take her in, her case will go to the family court and the most likely scenario is she'll go into foster care. Is that what you want for your goddaughter?'

'Of course it's not what I *want*,' I said, my voice rising. 'What I want is for her to live with her mother, for Juliet not to have died. But as that's not possible, I think Eloise is better off with foster parents. People who know how to look after children. Because, believe me, I struggle to keep houseplants alive.'

There was silence on the other end of the phone and for a moment I thought the social worker had hung up on me, but finally she said, 'It's a great shame. Eloise could do with some stability in her life. But I can't force her on you.'

'I think it's for the best,' I said.

'Yes, well, I won't make a start on the paperwork until the end of the week, so if you do change your mind…'

I repeated her phone number obediently, even though I wasn't writing it down. There was no point. I wouldn't be calling her.

We both started speaking at once.

'Please, go ahead,' Kirsty Meadows said.

'I was just going to say, will you tell Eloise I couldn't have her? Will she know?'

The social worker sighed. 'I don't see there's any point. She's just lost her mother. She doesn't need to know you won't take her in.'

Below the belt, but I probably deserved it.

'Thank you,' I said. 'I appreciate that.'

A week later, Eloise slipped her hand in mine as we stood shoulder to shoulder beside Juliet's grave. 'It's not fair,' she whispered. 'The court won't let me come and live with you.'

Kirsty Matthews had been as good as her word. Eloise would never know I'd rejected her. The relief made me lightheaded.

'I'm sorry,' I whispered back. 'I'm as disappointed as

you.' As the vicar glided towards us, I squeezed her hand. 'But if there's ever anything I can do for you, and I mean *anything*, you only have to ask. Will you remember that?'

She nodded solemnly and squeezed my hand back. Her palm felt sticky in mine and I fought the urge to pull my hand away and wipe it on my trousers.

'Don't worry, Auntie Rose,' she said. 'I'll remember.'

CHAPTER TWENTY-ONE

JULY 1991

Things were better after Danny's asthma attack. Once Juliet realised we weren't sleeping together behind her back, she calmed down, and when she heard how I'd saved her boyfriend's life, the chilly atmosphere between us melted away.

It didn't take long for Danny's swagger to return, but at least he tolerated my presence and he, Juliet, John and I made an unlikely foursome throughout the summer term.

Before I knew it, the other three were handing in their dissertations and cramming for their finals. And suddenly we were drinking shots in the student union bar to mark the end of their degrees.

Danny and Juliet had already booked flights to Ibiza, where they were planning to spend the summer, and John had found a job as a computer programmer for an investment company in the City. The three of them were in high spirits, clinking glasses and downing shots like vodka was going out of fashion.

I drank to drown my sorrows, because this was the summer Juliet and I should have gone on our Thelma and Louise road trip, and instead I had nothing to look forward to but week after suffocating week back in Kent. And that wasn't all. My tutor had summoned me to her office that afternoon to tell me I'd failed my end-of-year exams and had two choices: leave or repeat the year.

I was restless and on edge. I'd existed for the last month on a diet of coffee and Pro Plus while I'd revised for my exams, but far from helping me focus, the caffeine had made me irritable and unable to concentrate. I'd developed a twitch in my right eye. Even the vodka couldn't shift my sense of impending doom.

What the hell was I going to do? Even if I repeated the year, I'd still have another two to do after that, then the two-year post-grad foundation course. Five more years of struggling to keep my head above water. It sounded like a jail sentence. Panic gripped me, squeezing my chest so hard I felt as if all the air had been sucked out of my lungs. I clutched the edge of the bar stool to stop myself from toppling over. The floor swam in and out of focus, and a wave of nausea gripped me. I clamped a trembling hand to my mouth and looked around in desperation. John was at the bar getting the next round in. Opposite me, Juliet and Danny had their tongues down each other's throats, completely oblivious.

Breathe, Rose. Breathe.

Although every atom in my body screamed at me to gulp in air, I went against my instincts and slowed my breathing until the floor stopped pitching and my racing heartbeat eased.

After an age, John came back from the bar, a tray of drinks in his hands. He put a shot glass on the table in front of me and when I didn't pick it up, he peered at my face.

'Are you all right? You look a bit pasty.'

I was about to brush his concerns away when something stopped me. I liked John. He was a good egg. I could trust him.

'Think I've just had a panic attack,' I muttered.

His eyes widened. 'What's brought that on?'

'I've been burning the midnight oil revising for my end of years. Which I found out today that I've failed. I now have to decide whether I repeat the year or go home with my tail between my legs.'

'Shit,' he said, picking up his own glass and downing it. 'What are you going to do?'

A tear leaked out of the corner of my eye and trickled down my chin. 'I don't know.'

I glanced at Juliet as if she held all the answers, but she and Danny were still entwined. Danny's hand had disappeared up her skirt, and she was groaning softly. I rubbed my face and turned back to John.

'I can't cope any more. With any of it.'

He gave a knowing nod. 'You should see my GP. He's a good guy. He'll sort you out.' He pulled a pen out of his pocket and scribbled down a name and number on a beer mat.

I shook my head. 'I don't need to see anyone. I'll be fine.'

But John ignored my protestations and pushed the beer mat into my hand. 'He can't mend a broken heart, but he can help with your anxiety. Just phone him. And that's an order.'

Three days later, I picked up a prescription for amitriptyline from the local chemist. Two weeks after that, the little orange pills started working their magic, wrapping everything in a layer of cotton wool, helping me sleep and keeping my anxiety levels in check.

'Amitriptyline can cause side effects, such as a dry mouth, constipation and nausea,' the doctor had warned as I waited patiently for him to write out the prescription. 'And you'll need to come off them gradually as the withdrawal effects can include a fast or irregular heartbeat, flu-like symptoms and, in extreme cases, sensory disturbance, insomnia, mood swings and even mania.'

But I wasn't listening. I just wanted to put a stop to the anxiety that had plagued me for as long as I could remember.

Even so, a little part of me was ashamed I'd had to resort to medication to help me cope with life. So, I called them my vitamins, and I took them every day without fail.

CHAPTER TWENTY-TWO

I must have eventually drifted off because my alarm wrenched me from a deep sleep just before seven the next morning. I felt at once tired and restless, exhausted yet agitated, and I was regretting my promise to spend the morning helping Eddie with the charity's annual report when I could have slept in. I shuffled along the landing and down the stairs, almost tripping over Dinah, who was sprawled on the last but one step.

'What are you doing there, you silly cat?' I scolded, but I'd been out of favour the moment Eloise arrived and Dinah barely registered my presence.

Out of habit, I listened to the Radio Kent news while I made a pot of tea, relieved there was no mention of French chefs, missing or otherwise. While the tea brewed, I ran a cloth under the tap and wiped away the dusting of orange pollen the lilies had shed all over the kitchen table, then swore when I stepped in a pile of watery cat vomit by the fridge.

I mopped it up with a square of kitchen roll, decanted milk into a jug, and made my way into the hallway.

'Do you have to park yourself right there?' I asked Dinah, but she couldn't even be bothered to open an eye. 'Little madam,' I tutted as I stepped over her.

In her room, Eloise was already awake.

'Are you at work today?' she asked without preamble.

'Only for a couple of hours. Then we can do something together, if you like?' I said, setting her mug on the chest of drawers.

'Like what?'

'Lunch at the pub? A walk?'

'Sure, whatever.'

She picked up her phone and started scrolling, her eyes on the screen. Smarting a little at the obvious dismissal, I mumbled something about having a shower and left her to it.

As I stood under the lukewarm trickle of water, I told myself off for being so sensitive. *Don't suffocate the poor girl. She needs her space.* I turned the shower off and wrapped a towel around me. *Remember what happened last time.* I rubbed myself dry, feeling the beginning of a tension headache behind my eyes. I found some paracetamol in the mirrored cabinet above the sink and swallowed them with water from the tap. I hadn't lived with anyone since my father died. I was stuck in my ways and used to my own company. Of course living with Eloise would require some adjustment on my behalf, some give and take. But I was prepared to do whatever was necessary. Because one thing was for sure: she may have only been with me for a few days, but I knew the house would feel very empty without her.

Downstairs, I popped two slices of bread in the toaster and reached into the cupboard for my vitamins, only remembering once I'd pulled open the door that I'd thrown them away. The decision seemed rash in the cold light of day. I'd taken them for more years than I could remember, relying on them to keep everything on an even keel. Not to the point of dependency, obviously. That would be foolish. Just as an aid to navigating life without coming a cropper on the inevitable rocks. Anxiety blooming in the pit of my stomach, I pulled the lid off the swing bin, about to dive in and extricate them when I realised it was empty. Eloise must have put the bin bag in the wheelie bin. I was halfway to the back door before I stopped myself. I wasn't that desperate. I'd meant what I said when I told Eloise I didn't need them any more.

Instead, I opened a tin of cat food and spooned some into Dinah's bowl, tapping the rim of the bowl with the spoon as I put it on the floor. Normally, the sound summoned her from afar, but not this morning. I was about to check on her when my toast popped out of the toaster and the eight o'clock pips sounded, and I realised I would be late if I didn't get a wiggle on.

Forty-five minutes later, I pulled into the car park in town, locked the Land Rover and hurried down the alleyway towards the Sisterline offices. As I neared the building, my path was blocked by a red van parked at an angle outside the front door. Written in large white letters on the side of the van was *Paul Banks Glazing. 24-hour emergency service.* The doors of the van were open and a thickset man with a grey ponytail was pulling out a stepladder.

'What's happened?' I asked him.

'Some joker's lobbed a stone through the window,' he said, pointing at the small arched window above the door. A cobweb of shattered glass spiralled out from a hole in the middle. 'Still,' he said with a chuckle, 'keeps me in business.'

'Evidently,' I said, rolling my eyes as I took the steps two at a time. Inside, volunteers stood in huddles talking in hushed voices. 'Where's Eddie?' I asked the room in general.

'In her office with Dorothy,' said an earnest-looking woman called Irene. 'They're waiting for the police.'

'The police are coming here?'

'Eddie insisted,' Irene said. 'The forensic man's already been.'

'Seems over the top for a broken window.' I swept past her, knocked on Eddie's door, and walked straight in. She was deep in conversation with Dorothy, the chair of trustees, but broke off when she saw me and nodded to a spare chair.

'Rose, I'm glad you're here,' Eddie said. 'I'm going to need you to hold the fort while Dorothy and I speak to the police.'

'I'm surprised they're sending someone out. They never have before.'

'We've never received a threatening letter before,' Eddie said. 'I found this when I arrived this morning. Someone had pushed it under the door.' She picked up a plastic folder with a sheet of paper inside and passed it to me. An untidy scrawl covered one side of the lined A4 sheet. The same words had been written over and over, like lines meted out during detention.

You killed my baby girl, you bitch. But I know who you are and I know where you live.

You killed my baby girl, you bitch. But I know who you are and I know where you live.

You killed my baby girl, you bitch. But I know who you are and I know where you live.

As the lines marched down the page, the writing became more and more untidy until it was almost illegible. I held the plastic wallet to the window. The words had been scored so deeply that pinpricks of light peeped through. I became aware that Eddie and Dorothy were both watching me, waiting for a reaction.

'Someone's not a happy bunny,' I said, handing the sheet back to Eddie.

'Hence the visit from the police,' Eddie said. 'Whoever's sent this is probably all talk and no trousers, but we need to be sure. I can't have my staff and volunteers at risk.'

'You think it's a man?'

She and Dorothy exchanged a look. I scanned the page a second time. Something about the choice of words rang a bell. I frowned, chasing a memory, then nodded to myself.

'It's from that chap whose complaint you were dealing with the other day. India Matthew's father.'

'I don't remember telling you her name,' Eddie said, her gaze as piercing as a hawk's.

'I looked her up online.' I shrugged. 'I was curious. Her father called her his baby girl in one of the articles I read. Roy, his name was. It must be him. In which case,' I resisted the urge to rub my hands together. 'In which case, he's talking about Rhona. The poor thing.'

'It certainly seems that way,' Eddie said. She glanced at the door. 'But I urge you not to say anything until we've spoken to the police. I don't want to worry her unnecessarily.'

I kept my expression neutral. 'Your secret's safe with me.'

CHAPTER TWENTY-THREE

While Eddie was holed up in her office, I made a start on the annual report, although it was nigh impossible to concentrate on the charity's achievements and objectives, fundraising and media coverage over the past twelve months with all the kerfuffle going on around me.

Two police officers arrived just as the emergency glazier was leaving. Eddie ushered them into her office and closed the door. Wishing I was a fly on the wall, I wondered how seriously they would treat the incident. Roy Matthews hadn't directly threatened Rhona, after all.

How would I feel if I was told the father of a girl who'd killed herself on my watch was hellbent on revenge? Would I be worried he'd lash out again? I didn't think so. There was truth in the old saying, barking dogs seldom bite. In my experience, it was the quiet ones you had to watch.

Abandoning the annual report, I googled India Matthews, but other than a fundraising page set up by her friends, there was nothing new to see. Out of curiosity, I typed Roy Matthews into the search box, adding Teynham as an afterthought. India had lived in the village, according to the news reports.

A link to a story on the Kent Police website topped the list of results. Intrigued, I clicked on it, frustrated to see the words: `Webpage unavailable. This page may have expired.`

I clicked back and re-read the brief Google entry.

> `A Teynham man who threatened a woman with a baseball bat has been jailed for...`

All I could think was that the story was so old it had been taken down from the Kent Police website. I kept scrolling through the list of hits. Halfway down the page was a link to a Kent Online story. I clicked through and glanced at the date. Five years ago. My hunch was right.

> `A Kent judge has paid tribute to a brave victim who gave evidence against her baseball bat-wielding neighbour days before she was due to give birth.`
>
> `Judge Godfrey Lancaster said the victim's compelling evidence in the`

witness box helped convict 40-year-old Roy Matthews, who has since been sentenced to 15 months in prison.

Matthews, of London Road, Teynham, had denied affray and assault but was found guilty of both offences following a three-day trial at Canterbury Crown Court.

His heavily pregnant victim, Kerry Davis, 22, said her ordeal at the hands of the divorced father-of-one was 'the most terrifying five minutes of my life'.

The assault, described by police as a wanton act of intimidation, was the culmination of a three-month dispute between the neighbours over noise.

The dispute began when Ms Davis complained to the council about Matthews playing music in the early hours.

'He lost his job and would get drunk and play U2 at full volume until 2am or 3am every morning,' Ms Davis told the court. 'Whenever I asked him to turn the music down, he would give me an earful, so I reported him to the council. The day the council sent someone round to talk to him, he completely lost the plot and turned up on the doorstep later that night with a baseball bat.'

The court heard Matthews threatened to 'knock some sense' into Ms Davis before smashing her living room window. Another neighbour called the police and Matthews was arrested.

Sentencing him, Judge Lancaster said: 'Your bullying actions were designed purely to intimidate your heavily pregnant neighbour who was in fear for her life and that of her baby's, and to make matters worse, you have shown no remorse since. A custodial sentence is my only option.

'Furthermore, I would like to pay tribute to Ms Davis, who showed remarkable bravery coming to court to face you today just two weeks before her baby's due date.'

I was so engrossed in the story that I hadn't even glanced at the custody image that accompanied the article. When I did, I gasped. Staring at me from my computer screen was the spitting image of the man who'd harangued me in the car park. No, not the spitting image. Not quite. This man had more hair and was slimmer and slightly less jowly around the face than the man with the white SUV. Perhaps they were brothers? Cousins, even? I attempted to transpose the features of SUV Man onto the face of Roy Matthews. They were both more Neanderthal than Homo sapiens, that was for sure. They had the same piggy eyes, the same brutish jaws and heavy foreheads. In fact, the more I scrutinised the picture, the deeper the sense of foreboding grew, settling around my shoulders like a cloak.

My skin prickled as I struggled to join the dots. But deep down, I knew the truth. Of course Roy Matthews looked younger than SUV Man - the photo was taken five years ago.

It was staring me in the face. The man who'd threatened a pregnant woman with a baseball bat inside her own home was the same man who'd launched a diatribe against me, then slashed my tyre in a fit of rage. I took off my glasses and rubbed my face.

Just then, Eddie's door opened, and the two officers appeared, one of them holding the plastic wallet containing Matthews' note. I was about to jump up and pass on my vital new piece of evidence before I stopped myself just in time.

Careful, Rose.

I had Theo to think of. Theo, who was locked in a concrete bunker in the middle of my woods while I decided his fate. The last thing I needed was the police sniffing around.

Did it matter that Roy Matthews had ranted at me and slashed my tyre? With any luck, he'd soon be back under lock and key, anyway. He would get his just desserts. I clicked away from the news story and opened the Excel spreadsheet containing the charity's annual accounts. As I jotted down the headline figures, I reminded myself that sometimes it was best to keep a low profile.

Eloise greeted me at the back door with a smile that would warm the coldest of hearts.

'I've made vegetable soup,' she said proudly, taking my bag and coat and steering me towards the kitchen table. 'We can have it with cheese and crackers.'

'You didn't want to go to the pub?'

'I didn't fancy it. You don't mind, do you?'

'Of course not.' I picked up my spoon. 'It's a relief to stay in after the morning I've had. Remember SUV Man?'

Eloise frowned. 'The twat who shouted at you in the car park?'

'The very same.'

She listened as I described the broken window, the scrawled note, and my amateur sleuthing. 'He's a thug called Roy Matthews, who was jailed five years ago for threatening his pregnant neighbour. He's now gunning for the volunteer who spoke to his daughter.'

We ate in silence for a moment, lost in our thoughts. Then Eloise said, 'Does he know who the volunteer is?'

'I doubt it,' I said. 'All calls are anonymous to protect both the callers and our volunteers. He only knew she'd phoned us because the police gave him back her phone. He must have checked her call history and put two and two together.'

'Is it possible he followed you that day in the car park? Could he have seen where you went?'

'I don't think so. Why?'

'Because if he saw you go into the Sisterline offices, he might have thought you were the volunteer. In which case...'

'In which case what?'

'You need to be careful, Rose. People like him get fixated when they feel they've been wronged, and they get obsessed with the person they think has wronged them. I should know,' she added bitterly.

I reached across the table and patted her arm. 'I've told you, you don't need to worry about Theo any more. You're safe now.'

'But are *you*?' she asked. 'He said in the note he knows where you live. He must have followed you home.'

'Not me,' I reminded her. 'Rhona. Rhona's the one who took the call. She's the one he followed home.' But as I said this, I knew it was unlikely. There were over thirty volunteers at Sisterline and any one of them could have taken India's call. Roy Matthews had no way of knowing.

But what if Eloise was right? What if he'd chanced upon someone who worked at the charity? Might he have put two and two together and made five? Might he think I was the one who had whispered in India's ear seconds before she stepped into the path of a train? Might he think I'd killed his baby girl?

I tried to swallow a mouthful of cracker, but the dry pieces stuck in my throat like shards of glass.

CHAPTER TWENTY-FOUR

JULY 1991

I'd been home from university for a week when my mother marched into my bedroom one morning and yanked open the curtains, flooding the room with light.

'Do you mind?' I grumbled, burrowing under the duvet. 'I was still asleep.'

'It's half-past eleven. You may get away with lazing in bed all day when you're at university, young lady, but not under this roof. You can crawl out of your pit right now and help me with the hoovering.'

'I have coursework to do,' I said, scowling. Not quite true. I'd all but decided to drop out of my degree. I just hadn't plucked up the courage to tell my tutor or my parents. I couldn't bear to see the disappointment on my father's face, nor the triumph on my mother's.

'That can wait. Joyce from bridge club is coming over this afternoon. I want the place shipshape.'

'I'm not the hired bloody help. She's your friend. Do it yourself.'

My mother rose to her full height. 'Don't take that attitude with me, Rose Barton. Your father and I have sacrificed everything to send you to university. The least you can do is help around the house. And watch your language, please missy. I won't stand for that kind of potty-talk...'

As I glared at her, a strange expression crossed her face and the invective turned into an incoherent mumble. The left side of her face sagged, the side of her mouth drooping alarmingly. It was like watching a waxen figure melting in the sun. I leapt out of bed and thundered down the stairs and out of the back door, yelling for my father.

I found him in his vegetable garden, spraying the blackfly on his broad beans.

'Dad, you need to come. I think Mother's having a stroke. She started mumbling and her face has gone funny.'

The colour drained from his face and he dropped the bottle of insecticide he was holding. 'Have you phoned for an ambulance?'

I shook my head.

'Call one,' he said, jogging stiffly towards the house.

'She's in my bedroom,' I called after him. But he had already disappeared through the back door.

My mother spent the next month in hospital on the stroke ward, undergoing a plethora of tests and daily visits from a never-ending stream of speech and language therapists, physios and occupational therapists. But no amount of rehabilitation could repair the ravages the stroke had wreaked on her body. Her left side was paralysed, her speech slurred and her mind, once so sharp, was mired in confusion. The warfarin she was prescribed gave her nose-bleeds and bleeding gums, and ugly bruises bloomed on her papery skin if you so much as touched her.

When her consultant announced she was fit enough to come home, I was flabbergasted.

'We can't look after her!' I hissed to my father as we cradled polystyrene cups of weak tea in the hospital canteen.

'She belongs at home, Rose.'

'But I don't... I can't...'

He reached across the table and took my hands in his. 'It's all right, Rosie. I'm not asking you to. I'll look after her. And I'll have carers coming in every day to help. You have your own life to lead. I understand that. And you'll be heading back to university before you know it.'

I licked my lips. What with the stroke and the long hours at the hospital, I hadn't found the right time to tell him I wasn't going back. I couldn't face his disappointment when he learned I'd failed my exams, when he realised his golden girl wasn't clever enough to be a doctor.

But as I sat at the stained Formica table, the noises of the hospital echoing around us, I saw how I might wriggle out of my predicament, leaving his view of me untarnished.

I shook my head. 'I'm not going back to uni. You can't do this on your own.'

His eyebrows concertinaed. 'But Rose…'

'Don't you see?' I said urgently. 'I wanted to be a doctor so I could fix people. I can't fix Mother if I'm at university. I'm going to stay at home and help you. Help her. And there's no point trying to talk me out of it. I've made up my mind.'

A week later, my mother arrived home in an ambulance. My father had moved into the spare room so their old bedroom could be kitted out with all the equipment she'd need: a specialist hospital bed with side rails and chair and tilt functions, a commode, a walking frame and grab rails. He'd built shelves on the wall opposite her bed to accommodate her ghoulish collection of stuffed birds and had painstakingly cleaned every single display case, so the birds' glass prisons gleamed in the sun. Our bathroom was to be converted into a wet room, but until then the carers my father had organised to come in three times a day would have to wash her by hand.

She'd shrunk in the five weeks since her stroke. It was as if she'd folded in on herself. She was sixty-one but looked twenty years older. There was a look of bewilderment in her eyes, a look that said she couldn't quite understand how she, Shirley "Queen Bee" Barton, who played bridge four times a week and was chair of the local bowls club, had been reduced to a frail heap of bones and skin who spent her days staring aimlessly out of the window.

When my father's compassionate leave from the Post Office ended, he took early retirement to look after her.

'It's what you do when you love someone,' he said, when I questioned his decision. 'You'll find out for yourself one day.'

Little did he realise that I already knew all about love and the sacrifices it demanded. By then I hadn't seen Juliet for eight weeks and three days. The day after her graduation, she and Danny had flown to Ibiza, where they'd found jobs in a bar, working all day and partying all night. She sent me the occasional postcard, announcing in her familiar scrawl they were having a blast and might never come home. She never once said she wished I was there.

The days bled into each other, each as tedious and oppressive as the last. I'd been intent on becoming a doctor for so long that everything I'd done had been geared towards getting the grades, then winning - and keeping - my place at med school. Nothing else had mattered. Now, for the first time in my life, I had no goal, no purpose. I felt cast adrift on a flat sea. Directionless. Aimless. Useless.

And then Danny fucked up a second time, and suddenly I had hope.

CHAPTER TWENTY-FIVE

The moment I turned off my bedside light, my brain shifted gear into full-on paranoia. Downstairs, I had Eloise to distract me. Alone in my bedroom, I only had my thoughts to keep me company. Dark thoughts that crowded into my head one after the other, each more sinister than the last.

Faceless men with baseball bats; the pretty features of a pregnant woman smashed to a pulp; the grip of a claw-like hand on my arm, pulling me into a sinkhole whose depths I could only imagine. But one image kept forcing its way back into my brain, no matter how hard I tried to push it away: Theo's lifeless body growing cold in the stale, dusty air of the pillbox.

I'd dropped off his food just before dusk. Telling Eloise I was popping out to feed Mary's fish, I'd hurried through the woods, poked the bag of food through one of the window slits, and retraced my steps without even looking in on him. I knew I was burying my head in the sand, but

I couldn't deal with him alongside everything else. I just wanted to forget about him.

But of course I couldn't, and so for the second night running, sleep was impossible.

My limbs were heavy, yet my heart raced, the stress hormones cortisol and adrenalin surging through my bloodstream like an incoming tide. I tried counting backwards from a thousand but gave up at nine hundred and twenty-eight. I pictured sheep jumping over a stone wall, but that didn't work, either. I turned on the radio by my bedside, but even the soporific murmur of Today in Parliament failed to work its magic.

After a couple of hours staring, puffy-eyed, into the darkness, I swung my legs out of bed and went downstairs in search of a glass of water. As I felt my way along the hallway and into the kitchen, my foot came into contact with something warm and furry. Stifling a scream, I patted the wall, feeling for the light switch.

Dinah lay catatonic on the floor by my feet.

'Dear God, you scared the living daylights out of me,' I said, crouching down. She raised her head half-heartedly, then let it sink back onto her paws.

She offered no resistance as I scooped her into my arms and carried her into the kitchen, flicking on the light as I went. When she hadn't appeared for her tea, I'd assumed she was out hunting. It wasn't unheard of for her to disappear for a day or two, then turn up on the doorstep demanding attention as if she'd never been away. But she'd been listless that morning, I remembered. Hardly moving from the bottom stair. I glanced at her bowl. Her tea was untouched.

'We'd better get you to the vet's in the morning, old girl,' I said, stroking her under the chin. She began purring and, reassured, I deposited her gently into her bed by the radiator, ran myself a glass of water and went back up to bed.

This time, when I turned off the light and pulled the duvet under my chin, I didn't chase sleep. Instead, I tried to remember the visualisation technique a therapist had taught me when I was plagued with insomnia after my father died.

'Imagine there's a desk in front of you with lots of folders spread all over it,' said the therapist, a wide-hipped woman with a penchant for shapeless cardigans and a soft Aberdeen accent. 'Can you picture it?'

I nodded. 'Black lever arch files on a walnut desk with a green leather top.'

'Excellent,' she said. 'Keep that image in your head. Now imagine every file has something that is making you anxious written on its spine. An argument with a loved one that's preying on your mind. A time when you felt you let someone down. The grief you carry after the death of your father. Money worries. Fear of failure. Anything that makes you anxious, no matter how trivial it might seem, gets its own file.'

I closed my eyes and did as I was told, not because I was convinced it would work, but because I wanted to squeeze every penny out of the eye-wateringly expensive counselling session. I pictured the desk - my father's desk

- in a book-lined room with sunlight streaming through the window. I sprinkled in some dust motes for good measure. A cliché, but why not? On the desk was an untidy pile of lever arch files. I peered at the spine of the first. Grief, it stated in uncompromisingly thick black marker pen. All at once, a feeling of desolation swept over me, squeezing my heart until it threatened to burst. I took two deep breaths and looked at the next file. Medicine. Regret replaced the grief. Regret that I'd walked away from my degree, abandoned my dreams of becoming a doctor, choosing instead a stultifying, colourless life in which I was trapped in my childhood home like a prisoner in jail, but with no time out for good behaviour.

I moved around the desk to look at the next file. Juliet. More regret plus a stomach-churning embarrassment when I recalled the revulsion on her face when I kissed her the night of the Snow Ball. How naïve I'd been. I should have realised she would never love me the way I loved her.

'How are you getting on with those files?' the therapist said, startling me. I'd forgotten she was there.

'Just a couple more,' I said, picking up the next file in my mind's eye and lifting it to examine the spine. Smokey. No guilt or regret this time, just a low-level anxiety that at nineteen he didn't have long for this world, and when he died, I would well and truly be on my own.

And finally, the one file I didn't want to look at. But I took a deep breath and picked it up anyway, because I was paying seventy quid an hour to see this therapist and I wanted my money's worth.

I stared at the spine. Danny. The sight of his name still made me tremble, with anger or guilt I couldn't be sure. I replaced the file carefully on the desk and put him out of my mind.

'When you're struggling to sleep, I want you to picture the desk and all the files,' the therapist said. 'I want you to pick each file up, one at a time, acknowledge how important it is, and file it away for the night in a cabinet beside you.'

I pictured a pewter-grey filing cabinet, pulled open the top drawer and pushed the rack of dividers to the back.

'Upright or in a pile?' I asked.

'It doesn't really matter, Rose,' the therapist said. 'As you file away all the things that are on your mind, you are telling your brain that nothing is wrong, and you are giving yourself permission to relax and go to sleep.'

To say I was sceptical was the understatement of the year, but I was on my knees with exhaustion, so that night, feeling a little silly, I visualised the files strewn across my father's desk. One by one I picked them up and placed them in the filing cabinet, and before I knew it, my alarm was waking me at eight the next morning after the best night's sleep I'd had for months.

Now, with Dinah curled up in her bed downstairs and Eloise asleep across the landing, I conjured up my father's leather-topped desk and the heap of lever arch files. Curious to see what concerns they contained fourteen years on, I sifted through them. Medicine was still there, and so was Grief. I placed both files in the filing cabinet and picked up a third from the table.

Menopause. Fair enough. Because what woman over fifty didn't obsess about the hot flushes and night sweats, the palpitations and spikes in anxiety caused by their plummeting oestrogen levels? Into the filing cabinet it went.

I wasn't surprised to see a file each for Eloise and Theo. There was a fragility to my goddaughter that made me worry about her future happiness. And as for her psycho boyfriend, well, I felt little remorse for what I was doing, just unease that I might be found out.

I was clasping Theo's file to my chest and attempting to push the image of his huddled body to the back of my mind when the therapist's words came back to me as clearly as if she was sitting at the end of my bed. *Acknowledge how important it is and file it away.* I placed both files in the cabinet.

That left one file. I didn't need to pick it up to know what was in it. Because fourteen years may have passed since my sessions with the softly spoken therapist from Aberdeen, but there wasn't a day went by when Danny didn't dominate my thoughts and invade my dreams.

CHAPTER TWENTY-SIX

OCTOBER 1991

The trees that guarded our house were turning russet when Juliet and Danny flew home from Ibiza to start the next chapter of their lives. The country was in deep recession, yet they'd fallen on their feet. A friend of Juliet's dad had offered her a position as a gallery assistant at the Victoria and Albert Museum, and Danny had talked himself into a job in the gym of a Kensington health club.

I tried to sound pleased when Juliet rang to tell me they'd decided to flatshare with John and had found the "perfect, dreamy little maisonette" in Pimlico. 'Short commutes for us all. Honestly, Rose, I'm so excited.'

'Sounds ideal,' I said, waiting for her to ask how I was,

but she was too full of her plans for the flat. I let her ramble on, hoping some of her joy would rub off on me.

'Oh, I nearly forgot! You're not doing anything a week Friday, are you? We're having a flat-warming.'

I swallowed the snort of bitter laughter that threatened to reveal me and instead said casually, 'A week Friday? Um, no, I don't think so.'

'Cool.' She rattled off her new address. 'We'll see you about seven, yeah?'

And just like that, I had something to look forward to. I borrowed my father's Land Rover, drove into Canterbury, and spent the last of my grant on a haircut at the trendiest salon I could find. I ordered half a dozen new outfits from my mother's Kays catalogue and went on a strict thousand calories a day diet so I could fit into them.

The day of the party, my father dropped me at the station just after lunch. As the train pulled into the platform, I gazed at my reflection in the window. My hair framed my face pleasingly, and my white long-sleeved T-shirt, beige jacket and bleached jeans screamed smart-casual, which was the very look I was aiming for. My overnight bag felt as light as a feather as I slid it into the overhead luggage rack before settling into a window seat.

My confidence was given a further boost when a lad about my age boarded the train at Chatham and spent the rest of the journey chatting me up. As we approached Victoria, he asked if I fancied joining him for a drink.

'That would be lovely, but I'm going to a friend's flat-warming in Pimlico,' I informed him. I liked the way I sounded. Sophisticated, hip. Urbane. 'Maybe another time.'

He scribbled his number on the corner of an abandoned *Evening Standard*, tore it off, pressed it into my hand, and disappeared through the throng of people on the platform. I scrunched the paper into a ball and dropped it in the nearest bin, then headed for the underground. One stop later, I emerged at Pimlico. From there it was a short walk to the stucco-fronted, four-storey building in Claverton Street that Juliet, Danny and John now called home. Juliet had told me their maisonette was on the top two floors. I stared up at the windows looking for signs of life, then ran my hands through my hair and pressed the buzzer.

'Yes?' said a familiar voice through the intercom.

'John, it's me, Rose,' I said.

'Rose!' he said, with such warmth in his voice that I forgot about my nerves. 'Come on up.'

The door clicked. Pushing it open, I stood in the narrow hallway for a moment, taking in the scuffed terracotta tiled floor, the high ceilings and the dusty chandelier. The place would have been grand once. Now it was a little shabby around the edges, but I liked it all the more for it. I wondered what it would be like to work in London and to live at the top of this down-at-heel yet genteel building. I pictured myself arriving home from my stressful but rewarding job, a tissue-wrapped bottle of wine in one hand, my briefcase in the other. I imagined climbing the stairs to a flat filled with voices and laughter. The clink of glasses.

Dissecting my day over a Rioja or three with my flatmates. Easy banter between old friends. Being independent. Confident. Capable. Responsible for no one but myself.

But the vision blurred, then vanished before I could lock onto it, because it was nothing more than a chimera, so far removed from my day-to-day life that it could never be. Reality for me was a suffocating existence in a damp, dingy cottage in the middle of the woods with my aged parents for company. Financial dependence. No job. No future. Nothing.

'There you are!' John cried, bounding down the stairs and jerking me from my self-pity fest. He held out his arms and I let him hug me. He drew back and regarded me, his hands still clasping my shoulders, then gave an appreciative nod. 'Nice hair,' he said. 'Suits you. In fact, you look amazing. Very chic.'

I could have kissed him, but instead I let him take my case and I followed him up the stairs to the flat he shared with the person I loved most in the world, and the person I most despised.

'Jules and Danny are on a booze run. They won't be long,' John said as he pushed open the door to the flat.

'I'm a bit early,' I admitted. 'But I thought I could help with nibbles and things.'

'No nibbles tonight. It's strictly alcohol only.'

I plonked my handbag on the kitchen counter next to a

couple of packets of plastic glasses and some cocktail umbrellas. 'Are many coming?'

'About thirty if everyone shows. A few nerds and some traders from my place, some of Danny's workmates and clients at the gym, and some people from Juliet's new work. She said something about her old school crowd dropping in later, too.'

I groaned inwardly. I'd met a few of Juliet's school friends while we were at uni. They all had swishy hair, white teeth, braying voices and a propensity to look right through me as if I was invisible.

'I assume the bag means you're staying the night?' John asked.

For a moment, I was filled with doubt. Juliet hadn't actually offered to put me up, but surely she wasn't expecting me to catch the last train home on my own? It would be full of sleazebags and drunks. I told myself not to be so stupid. This was Juliet we were talking about. My best friend. Of course she wasn't.

'Yes, I'm staying,' I said. 'She mentioned something about a box room?'

'It's full of Danny's crap, but I'm sure we can squeeze you in.'

John led me up a second flight of stairs. 'My room's on the right and yours is here,' he said, opening a door to his left. 'It's supposed to be Danny's, but he shares Juliet's, obviously.'

'Obviously,' I said, gritting my teeth.

Danny's room was kitted out as a home gym, with a rowing machine, workout bench, freestanding punch bag and an array of barbells and dumbbells. A sink was tucked behind the door and the single bed was almost hidden under a pile of sports clothes and kit bags, a couple of pairs of boxing gloves and a stack of bodybuilding magazines. I shuffled around the clutter on the floor to the sash window. It looked out over a vast red-bricked block of flats.

'That's Dolphin Square,' John said, joining me. 'It's art deco. Quite famous. Here's an interesting fact: Oswald Mosley and Christine Keeler both lived there.'

'Not at the same time, I hope,' I said, tugging the window open to rid the room of the sour smell of Danny's stale sweat.

'Fortunately not. Look, I need to pop out for half an hour. Will you be all right on your own?'

'Of course.'

'The bathroom's next to Juliet and Danny's room if you want to freshen up. Won't be long.'

I waited until I heard the door to the flat close, then opened my case and took out the black velvet dress I'd ordered from Kays for tonight's party. I'd chosen it partly because the model wearing it had the same shade of red hair as me and partly because even I knew every girl needed a little black dress. I hung it on the back of the door and went to explore the rest of the flat.

John's room was painted dove grey with a darker grey duvet cover on the double bed. There were film posters on the walls, cotton rag rugs on the floor, a guitar on a stand and an Amstrad computer on a desk in the corner. I closed the door softly behind me and headed downstairs. The first door opened onto a cramped, windowless bathroom with rust stains on the bath and a shower curtain that smelt of mildew. My heart beat a little faster as I opened the door to Juliet and Danny's room. It was easily the nicest room in the flat, with high ceilings, decorative coving and two sash windows with a view of Claverton Street, yet it was a tip, a virtual facsimile of Juliet's room in our student digs. As I scanned the unmade kingsize bed, the jumble of makeup and jewellery on the dressing table and the clothes strewn everywhere, I was reminded of the jumble sales my mother used to drag me to before her stroke, only Juliet's clothes were from Whistles, Hobbs and Jigsaw, not British Home Stores and Marks and Spencer.

Danny's side of the bedroom was no less messy and for the first time I wondered if they were better suited to each other than I'd always thought. No neat freak could put up with Juliet's chaos, that was for sure. I poked around in Danny's underwear drawer and picked through the detritus on his bedside table. A mouldy apple core, a used tissue, a pile of coppers and a black leather Filofax. Without thinking, I flicked through the pages, beginning with the diary. On Friday the twenty-fifth of October Danny had written, *Housewarming, ours*. I thumbed through a few more pages. My heart rate quickened as I noticed that on four separate days over the next three weeks, he had written a woman's name. Tania. Different times had been scribbled beside her name each time, but they were always in the evening, anywhere between 7pm and 9.30pm.

Who the hell was Tania, and why was Danny meeting her? I rifled through the pages until I came to the address book at the back of the Filofax, running my fingers down several pages of names until I came to a Tania Emery, an address in Knightsbridge and a phone number.

I held the Filofax in front of me almost reverentially, like I'd just unearthed the Holy Grail. Could this be evidence that Danny was having an affair? I didn't have a chance to ponder further because at that moment I heard a door opening and Juliet's laughter ringing through the flat. I dropped the Filofax like a hot coal and scooted out of the room.

'Rose!' Juliet exclaimed as I wandered into the kitchen, where she and Danny were unloading bottles of wine from Tesco carrier bags. 'I thought we said seven?'

'I thought I'd come early to give you a hand.' I picked up a carrier bag from the floor and was about to set it on the counter when Danny swiped it out of my hands.

'No need,' he said. 'We have everything covered.'

'I also thought it would give us a chance to catch up before everyone else arrives. I'm dying to hear about Ibiza.' I hated the pleading tone to my voice, but Juliet's face softened, and she dumped the bag she was holding and crossed the room.

'You're right,' she said, linking arms with me. 'There's plenty of time for a chinwag and a cuppa.' She glanced back at Danny. 'Stick the kettle on, will you, Daniel? A girl could die of thirst around here.'

Danny sighed audibly. Juliet gave me a conspiratorial wink and something tight inside me unfurled.

CHAPTER TWENTY-SEVEN

Fatigue settled on me like a blanket as I sat in the vet's waiting room with Dinah's cat basket at my feet, waiting for her name to be called. Swallowing a yawn, I bent down and peered through the basket's wire door. My little grey and apricot cat was curled like a full stop at the back of the basket, as still as a stuffed toy. Only the faintest rise and fall of her flank signalled she was still breathing. I pushed a finger through the wire and waggled it, calling her name softly. One crocodile eye flickered open, then closed again.

I sat back up, stifled another yawn and scanned the room, taking in the displays of veterinary-approved cat and dog food, a stainless steel set of scales and a notice-board covered in thank-you cards.

I stood up, stretched my back and wandered over to a poster on the opposite wall showing the body condition scores for cats, from one - too thin - to nine, obese. My hand subconsciously crept around my own thickening midriff as I read the descriptions. Were Dinah's ribs palpable under her fat? Debatable. Was her waist visible? Not these days. Did she have a slight abdominal distension? Didn't we all? Taking all that into account, she scored an eight despite the weight she'd lost in the last couple of days.

'Dinah Barton?' said a voice, and I turned to see a middle-aged man in blue scrubs holding open the door to a consulting room on the far side of the waiting room. I picked up Dinah's basket and hurried over. Once inside, I placed the basket on the examination table.

'What seems to be the problem?' the vet asked with a businesslike smile.

'She's been a bit under the weather. Lethargic. And she's not interested in her food, which isn't like her,' I said, my fingers trembling as I fumbled with the basket's leather straps. 'I gave it a couple of days hoping she'd get better, but if anything, she's worse.'

'Is she up to date with her vaccinations?'

'She had her booster in February,' I confirmed.

'Worm and flea treatment?'

I nodded.

'Let's have a look.' He reached into the basket and lifted Dinah out. She was as floppy as a rag doll. I held my breath as he examined her eyes, ears and teeth, listened to her heart and felt her stomach. Dinah barely seemed to register him.

'When did she last have anything to eat?' he asked, placing his stethoscope on the counter behind him.

'A couple of days ago.'

'Has she been drinking more than usual?'

'She does seem quite thirsty,' I said.

'And has she vomited?'

I pictured the pile of watery sick. 'Yesterday morning.'

'Right.' He rubbed his face. 'Has she ever had problems with her kidneys?'

It was the question I'd been dreading. Lethargy, loss of appetite, vomiting and dehydration were all symptoms of renal failure, a common condition in older cats. But Dinah was only seven.

'No,' I said. 'She's always been a healthy little thing.'

'It's a long shot, but I don't suppose she could have come into contact with antifreeze or lilies?'

I stared at him. 'Why?'

'They're both highly toxic to cats. Ingesting them can cause the kidneys to shut down.'

I held onto the examination table to steady myself. 'Someone bought me a bunch of lilies,' I said. 'But they were on the kitchen table. Dinah wouldn't have eaten them.'

'She wouldn't have needed to,' the vet said. 'She could have simply brushed past the flowers, then groomed the pollen off her coat.'

My blood ran cold as I remembered wiping a dusting of pollen off the table.

The vet listened to Dinah's heart again. 'When a cat has recently come into contact with lilies, we induce vomiting and feed the cat activated charcoal to reduce them being absorbed further. Treatment should ideally start within six hours. When were they brought into your house?'

'The day before yesterday.'

'Right. In that case, our only course of action is to give her intravenous fluids.'

'A drip?'

He nodded. 'We want to reduce the long-term impact on her kidney function and try to clear her body of toxins. It'll mean her staying for a few days. While she's with us, we'll carry out kidney function blood tests and monitor her blood pressure and urine output.'

'Does it work, flushing the toxins out of her system?' I asked.

He couldn't meet my eye. 'Sometimes,' he said.

I left Dinah at the vet's and drove home, wishing I'd brought her in sooner, wondering who the hell had left the deadly bouquet of lilies on my doorstep.

Who could hate me so much that they would poison my cat? Three people came to mind: Rhona Richards, Roy Matthews… and Theo. Rhona had loathed me from the day I'd started volunteering at Sisterline, and now I was about to steal the top job from right under her nose. Roy Matthews thought I was the last person his precious daughter had spoken to before she killed herself. And Theo, well, Theo had more reason to hate me than the other two put together.

The flowers hadn't appeared out of thin air. Someone

had left them on the doorstep. Someone who knew where I lived. Would Rhona have accessed my personnel file to find my address? My mind whirring, I realised she didn't have to. The charity's Christmas party the previous year had been held at a pub in Faversham. Dorothy had given Rhona and me a lift home, dropping me off first. What about Matthews? Had Eloise been right? Had he followed the recovery truck home the day he'd slashed my tyre?

Theo knew exactly where I lived, but he hadn't left the pillbox in five days. It couldn't be him. I erased his name from my list of suspects.

As I approached the junction with the A2, I glanced in the mirror, my heart lurching as I saw the sun glinting off a white bonnet behind me. I pressed hard on the brakes, and the Land Rover shuddered to a stop. I looked left and right, searching for a gap in the traffic, hoping someone would let me out. But the steady stream of cars surged past, a river of steel and glass, as impenetrable as a wall. I dragged my gaze back to the rear-view mirror, but the sun shone on the tinted windscreen, hiding the driver's face, and the car was too close for me to see the badge on the bonnet.

All at once it seemed unbearably hot in the Land Rover and I turned off the fan heater with a flick of my wrist. But still heat suffused me, beads of sweat breaking out across my brow, my fingers slippery on the steering wheel. Too late, I realised I'd missed a chance to pull out and the car behind blared its horn and edged closer to my back bumper. My heart beat faster.

I was gripped with paranoia. Had I somehow conjured

Roy Matthews up just by thinking about him? Or, more likely and infinitely more disturbing, had he been following me all this time, unnoticed until now?

I felt claustrophobic in the airless Land Rover, but I didn't dare open a window in case Matthews appeared by my door brandishing a knife. Instead, I plucked at the neck of my blouse, leant back against the headrest and forced myself to breathe deeply. But it was impossible through clenched jaws, and my breathing grew shallower still.

Another toot of the horn made me jerk forwards, and I gripped the steering wheel, my eyes darting left and right. At last, I spied a break in the traffic and hit the accelerator. As the Land Rover bunny-hopped forwards and was swallowed up into the line of traffic, my heart rate slowed and my grip on the steering wheel eased.

But my relief was short-lived. As I turned onto the Eastling road, I realised the white car was still following me. *Shit.* I stamped on the accelerator and the Land Rover shot forwards, the seatbelt tightening across my chest. Dizziness made my head spin, and I closed my eyes to ground myself. When I opened them again, I saw a line of parked cars bearing down on me, and I wrenched the steering wheel to the right, missing them with seconds to spare.

The car behind was flashing me now, and the driver had stuck his arm out of his window and was gesturing me to pull over. I ran through my options. The shops and café at Brogdale were coming up on my left. I could stop in the busy car park and see what Roy Matthews' problem was in front of a dozen witnesses, or I could drive back to my cottage in the middle of the woods with him tailing me.

I indicated left and turned into the car park, the car behind still following. I pulled into a space but left the engine running. Winding down the window, I waited, my heart in my mouth.

CHAPTER TWENTY-EIGHT

'One of your brake lights isn't working,' said a polite voice. I stared at its owner. A slight man in his eighties was smiling at me through the window. As I stared, his smile faded, and his brow creased. 'Are you all right?'

I found my voice. 'I thought you were someone else.'

'Sorry to disappoint,' he said, the smile back in place. 'Only Jeanie - my wife,' he turned and waved at the woman in the passenger seat. 'Jeanie said we ought to let you know. She said she'd never forgive herself if the police stopped you.'

'The police?' I said, only half-listening. I was too busy gaping at the man's car. It was a silver Fiat Doblo, one of those ones that takes wheelchairs in the back. As I stared, Jeanie waved at me through the window. I gave a half-hearted wave back.

'It's the left one,' the man said.

'The left what?'

'The left brake light that's not working. Are you *sure* you're all right?' he asked, peering at me.

'Sorry, yes, I'm fine. I'll see it's fixed. Thank you,' I added as he headed back to his car. 'You're very kind.'

He waved my thanks away, climbed back into his silver car, and drove out of the car park. I pulled a handkerchief from my bag and dabbed at the sheen of sweat on my forehead. Had a trick of the light made me think the car was white, or was I becoming paranoid, seeing things that weren't there? Of course Roy Matthews wasn't tailing me. To think it was even a possibility said more about the state of my mind than his. I suddenly craved my vitamins and the way they calmed my racing thoughts, blunting the rough edges and dulling my emotions.

'Pull yourself together, Rose,' I muttered, slamming my foot on the clutch and thrusting the gearstick into reverse.

The stench of faeces hit me the moment I pushed open the door of the pillbox, and I gagged. Theo watched from the corner as I pinched my nose with one hand and gingerly picked the bucket up with the other. When I returned a moment later, the bucket empty, he had bum-shuffled halfway to the door.

'If you want this, you'll get back right now,' I growled, dangling the bag of food in front of me.

For a minute he held my gaze, his eyes burning with defiance, then he lowered his head and slowly retreated until his back was once again against the wall. I dropped the bag on his lap, and he scrabbled through it, pulling out a packet of pork pies. His wrists were still bound, so he ripped off the plastic wrapping with his teeth and, with a small moan, rammed one of the pies into his mouth.

He must have seen the revulsion on my face because he finished his mouthful and said, 'You look at me as if I am an animal.'

I said nothing.

He took a huge bite out of a second pork pie. This time he spoke with his mouth full, spraying crumbs towards me. 'You look at me as if I am an animal, yet that is exactly how you are treating me. A caged animal. What have I done to deserve such treatment?'

I shook my head. 'If you don't know, then you are a fool.'

He took the bottle of water from the bag and cursed roundly in French as he struggled with the screw-cap lid. I would have opened it for him if he'd asked, but he was too proud for that. Eventually, he managed it, raising the bottle to his mouth and drinking deeply.

'I have a lot of time to think in here,' he said. 'And I have been thinking about you. Who you are. Why you are punishing me.'

I picked up the pork pie packet, folded it into eight and popped it in my pocket.

'You cannot be Eloise's mother, because Eloise's mother is dead. Unless that was another of her lies.'

Blood pounded in my ears. 'It wasn't a lie.'

'So perhaps you are an aunt, or a friend, or someone

she paid,' he continued. 'Because I know she is behind this.'

'How dare you blame Eloise when she's the victim?' I exploded.

His eyes widened. 'Eloise, a victim?' He shook his head ruefully, then met my gaze. 'Eloise is a bad person.'

I knew I should walk straight out without listening to his lies, but I couldn't bring myself to move.

'What d'you mean, bad?'

He held up his hands and started twisting his wrists against each other, so the sleeves of his chef's whites slipped down.

'Look,' he said, holding both hands towards me. 'See that?'

Curiosity got the better of me and I bent down to look. There were small areas of red, puckered skin on both his wrists, just above his cuffs.

'They are burns,' he said. 'She flicked hot oil at me because she thought I was having an affair with someone at work.'

'I don't believe you. You're a chef. You work in a kitchen. You must burn yourself all the time.'

'I was holding up my hands to protect my face. That is why the burns are on the insides of my wrists. When I asked her to move out, she poured acid over the bonnet of my car. She is fou.' He shook his head. 'It means crazy in French. Insane.'

'You're the crazy one if you think I'm going to believe this codswallop. You were the jealous and controlling one.

You were the one who was violent towards her. She told me everything.'

'Did she tell you about the time she smashed a mirror over my head? The plates she threw at me? The black eye she gave me on my birthday because I went to the pub after work without her?'

'She said you were the one who gave her a black eye.'

'She was lying.'

'If what you say is true, why didn't you call the police?'

'I did not think they would believe me. Women do not attack men.' He exhaled loudly. 'Also, I was ashamed. What kind of man lets his girlfriend scratch him, hit him, kick him?'

I shook my head. 'I've had enough of your bullshit.' I headed for the door.

'You say I am the fool,' he said calmly. 'Trust me. If you believe Eloise, you are the bigger fool.'

Eloise's face crumpled when I relayed the vet's prognosis. She turned away, shielding her face so I wouldn't see her tears. I laid an arm around her shoulder and pulled her awkwardly towards me, holding her tightly as her whole body shuddered.

'There, there,' I soothed. 'She'll be OK. You know our Dinah. She's a feisty little bugger.'

My words triggered a fresh storm of tears and I rubbed her back until the sobs subsided.

'Come and sit down,' I said, leading her to the kitchen table and pouring her a glass of water from the tap. She took a couple of sips, then looked at me with bloodshot eyes.

'I had no idea lilies were poisonous.'

'Only to cats, it seems.' I handed her a tissue.

'I thought someone was trying to send you a warning.'

'What do you mean?'

'They're the flowers everyone has at funerals, aren't they? Mum had them.'

I thought back to her mother's funeral, trying to picture Juliet's coffin as the pall bearers lowered it into the earth. Stargazer lilies had been the centrepiece of the pink and white wreath on top. 'You're right,' I said, surprised Eloise remembered. 'She did.'

A coincidence, I wondered? But no. I'd chosen lilies for both my parents' funerals. White ones with wax-like petals and a heavy scent, symbolising the innocence restored to the souls of the departed. Eloise was right. They were a funeral favourite.

I became aware that she was speaking.

'Sorry, honey, you'll have to say that again.'

'I should never have left them,' she wailed.

I looked at her, not understanding.

'On the kitchen table. I should never have left them on the kitchen table. I should have put them somewhere she couldn't reach or, better still, thrown the fucking things straight in the bin.'

'Don't blame yourself, it's not your fault. It's just one of those things. Dinah will be fine. And we'll both know for next time, won't we, eh?' I said, thumbing away the tear sliding down her cheek. 'I tell you what, why don't we go for a nice long walk to take our minds off it all?'

Eloise shook her head. 'I don't feel like it. But you should go. I'll be fine here.'

'Are you sure?' I said. The urge to be outside, striding through the trees and breathing in the damp, earthy woodland air, was like an itch waiting to be scratched. 'I won't be long.'

'Take as long as you want. I'll be here if the vet rings.'

I pulled on my wellies and coat and walked the length of the woods and back, nervous energy zipping through me like the buzz from an electric current. I walked until my legs were heavy and dusk was darkening my view. And when I went back indoors, Eloise was in the kitchen peeling potatoes. We ate cottage pie in silence and watched crap on the television until it was time to go to bed. I was going through my nightly routine of closing windows and locking doors when the phone rang.

'Miss Barton? It's Pete Harris from the veterinary practice. I'm calling about Dinah.'

I sucked in air. 'How is she?'

His pause told me everything.

'I'm afraid it's bad news,' he said finally. 'We gave Dinah intravenous fluids, but her kidneys were already failing. Despite our best efforts, she passed away about ten minutes ago.'

'I understand.' My voice cracked. I swallowed, cleared my throat and said, 'Was it peaceful, the end?'

'It was. The vet nurse and I were both with her. She just slipped away.'

'Good.' I glanced up the stairs and wondered how I would break the news to Eloise. 'Can I bring her home?' I asked. 'I'd like to bury her in the garden with the others. The other cats,' I added hastily. 'They're all buried under the apple tree.'

'Of course. Just phone to let us know you're coming, and we can make sure she's ready. I'm very sorry we couldn't save her, but the damage had already been done.'

'You did your best,' I said, because it seemed like the right thing to say. 'Thank you for letting me know.'

'That's all right. I'm on call tonight. I was here anyway.'

I stumbled across the room to the sofa and sank down, cradling my head in my hands as I tried to imagine life without my insouciant little cat. Out of nowhere, I remembered something Juliet once said to me.

You reap what you sow, Rose.

Was it my fault Dinah died? Had my actions been the catalyst for her death by poisoning two decades later? Was it payback for my crimes?

There was a time I'd have dismissed such a notion as far-fetched. Ridiculous, even. But doubt clouded my certainty. I wasn't sure of anything any more.

CHAPTER TWENTY-NINE

OCTOBER 1991

Seven o'clock came and went. At ten past seven, a couple of John's pale-faced computer nerd work-mates arrived at the party, dressed in head-to-toe black and clutching cans of lager and cider. Just after eight a contingent from Danny's gym turned up, all tight T-shirts and taut muscles. At nine, a dozen traders from John's bank bowled in, besuited and brandishing bottles of Dom Perignon and Bollinger. A pack of Juliet's old school friends arrived soon after and suddenly it was standing room only, bodies crushed against each other, the whole flat pumping with the music of Sisters of Mercy and Bauhaus. John's choices, because although he dressed like the traders he wanted to become, he was also a sad goth at heart.

I found myself discussing the difference between Pilates and yoga with a sinewy American girl called Honey, although I would have bet my last pound that wasn't her real name. And we could have been talking about the difference between William Shakespeare and Christopher Marlowe for all I could hear over the pounding beat of the music.

'D'you know Tania?' I shouted in her ear during a lull in the conversation.

'Tania Emery?'

I nodded, unable to believe my luck.

'Sure,' Honey said. 'She's right over there.'

I followed her gaze to an arrestingly beautiful black girl in a red stocking of a dress that fitted her like a second skin. She had almond-shaped eyes and straight hair worn in a single plait down her back. Two of the bankers were vying for her attention, but the bored expression on her face hinted they were both failing miserably.

'Does she work at the gym?' I asked, surprised. She seemed too slender, too fragile, to be a personal trainer.

'She's one of Danny's clients,' Honey said. 'Used to be mine, but I've cut back my one-to-ones to concentrate on my Pilates classes.'

But I wasn't really listening because I was too busy chastising myself for jumping to the wrong conclusions. Of course Danny wouldn't write dates with his lover in his diary. Of course Tania was a client. It was obvious when I thought about it. My brain had made the leap because I so desperately wanted Juliet to see Danny for what he was: a liar and a cheat. A love rat.

I scanned the room searching for Juliet, spotting her with her arms draped around Danny's neck, her upturned face gazing into his. As I watched, he cupped her chin and kissed her deeply. Their bodies melded as she kissed him back. Who was I kidding? Any fool could see they were crazy about each other. A crushing disappointment knocked the breath out of me, and I swayed like a sapling in the wind.

Honey frowned in concern. 'Hey, are you OK?'

I muttered something about needing the loo and stumbled from the room.

I sought sanctuary in Danny's bedroom, sweeping the clothes, kit bags and magazines from his bed onto the floor and burrowing under the duvet like a small nocturnal animal. Only then did I allow the tears to fall. I stuffed a corner of the pillow into my mouth, so I didn't make a sound as the sobs shuddered through me. I didn't want anyone seeing me in this state, least of all Juliet. The look of disgust on her face when I tried to kiss her after the Snow Ball swam before my eyes and I cried even harder. I was gripped by self-loathing. I was such an idiot. Juliet and Danny were a couple, and the sooner I accepted it, the better. The blonde DJ had been an aberration for which Danny had apologised. It was clear he was besotted by Juliet and if I truly loved her, I would be glad. And I did truly love her.

Slowly, my sobs subsided, and I sat up and wiped my

eyes. Downstairs, the party was clearly still in full swing if the volume of the music was anything to go by. I checked the time, surprised to see it was already almost one in the morning. I debated whether or not to attempt to repair my makeup and go back down or hide up here until everyone had gone home. I decided to stay put. If anyone asked, I'd feign a headache. I could always pee in the sink if I needed to.

I was climbing out of bed when I heard the creak of a stair and a stifled giggle. My eyes widened. Had John actually pulled? Shaking my head in disbelief, I ferreted through my overnight bag, looking for my nightie. I was hoicking it out when there was another creak and a man said silkily, 'In here.'

A sixth sense told me he was talking about Danny's room, not John's, and I darted back under the duvet, pulling it over my head and making myself as flat as possible as the doorknob turned, and the door swung slowly open.

I lay as still as a corpse as the door clicked shut again. There was another giggle, then a muffled thud, as if a body had been pressed up against the stripped pine door. Then the unmistakable sound of kissing. Lips against lips, caught breath and smothered groans. A voice whispering, 'Fuck, you're driving me crazy. I want you so much it's killing me.' Not just any voice. Danny's voice.

Under the duvet, I pulled a face. Wasn't necking Juliet on the dance floor enough for him? Couldn't the man wait until the last guests had gone before he dragged her upstairs and shagged her? What was the urgency?

And then I realised with horror that I was going to be forced to listen to every grunt, every moan, every whimper as they had sex a few feet away from me. And what if they retired to the bed? I imagined the mocking curl of Danny's mouth as they discovered me hiding. He'd probably accuse me of voyeurism. But I was no peeping tom. I'd rather walk naked down Oxford Street than have to endure listening to them going at it like rabbits.

I wanted to clasp my hands over my ears to drown out the sound, but I couldn't risk being seen. So, I concentrated on breathing as shallowly as I could. And then Danny's voice again.

'I'm going to do unspeakable things to you,' he murmured. I caught the almost imperceptible sound of a zipper being undone. 'Unspeakable things.'

'What about your girlfriend?' said a woman's voice and my stomach flipped like a pancake because I'd been wrong. Correction: I'd been right. Danny *was* a bastard. He was a love rat and a lying, dirty cheat, and the woman he was about to have sex with wasn't Juliet. It was someone else entirely.

He laughed, and under the duvet, my hands curled into fists.

'She's as pissed as a fart. She won't even notice I've gone.'

'Well, in that case…' the woman cooed.

Pictures of You by The Cure had been playing, but someone turned the volume down and Juliet's voice rang up the stairs.

'Danny!' she called. 'Oh, Danny Boy! Kim and the gang

are off to Annabel's and want to know if we'd like to go with them. Can we? Can we please?'

'Shit!' Danny hissed. 'Get dressed!'

I pictured a pair of jeans being dragged up and a dress being tugged down. Hair smoothed and lipstick wiped off. Smiles painted on faces. Excuses at the ready. Then Juliet cried, 'Where in heaven's name *are* you?' And the door burst open and even through the duvet I sensed the light from the landing illuminating Danny and the mystery woman as if they were actors on a stage and for a moment, no more than a second or two, everything was silent.

And then Juliet howled, 'You bastard! You utter fucking bastard! How could you? How *could* you?'

I'd been right all along. The mystery woman was Tania Emery, Danny's newest client. When Tania had legged it out of the room and down the stairs with both Juliet and Danny in hot pursuit, I'd seized the opportunity to sneak out of Danny's room into John's, where I emerged moments later, my face a picture of innocence. Juliet was sitting, white-faced, at the bottom of the stairs.

'I was just seeing if John had any painkillers,' I said, joining her. 'Then I heard a kerfuffle. What on earth's going on?'

'Danny's... Danny has...' She gulped. 'There was another girl. He was with another girl.' Tears streamed down her face and she pointed to the door that separated the hallway from the rest of the flat. 'Make everyone go home, Rose. Please make them go.'

I nodded. 'On it like a car bonnet.'

John and I spent the next ten minutes chivvying everyone out of the flat. Once they'd gone, I climbed wearily up the stairs to John's room, where I'd left Juliet with a pint glass of water and a box of tissues.

Her tear-blotched face jerked towards me as I let myself in and as she stared over my shoulder, I thought I saw a flicker of hope in her pink-rimmed eyes.

'He's gone,' I told her. 'Said he'd be back in the morning when you were in a fit state to listen to him. Went off with that girl from the gym, Honey, and another girl. I think she was a client? Tammy or Tara or some such.' It wasn't quite the truth. I'd found Danny pushing his way through the scrum of partygoers leaving the flat, heading for the stairs and Juliet. I'd grabbed his arm and pulled him into the kitchen, where I'd told him in no uncertain terms to piss right off.

'But I need to see Jules. Explain that it wasn't what she thought it was.'

'Oh, come on,' I said with a snort of derision. 'She caught you red-handed. How are you going to explain that away?'

'But I've signed the tenancy here. I don't have anywhere else to go.'

I narrowed my eyes. 'Then perhaps you should have told your cock that, arsehole.'

For a moment he looked as if he was about to retaliate,

but then he hung his head and said, 'I'll come around in the morning. Talk to her then.'

'You can try,' I said. 'But don't hold your breath. She won't forgive you this time. Not in a million years.'

Next to me, Juliet had broken into a fresh storm of tears. I leaned towards her, about to put my arm around her, but thought better of it. Instead, I pulled a tissue out of the box and pressed it into her hand.

'I feel so stupid,' she sobbed.

'Don't be so hard on yourself. He's the one who's in the wrong.'

'I know, but I should have realised I couldn't trust him after last time.'

'Once a cheater, always a cheater,' I agreed. I handed her another tissue. 'What will you do?'

Juliet blew her nose noisily, jutted out her jaw and looked me straight in the eye. 'I'm going to chuck him out. You were right all along, Rosie. He's not worth it.'

CHAPTER THIRTY

Eloise was sleeping when I let myself into her bedroom the next morning. I hovered just inside the door, her mug of tea in my hand, wondering if I should wake her. She was on her side facing me, one hand tucked under her chin, one slender arm on top of the covers. Her face was strangely blank in repose, the face of a mannequin. Her chest rose and fell as she sighed, stretched her legs and turned onto her other side.

I hadn't believed a word of the nonsense Theo had fed me the previous day. From what Eloise had told me, it was clear he had psychopathic tendencies, and everyone knew psychopaths were pathological liars. They simply didn't care about the truth. It suited him for me to believe Eloise was the enemy. Simple as.

I knew Eloise. I had seen her need to be loved. I had glimpsed the vulnerability at her core. She was her mother's daughter through and through.

For the first time in my life, I wondered what would

have happened if I'd told Eloise's social worker that I wanted her to come and live with me. I'd said no because I hadn't wanted anyone to upset my prissy, ordered life. I hadn't given a toss about poor Eloise, orphaned at eleven, and teetering on the brink of a life in care. In the dark days after her mother's death, she'd had the courage to find my number and phone me, a woman she barely remembered, because she had no one else. No one. But her pleas had fallen on deaf ears because I was a self-centred bitch.

What if I had taken Eloise in? We could have been a family of two, just as Eloise and Juliet had been. The walls of my shabby, forlorn, creeper-covered cottage would have rung with the sound of laughter, of life. Yes, there would have been teenage strops, cross words and maybe even stand up rows, but the house would have been a living, breathing place, not the silent mausoleum I'd rattled around in for the last fourteen years, the only noise the depressing drone of Radio 4 and my one-sided chats with the cat.

There would have been parents' evenings to attend and school discos to find outfits for. Dentist appointments to meet and friendship dramas to dissect. First boyfriends and spots; driving lessons and periods. Eloise had to navigate them all alone, when I could have been by her side.

The tea was growing cold in my hand as a swell of self-loathing rose like bile at the back of my throat. 'I'm sorry,' I whispered to her sleeping back. 'I am so sorry.'

I froze as she shifted in the bed, then rolled onto her back and gazed at me blearily.

'Rose, is that you? Have you heard from the vet?'

I set the tea on the bedside table, perched on the side of the bed, and took her hand in mine.

'He rang last night after you'd gone to bed.'

'Is she going to be all right?' she said, her voice as hopeful as the day she'd phoned asking if she could come and live with me. I swallowed. I'd dashed her hopes then; I was about to do so again.

'I'm afraid it's bad news,' I said, echoing the vet. 'Dinah didn't make it. She died last night.'

Her eyes widened, and a sob escaped her lips. 'No!' she cried. 'She can't be dead. She can't be!'

'I'm so sorry,' I said again. 'They did everything they could.' I held out my arms, inviting Eloise in for a hug, but she shook her head, hunkered under the duvet, and turned back to face the wall.

My heart was heavy as I drove into Faversham an hour later. I hadn't wanted to leave Eloise on her own, but she'd insisted, assuring me she would be all right.

'They can manage without me for one morning,' I told her.

'I'll be fine,' she said firmly. 'Anyway, you need to see if you've got the job.'

Rhona was in with Eddie when I arrived, so I busied myself by tackling the inbox and drafting a press release for a joint initiative with the police in which we were planning to visit schools to talk to students about identifying people in crisis. But I'd barely written the first paragraph when the door to Eddie's office flew open and Rhona stalked out, thin-lipped and frowning.

A couple of minutes later, Eddie popped her head around the door.

'Rose, do you have a minute?'

I saved my document and followed her into her office, pulling up a chair. She regarded me for a moment.

'You look tired,' she said.

Taken aback, I took my glasses off and cleaned them on the corner of my cardigan.

'I'm not sleeping very well at the moment,' I admitted. 'I keep waking up in the middle of the night drenched in sweat with my heart racing nineteen to the dozen.'

'Bloody menopause,' Eddie said, shaking her head. 'Men don't know how lucky they are. Anyway, that's not why I asked you in. I wanted to let you know that Dorothy and I have reached a decision about the chief executive role and we're delighted to offer you the position.'

Happiness stole my voice for a moment, and I tipped my head back and stared at the ceiling while I composed myself.

'Thank you,' I said at last. 'You don't know how much this means to me.'

Eddie smiled. 'It was a unanimous decision. We both felt you're exactly what we need to take the charity to a new level. I'll email your formal offer with all the terms and so on. As you know, the post is currently vacant, so from our point of view the sooner you start the better.'

'Of course. How did Rhona take the news?'

'How did you know Rhona was the other candidate?' Eddie asked.

'Call it a lucky guess.'

She nodded and glanced at the door. 'Not terribly well.'

'I can imagine,' I said, trying to hide my smile. 'Poor Rhona.'

'Quite. I'll announce our decision shortly, so if you could keep the news to yourself until then I'd appreciate it.'

'Absolutely,' I said, standing and drawing my thumb and forefinger across my mouth. 'My lips are sealed.'

At eleven, Eddie came out of her office and called for everyone's attention.

'I wanted to share some wonderful news with you all. Sisterline has a new chief executive, and she's one of our own. We had some excellent candidates.' She glanced at Rhona, who was staring blankly out of the window. 'But after much deliberation, we have asked Rose to join the leadership team as chief exec. She'll be starting proper on Monday. Rose,' she said, beckoning me to join her, 'come and say a few words to the team.'

Shit, I wasn't expecting that. I made my way to Eddie, cleared my throat and said, 'Someone once said that the definition of insanity was doing the same thing over and over again and expecting different results.' I paused. A couple of the volunteers exchanged glances and beside me, Eddie shifted her weight from one foot to the other.

'What I'm trying to say is that we need to embrace change when it happens, for another wise soul, Winston

Churchill in fact, said, "To improve is to change; to be perfect is to change often". And I'm aiming for perfection at Sisterline. Nothing else will do. So, expect some changes. But they will all be for the greater good.'

My gaze flickered to Rhona, who was no longer staring out of the window but was scowling at me, her eyes filled with hatred.

CHAPTER THIRTY-ONE

Any jubilance I'd felt about getting the chief executive's job leached away as I left the office just after half-past four. Dusk was already falling, and instead of taking the direct route along the alley to the car park, I walked through town, my eyes darting left and right.

Bravado was easily come by in a strip-lit room full of people. It was harder to find in a deserted town centre on a murky November afternoon. Fear fluttered in my chest as I scurried along the road. I didn't think for a moment that Rhona would attack me, but Roy Matthews was another matter. He was a convicted criminal who hadn't thought twice about assaulting his heavily pregnant neighbour. My skin prickling, I quickened my pace. Hearing a scrabbling noise, I glanced to my right, but it was only a couple of pigeons tussling in the guttering of the Oxfam shop. My gaze fell to the hunched, timid-looking woman reflected in the shop window, then I realised with a start that it was me.

I recalled a talk given by a self-defence expert at the women's refuge I'd volunteered at years ago. He was a former police officer and judo coach and he'd spent a couple of hours teaching us tactics to use if we were attacked.

He'd also drilled into us the importance of not walking like a victim.

'Someone with a slumped posture and a lowered gaze who drags their steps and has their arms pressed to their sides sends out a message that they are less likely to fight back,' he said. 'But if you hold your chin high, straighten your back, swing your arms and take forceful, dynamic steps while looking around and taking notice of your surroundings, you are telling people you are assertive and confident.

'It takes seconds for a seasoned criminal to size someone up and decide if they would be easy to rob, assault, or worse. Don't take my word for it. Remember the serial killer Ted Bundy? No? He was executed after confessing to thirty murders in the States in the seventies. He claimed he could tell a victim by the way she walked down the street, the tilt of her head, the manner in which she carried herself…'

'Excuse me,' I'd said, raising my arm.

He looked at me in surprise.

'I know you're trying to be helpful, but I take exception to what you're saying. It isn't a woman's responsibility to defend herself. It's a man's responsibility not to attack her in the first place.'

My outburst was greeted with murmurs of assent.

Many of the women in the room had suffered at the hands of their husbands or boyfriends.

'I agree with you a hundred per cent,' he replied. 'And in an ideal world, I wouldn't need to stand here and tell you how to defend yourselves against attack. No one's arguing that we need to make a cultural shift, but we need to be realistic. It won't happen overnight. I want to give you the skills to protect yourselves in the meantime. After all,' he said mildly, 'telling a woman not to learn self-defence because it's not her responsibility is like saying don't lock your doors because burglars shouldn't steal. Yet we all lock our doors when we go out. It's common sense.'

I couldn't argue with that, so I flopped back in my chair and listened to the rest of the talk without passing comment.

Remembering his advice now, I hitched my shoulders back, lifted my chin and lengthened my stride, my arms swinging by my sides. A couple of decades on, society was still fucked up and women were still worrying about their personal safety. We shouldn't have to. But I wasn't taking any chances.

I reached the Land Rover without incident and had the key in the ignition when my phone rang. I checked the screen. *Home*.

'Rose?' said a breathless voice before I had a chance to speak. 'Someone's here.'

'Who?'

There was a clunk and an intake of breath. 'Someone's in the house!' Eloise whispered. 'I can hear them.'

Terror tightened like a noose around my neck. He wouldn't, would he?

'Where are you?' I said urgently.

'In my room. But I can hear them, Rose. They're downstairs…' her voice tailed off, and I heard a muffled sob.

'Eloise,' I said. 'El. Listen to me. I want you to run into the bathroom and lock the door. Do you understand? Lock the door and drag the chair in front of it,' I instructed.

'Now?' she gasped.

'Yes. I'll stay on the line.'

She whimpered, then everything went quiet. I clutched my phone with trembling fingers. Common sense told me I should end the call and dial 999, but gut instinct screamed at me to wait until I knew she was safely in the bathroom. I held my breath and listened, but the only sound was the pounding of my heart.

Then, finally, Eloise's voice. 'I'm here. I've locked the door.'

'The chair?'

'Yes, it's jammed against the door handle.'

'Stand back from the door just in case he…' I broke off.

'Just in case he what?'

'Just do it,' I said. 'The window opens onto the flat roof over the kitchen. You can get out that way if you have to. I'll be home in ten minutes.'

Another sob escaped her lips. 'Rose?'

'Yes?'

Her voice cracked. 'Please hurry.'

The 20mph speed limit was forgotten as I drove home like the clappers, every sinew of my body desperate to protect my goddaughter. But from who - Theo or Roy Matthews?

I could only hope it was Matthews, because his hatred was focussed on me, not Eloise. It was another story if Theo had somehow broken out of the pillbox and come crashing through the woods to the house. I gripped the steering wheel tighter. Letting him live was the biggest mistake I'd ever made. I should have finished him off for good when I'd had the chance.

After what felt like the longest journey of my life, I arrived home. The Land Rover rattled as it negotiated the bumpy drive and slew to a stop in front of the coal bunker. My gaze swivelled this way and that. There was no sign of a white SUV. I glanced at the back door. It was swinging open.

'Shit,' I muttered, yanking the handbrake up. I blundered out and was about to race into the house when I stopped and changed direction to the shed. I threw open the metal trunk, snatched my father's air rifle, and ran back to the house. Stopping at the back door, I cocked my head, listening for signs of life. Silence. I tip-toed through the kitchen and into the hall. Still nothing. I ducked under the stairs and texted Eloise.

I'm downstairs. You OK?

The text immediately showed as read and I watched the ellipsis in the speech bubble as Eloise typed her reply.

Still in bathroom. Haven't heard him for a bit. Should I come out?

No. Wait till I've checked the house.

Happy that she was safe, I crept into the front room. My eyes widened as I took in the upended furniture, the smashed lamp and the broken mirror above the log burner. I could almost taste the loathing, the rage, behind the shattered glass, the overturned coffee tables, the ripped cushions, and I turned away before the image burnt on my retinas.

The scrape of a chair on the wooden floor above my head galvanised me, but before I headed upstairs, I checked the dining room and library. Both rooms had been ransacked: books ripped off shelves, chairs pulled over and pictures wrenched from walls. It was carnage, and as I went from room to room, my hand tightened on the air rifle, but there was no sign of our intruder.

I climbed stiffly up the stairs, checking each bedroom, relieved to see these hadn't been touched. Once I was satisfied we were alone, I knocked quietly on the bathroom door.

'Eloise, it's me, Rose. It's all right. It's safe to come out.'

The door opened at once, and Eloise peered around the jamb.

'Are you sure?' she whispered.

'I've checked the whole house.'

Nodding, she pulled open the door, then her mouth fell open when she saw the rifle.

'Christ, Rose, you've got a fucking shotgun!'

I stared at the gun bent over my arm.

'It's only an air rifle. Are you OK?'

She sniffed. 'I haven't heard him since I rang you. Either he heard me phoning for help or he couldn't find what he was looking for and cleared off.' Her voice quivered. 'I was so scared.'

I held out my free arm and she flung her arms around me, burying her face in my neck. A wave of tenderness threatened to overwhelm me, and, in that moment, I realised I would do anything for my complicated, unworldly goddaughter.

CHAPTER THIRTY-TWO

Eloise looked at me in surprise when I was the first to pull away. I smiled to show her nothing was wrong.

'I need to put the gun back. Will you be all right on your own?'

She sniffed, then nodded.

Promising not to be long, I hurried downstairs, shoved a couple of bananas, half a packet of digestives and more water in the pockets of my coat, grabbed a torch and set off through the garden to the woods. As I neared the pill-box, I stopped and shone the torch at the door, letting out a breath when I saw the bolts were closed.

But that didn't mean Theo hadn't kicked down the door and bolted it closed from the outside to fool me. I battled through the brambles to the nearest window slit and was about to shine the torch inside when something fluttered past my face. I dropped the torch and swallowed a scream, flapping my hand in front of my face as I felt another swish of air that stiffened the hairs on the back of my neck.

It was only when I caught a movement in the corner of my eye that I remembered the pipistrelles. I'd assumed they'd be hibernating, but perhaps the mild night and the promise of food had lured them out.

I pricked my thumb on a thorn as I scrabbled around at my feet for the torch and swore under my breath.

'Who is that?' Theo called. He sounded groggy, as if he'd just woken up.

I pushed the food and water through the slit with the muzzle of the gun, careful to keep my finger well away from the trigger. I rechecked the bolts and turned back to the house.

After I'd put the rifle back in its trunk in the shed, I went in search of Eloise, finding her in the library.

'It's not as bad as it looks,' she said, a copy of Maigret's *Dead Man* in her hand. She slotted the book neatly into the bookshelf. 'Why don't I make us a cup of tea before we start on the lounge?'

As we sat at the kitchen table nursing our mugs, she said, 'Since when have you had a gun?'

'It's my father's. He used it to shoot rabbits. I should have handed it in with his shotgun when he died, but it wasn't on his firearms certificate, so I kept it. Don't look at me like that.'

'Like what?'

'All disapproving. I live on my own in the middle of the woods. It's a deterrent. You can't be too careful these days. And, anyway, it's pretty harmless. It only shoots pellets. And I don't keep it in the house. It lives in a trunk in the shed.' I eyed her. 'Are you sure you're all right?'

She nodded, then looked as if she was about to say something.

'What is it?' I asked.

She shook her head. 'Nothing.'

'Come on, Eloise. Spill.'

Sighing, she said, 'I was wondering who the intruder was.'

'An opportunist burglar, I'd imagine. Maybe Jaden and his dodgy mate?'

'But nothing's been stolen. Whoever did this was sending you a message, a warning.' She paused. Scratched the side of her neck. 'I think it might be the road rage guy.'

'SUV Man?' I tried to keep my voice light. 'Don't be silly. And, anyway, he doesn't know where I live.'

'You keep saying he doesn't, but someone was downstairs, Rose. And someone left those lilies on your doorstep. If it wasn't him, who was it?'

'I don't know,' I said, draining my cup. 'But sitting here talking about it won't get the front room shipshape, will it?'

Eloise took the two mugs, rinsed them under the tap, then turned back to me. 'I just think you need to be careful, that's all.' To my surprise, a tear rolled down her cheek. She wiped it away with the back of her hand and gave me a watery smile. 'Because I couldn't bear to lose you, too.'

That night, as I tossed and turned in bed, it was hard to downplay Eloise's fears. What if she was right? What if the intruder had been Roy Matthews seeking vengeance? What would he have done if I'd been home? He'd threatened Kerry Davis with a baseball bat for complaining to the council about his music. What would he do to the woman he clearly blamed for his precious daughter's suicide?

I shivered under my duvet as an unwelcome thought struck me. What if Matthews was prowling around the house right now, biding his time before he broke in, crept up the stairs and attacked me in my bed? My breathing quickened as I pictured the door crashing open and Matthews bursting in, his face tight with rage, his baseball bat swinging by his side. Raising a muscular arm, bringing the bat down in an arc. It would be like swatting a fly.

But I was being ridiculous. Paranoid. Of course he wasn't outside. *But if it wasn't Theo, and it wasn't Roy Matthews, who was it? Who trashed the house? Who left the lilies?*

Now the doubt had taken root in my brain I knew sleep was impossible. I threw the duvet off, swung my legs out of bed and clomped over to the window, peering through a crack in the curtains. A full moon blinked back at me, its pale yellow light casting long, undulating shadows on the grass. Funny how the trees seemed to press into the old house at night, squeezing the oxygen out of the place like the hug of an overbearing aunt. My house, caught in a stranglehold. Even though I knew that by morning the trees would have retreated to a respectful distance, it didn't stop my scalp tingling.

I scanned the garden left to right, checking everything was where it should be. The Land Rover, its bulk reassuringly solid. Three wheelie bins. The squat squareness of the coal bunker. A row of hydrangeas with flower heads like crinkly brown greaseproof paper. Nothing untoward. I was about to head back to bed when a movement in the trees caught my eye. The flit of a shadow, dark, menacing. For a moment, I was rooted to the spot, paralysed by fear. But then I felt a rush of something hot, fierce, pulse through my veins.

Anger.

Fear would *not* hold me prisoner. Because avoiding danger was no safer in the long run. The fearful were caught as often as the bold. If Roy Matthews was coming for me, I would be ready for him.

My mind made up, I grabbed a fleece and headed downstairs, careful to avoid the creaky floorboard outside Eloise's room. As I passed through the kitchen, I stopped by the sink and stared out of the window into the night, wondering if Matthews, cloaked by the trees, was staring back at me in a sinister game of cat and mouse. With a pang I thought of Dinah, my beautiful, spirited cat, lying dead on the cold slab of the vet's examination table, the life sucked out of her by Roy fucking Matthews, and my resolve strengthened.

Pulling on my wellies, I picked up my keys and let myself out of the back door. Mindful that Eloise was now alone, I locked the door behind me. Once outside, I paused and listened while my eyes adjusted to the dark. But the only sounds were the rustle of leaves, the soft soughing of branches, and the occasional hoot of a barn owl. Noises I had grown up with, as familiar to me as the pounding of my heart.

Satisfied Matthews wasn't about to leap out of the trees and grab me around the neck, I made my way towards the shed. My bare feet slid in my wellies, and my wellies slid in the mud, giving the disconcerting sensation that I was skating on ice. Ice so thin it could shatter under my weight at any moment.

I made it to the shed unnoticed and in one piece. Before I pushed the key into the lock, I looked around again, straining to hear a twig snap or the low hawk of a throat being cleared. Nothing. I turned the key and pushed open the door, my focus on the trunk.

I'd been lying when I'd told Eloise my father's old rifle was harmless. OK, so it wasn't a twelve-bore shotgun, but in the wrong hands, air rifles could be lethal. A pellet could perforate a lung, killing someone in minutes. A chest wound might lead to heart failure. Hitting a major artery or blood vessel would almost certainly cause catastrophic blood loss. And bleeding out was never a pretty way to die.

Not that I wanted to kill Roy Matthews. Of course I didn't. The gun was merely a deterrent to show him he couldn't intimidate me. I would sleep better at night knowing it was under my bed, loaded and ready.

Just in case.

The metal trunk was cold to the touch, and my fingers fumbled with the catch. There was a knack to it. You had to press the lid of the trunk down, and only then could you prise the latch from its keeper. Eventually the catch sprang open, and I lifted the lid and stared into the blackness.

Suddenly, I was transported to the side of the sinkhole, a spade in my hand and the dank scent of mud in my nostrils. And then time and place shifted again, and I was gazing into another gaping chasm. Juliet's grave. A warm hand in mine. A promise. A second death on my conscience.

My head reeling, I stepped back, colliding with a set of shelves and knocking a stack of plastic plant pots flying. The sound of them clattering to the floor was unnaturally loud, and I stood like a statue and held my breath and listened for Matthews, aware that I might as well have erected a neon sign over the shed screaming, SHE'S IN HERE!

I counted to twenty, then reached into the trunk, the tips of my fingers walking over the contents, feeling for the rifle's smooth wooden stock or its cylindrical metal barrel, keen to feel the weight of the gun in my hand, even though I knew I would never use it.

Would I ever use it?

But the question was irrelevant, because someone had beaten me to it.

The rifle wasn't there.

CHAPTER THIRTY-THREE

JUNE 1999

It took eight whole years for Danny to creep back out of the woodwork.

Juliet was working in a small art gallery in Marylebone High Street by then, living in a pretty mews house a five-minute walk away. Her parents had bought her the house for her twenty-fifth birthday.

'They've given you a house?' I said incredulously when she told me. 'I got a twenty-pound gift voucher for BHS.'

'They're worried about me. They think I've been left on the shelf.'

'Left on the shelf?' I spluttered.

'They were married at nineteen. They think I should have settled down and started a family years ago.'

'I don't know why you haven't. It's not like you don't

get enough offers.'

It was true. The rich City types who frequented the gallery were always asking her out, but she rarely accepted, and the few men she did date never lasted long.

'It didn't feel *right,*' was her constant refrain, and I was happy, because when Juliet was single, she had time for me, and that was all I ever wanted.

I was still living at home and working as a volunteer in a local charity shop. It was dull, uninspiring work, and I was the youngest there by almost forty years, but it saved me having to look for an actual job. Because the unpalatable truth was that I didn't have the confidence to find proper paid work, let alone fly the nest. It may have been eight years since I'd dropped out of med school, but my self-esteem was still at an all-time low.

I couldn't blame my mother any more, either. Although she'd clung onto life for six miserable years after her stroke, she'd finally succumbed to a nasty bout of pneumonia two years previously. Her death could have set me free, but instead I chose to stay at home with my father. The only thing that kept me sane were the weekends I spent in London with Juliet, when we drank Chardonnay by the gallon and pretended we were Bridget Jones.

More often than not, our drunken musings turned to Danny and what a prick he was. According to John, now a Porsche-driving City trader, Danny had spent a year travelling around Australia after Juliet kicked him out, settling in Melbourne where he worked as a personal trainer.

'Such a twat,' Juliet would say, tipping wine down her

throat. 'What a lucky escape.'

'Amen to that,' I'd agree, clinking glasses, and although we'd laugh and move on, I'd sense a certain wistfulness in her expression for the rest of the night.

I didn't think much of it when Juliet casually mentioned one day that John had told her Danny was back in the country. I was confident that even if he dared show his face, there was no way she'd forgive him for cheating on her twice.

Two weeks later Juliet cancelled our weekend because she had a last-minute exhibition to prep for.

Two weeks after that, she said she was coming down with a migraine and needed to spend the weekend in bed.

The week after that, the gallery's ceiling fell down after a water leak in the flat upstairs.

'You'll be washing your hair next. Anyone would think you didn't want to see me,' I joked. But inside I was seething. If Juliet had a boyfriend, why didn't she just tell me? I wouldn't have minded. Much.

I decided to surprise her the following Friday. I left the charity shop just after lunch and bought flowers and a bottle of wine on my way to the station. The Victoria Line was already busy, and it was standing room only. I jumped off at Oxford Circus and followed signs for the Bakerloo Line, this time finding a seat between a teenage boy listening to his Sony Walkman on one side and a man reading the *Financial Times* on the other. I clutched the wine and flowers close to my chest as the tube click-clacked towards Marylebone, wondering if I should have phoned Juliet to warn her I was coming.

Too late now, I thought, as the train lurched to a stop and I jumped onto the platform.

I called in at the gallery first. It was an exclusive place that specialised in the work of the new breed of conceptual artists taking the country by storm. The kind who thought a series of black and white photographs of a man eating a Fray Bentos steak and kidney pie was of more artistic merit than the Mona Lisa. The gallery itself was a white cube-like space where a wire bin filled with screwed up bits of paper could just be a wire bin filled with screwed up bits of paper or it could be a piece of art with a price tag that would make your eyes water.

'She took today off,' an effete young man dressed in a candy-pink pinstripe suit informed me. 'Won't be back in till Monday.'

I thanked him and turned right out of the gallery towards the cobbled mews where Juliet lived. It was a warm summer's afternoon and Marylebone High Street was teeming with tourists and office workers.

Juliet took so long answering her door that at first I thought she might not be in at all, and I was about to retrace my steps to the cafe around the corner and grab a coffee when I saw a figure come down the stairs and the door swung open. Juliet was wearing a satin dressing gown I hadn't seen before and her hair was scraped into a bun at the top of her head.

'Surprise!' I said, handing her the flowers.

'Rose!' Juliet cried. 'You didn't tell me you were coming.'

'It was a last-minute thing,' I said, holding up the wine. 'Shall I put this in the fridge?'

'Um, yes, of course.' She followed me through to the kitchen and opened the fridge door. I slotted the bottle between a two-pint carton of milk and a bottle of champagne.

'Special occasion?' I asked, looking in the cupboards for a vase.

'What?' Juliet's head snapped around.

'The Moët.'

'Oh that. No. We were all given one as a thank you for the exhibition the other week. It sold out. Tell you what,' she said. 'We should drink it now. We are celebrating, after all.'

'Are we?' I raised an eyebrow. Her welcome had been lukewarm, bordering on perfunctory.

'Of course we are. It's such a lovely surprise to see you. Why don't you sit in the garden while I take a quick shower?'

I elbowed her playfully. 'Yes, why *are* you still in your dressing gown in the middle of the afternoon?'

A dark flush crept up her neck. 'Thought I'd make the most of my day off. Have a duvet day, you know?' She thrust the Moët and two glasses into my hands, opened the back door, and ushered me out. 'Make yourself comfortable. I won't be long.'

The door closed swiftly, and I was alone. I crossed the small courtyard garden, plonked the glasses on the bistro table in the sunny far corner, and set about opening the champagne. As I twisted the wire, a movement upstairs caught my eye. My grip on the neck of the bottle tightened as the curtain in the top window - Juliet's bedroom - twitched and a silhouette appeared. Juliet? I shook my head. No one could have sprinted up two flights of stairs that quickly. I stiffened as I realised I wasn't the only one making myself comfortable at Juliet's place this afternoon.

Why couldn't she just tell me she had someone round? I wouldn't have minded. Unless… The thought made my stomach flip. Unless it was a woman. But no, Juliet was straight. She had to be. She wouldn't have rejected me otherwise.

Self-doubt gnawed at my insides as I gripped the cork and twisted the bottle towards me. Just as the cork popped out, the front door slammed. Whoever Juliet had been having a duvet day with had gone.

I poured two glasses and downed mine in three painful gulps.

Juliet appeared, fresh from the shower, fifteen minutes later. She was glowing. Tanned and luminous, her tawny eyes sparkling and her newly washed hair a curtain of spun gold across her bare shoulders. Beside her, I was pale and drab and one-dimensional. I let out a long sigh.

'Penny for them,' she said, refilling my glass.

How could I tell her that the thought of someone kissing her neck, her breasts, the deepest parts of her, sent me crazy with jealousy? That I couldn't bear the thought of sharing her? That if she only opened her eyes and looked at me… *properly* looked at me… she'd see what I'd seen the moment she burst into my room at university, that we were meant to be together. But it was useless because I'd never tell her, because I was a coward. And platonic love was better than no love at all.

'They're not even worth a penny,' I said, pushing my chair back. 'I need a pee.'

In the bathroom, I splashed water on my face and stared at my reflection as the drops trickled down my cheeks like tears. I needed to get a grip. I needed to be acerbic, caustic Rose, queen of the quip, master of the pithy aside. That was the Rose Juliet loved, not woebegone Rose, wallowing in self-pity. I dried my face on the hand towel, slapped my cheeks to get some colour into them, and left the bathroom.

At the top of the stairs I paused, one hand on the white-gloss newel post. Something was drawing me towards Juliet's bedroom at the top of the house. Maybe it was morbid curiosity. Maybe I was tormenting myself with what could never be mine, but the pull was irresistible and could not be ignored. I sidled along the landing to the narrow staircase at the back of the house that led to Juliet's bedroom and en suite.

The stairs were steep, and I was puffing when I reached the top. Stopping to catch my breath, I glanced out of the window. Juliet was still sitting at the table sipping her champagne. Reassured, I pushed open her bedroom door.

The bed was rumpled, the smell of sex heavy in the dimly lit room. On Juliet's side of the bed, a copy of *Captain Corelli's Mandolin* had been left open and face down on the bedside table next to an empty coffee cup. I picked up Juliet's pillow and held it against my cheek, breathing in her scent. Next, I shuffled around the bed, looking for anything that might identify her lover.

This pillow smelt of cologne. I inhaled deeply. Citrus and cedar wood. The unmistakable aroma of CK One. But that told me nothing. Everyone knew it was a unisex fragrance. *Leave it, Rose,* said the voice in my head. I dropped the pillow and was about to leave the room when I spied a glint of metal peeking out from under the bed. The strap of a chunky steel watch. A man's watch. I stooped down and picked it up, looping it around my wrist and fixing the catch. It was a Tag Heuer, so big the metal links flapped loosely around my wrist.

As I slid the watch off, the tightness eased in my chest. I closed my eyes and exhaled slowly. Juliet might have taken a lover, but it wasn't a woman, and that made it bearable.

I was about to head downstairs when I remembered I still hadn't peed, so I slipped into the en suite. I was washing my hands when I saw it. A blue inhaler, next to a tube of toothpaste for sensitive teeth. The type of inhaler used to treat the symptoms of asthma. And I only knew one person with asthma.

Danny.

CHAPTER THIRTY-FOUR

I felt discombobulated as I staggered back to the house. I was certain I'd put the rifle back in the trunk in the shed. For one bewildering moment, I wondered if the lack of sleep was messing with my head and the intruder had been a figment of my imagination, too. But no, Eloise had heard him and had called me. And the house had been turned upside down. I hadn't imagined that. Nor the couple of hours we'd spent setting everything straight.

Even so, I reached for my phone and checked my call log to confirm Eloise had phoned me. And she had, at ten to five, just as I remembered. Of course I hadn't imagined it. Any of it. The fact that I'd doubted myself was almost as terrifying as the possibility I'd made it up.

No, I reasoned, as I let myself in the back door and kicked off my boots. There would be a perfectly reasonable explanation for the gun not being in the trunk. Like I had meant to put it back but had been distracted by something and had clean forgotten. It wouldn't be the first time, and

I was sure it wouldn't be the last. I was always walking into rooms only to wonder what the hell I'd gone in them for.

I locked and bolted the back door and then walked from room to room, pulling curtains and checking every window was closed. As I passed the mirror in the hallway, I glimpsed my reflection. My hair was awry, and my face was gaunt, apart from the puckered pouches beneath my eyes. I looked like the crabby and eccentric inhabitant of Alan Bennett's driveway in *The Lady in the Van*.

I ran my fingers through my hair and slapped some colour into my pale cheeks. The pain felt good, sharp and stinging, and I slapped them again, harder. As I stared at my reflection, I became aware that my right eye had begun to twitch. A spasm caused, no doubt, by exhaustion. Wearily, I trudged up the stairs to bed.

It was only as I pulled back the covers and was about to climb into bed that I stubbed my big toe on something cold and hard behind the ruffled valance. Mystified, I bent down and peered under the bed, my eyes widening when I realised I was staring down the barrel of a gun. My father's rifle. I would recognise it anywhere. Carefully, I spun the rifle round so it was facing away from me, then pulled it out. I rocked back on my heels, uncocked it and checked to see if it was loaded. Sure enough, the skirt of a little lead pellet was visible in the chamber, just waiting for someone to pull the trigger.

I pushed the rifle back under the bed and contemplated the very real possibility that I was losing my mind. But no, my memory was playing tricks on me, that was all. Even though I could have sworn I'd put the rifle back in its trunk in the shed, I must have stowed it here after all. No matter. At least I knew it hadn't fallen into the wrong hands. My eye twitched again, and I rubbed my face before hauling myself up from the floor. All I needed was a good night's sleep. A deep, dreamless sleep from which I'd wake up calm and refreshed, not jittery and paranoid.

Not for the first time, I wished I hadn't chucked my stash of vitamins. Had I been arrogant to think I could manage without them?

I didn't mention the rifle to Eloise when I took her a cup of tea the next morning. I didn't want her to think I was going doolally. So, I painted a smile on my face and wittered on about the garden and how I needed to get on with cutting back the Virginia creeper before it covered every window in the house.

'Are you going into work today?' Eloise asked, interrupting.

I shook my head. 'I don't go in on a Saturday. But I do need to pop out this morning. Will you be all right here on your own?'

''Course,' she said, as if I was mad to suggest otherwise.

'Promise you'll ring if you need anything?'

She sighed and reached for her phone. 'I promise.'

'OK, well, I'll leave you to it,' I said, shuffling out of the room.

At the top of the stairs, I paused, wondering if I should give the gun to Eloise while I was out. But I didn't think Roy Matthews would show his face here again. For all he knew we'd called the police, they'd dusted the place for prints, found a match and were about to turn up on his doorstep to arrest him for breaking and entering. Eloise had promised she'd call me if anything happened and if she did, I would tell her where the gun was.

It was one of those bright but still late autumn days that felt like a caress before winter's penetrating grip. The trees had retreated as the sun had risen, maintaining a polite distance between them and the house once more. In the weak sunshine, my fears that Roy Matthews had been hiding in the woods the previous night seemed irrational, but I still locked the back door behind me.

I'd only slept in snatches despite my exhaustion, and the twitch above my right eye was more pronounced than ever as I steered the Land Rover through the back lanes towards Teynham. As I'd tossed and turned in bed, I'd reached a decision. If I was to stand up to Roy Matthews, I had to know my enemy. I needed to find out if there was a chink in his armour I could use against him, and there was one person who might help me there - his victim and former neighbour, Kerry Davis.

I knew from the court report that Kerry lived in London Road, Teynham. Although the road stretched the length of the village, I felt confident someone would remember the day a man wielding a baseball bat turned up on a pregnant woman's doorstep and started smashing windows, even if it had happened five years previously.

I parked on a side road, picked up the string shopping bag on the passenger seat, and headed for the Co-op, which seemed as good a place as any to start. I meandered up and down the aisles, picking up tins and packets and inspecting their labels before replacing them. I knew I was procrastinating, but I was beginning to doubt the wisdom of my mission. Kerry Davis probably didn't live in Teynham any more. And even if she did, I doubted she'd talk to me. Why would anyone want to be reminded of such a terrifying ordeal?

'Are you lookin' for somefing in particular?' said a voice. 'Only you've been picking up and putting back stuff for the last ten minutes.'

I looked up to see a girl in her twenties giving me an appraising look. She was wearing a Co-op uniform and was clutching one of those handheld scanners supermarket staff used for stock control.

'So sorry,' I said. I glanced at the shelf. 'I was just looking for… tinned artichokes in brine. And would you believe my luck? Here they are!'

'Right,' the girl said doubtfully. 'Till's that way.' She pointed a thumb towards the door.

I picked up the tin and was about to sidle off and pay when I realised the girl must be about Kerry's age.

'Um, I don't suppose you know Kerry Davis, do you?'

Her brow knitted. 'Why?'

'I'm researching my family tree,' I improvised. It was

the kind of thing a woman my age would do. 'I think she might be related to my great aunt twice removed.'

The girl's face cleared. 'Kezza might be part of your family?'

'That's right.'

'I went to school wiv her.'

'She still lives in Teynham?'

'In the house opposite the crossing. Number forty-six. Tell her Sammy says hi.'

'I will.' I made to leave, but quick as a flash, Sammy grabbed my forearm.

'Don't forget to pay for that though, will you?'

'Silly me.' I smiled and checked the label, wincing inwardly when I saw the artichokes were almost three pounds. And I loathed artichokes. But Sammy was watching me keenly, so I tramped up the aisle to the till, handed her colleague a crisp ten-pound note, dropped the tin in my string bag and headed out of the shop.

On the journey over, I'd painted a picture of a careworn council house with grubby windows, overflowing wheelie bins and an old banger on bricks in the front garden, snobbery being an unattractive trait I'd learned through osmosis from my mother.

In reality, number forty-six London Road, Teynham, was a narrow red-bricked Victorian terraced house with gleaming white uPVC windows and a sage-green uPVC front door. Two bay trees shaped like pyramids sat in terracotta pots on either side of the door. I loitered on the other side of the road by the pedestrian crossing and gazed at the two houses on either side. Number forty-eight was also red-bricked and well-cared for, although its door was a smart navy blue. But number forty-four, the house to the left of Kerry's, was another story. Pebble-dashed and rundown, it had a neglected air. A length of guttering had come free of its fixing and was hanging precariously from the fascia board, and the windows were opaque with grime. That, I decided, must be where Roy Matthews had lived.

I rehearsed what I was going to say one last time before pressing the button on the pedestrian crossing. When the green man appeared, I hurried across, my eyes firmly fixed on Kerry's sage-green front door. Before I could change my mind, I rapped the silver door knocker and waited for her to answer.

CHAPTER THIRTY-FIVE

I didn't have to wait long. The door opened an inch and a girl with an elfin face and unfeasibly long eyelashes stared at me around the door jamb, chin defiantly high and her eyes narrowed.

'Kerry Davis?' I asked.

She gave the tiniest of nods. 'Who are you?'

I'd been planning to regurgitate the family tree story just to get a foot in the door, but something about the determined jut of the girl's jaw made me stop. She deserved the truth.

'It's about Roy Matthews,' I said.

'Roy Matthews?' she repeated a little breathlessly. Her eyes darted behind me. 'I'm sorry but I don't know anyone of that name.'

'Come on, Kerry. Everyone knows what he did to you. How brave you were, giving evidence against him in court.'

'Are you a reporter?' she asked.

I shook my head.

'Then who are you?'

I looked her square in the eye. 'Someone Roy Matthews has a grudge against.'

'Why, what did you do to him?'

'If you let me in, I'll tell you.'

The door started closing, and I thought she was about to shut it in my face when I heard the clink of a safety chain. The door swung open, and she ushered me in, replaced the chain and turned the key in the mortice lock. Sensing me watching her, she shrugged and said, 'Old habits.'

I followed her through the front room into an immaculate kitchen at the back of the house overlooking a small rectangular lawn. A baby was sitting in a high chair, a rattle in one chubby fist and a rich tea biscuit in the other. The baby broke into an uncomplicated smile as I walked into the room, and banged the rattle on the high chair's plastic tray in excitement.

'This is Eva,' Kerry said, bending down to tickle the child's cheek. Eva broke into a gale of giggles.

'You had another baby,' I said. 'After the attack.'

Kerry nodded. She pulled up a chair at the kitchen table and motioned me to do the same. 'Luke's five now. His dad takes him swimming on a Saturday morning.' She was watching me like a hawk. I had the impression she didn't miss much. 'So now you know who we are. But we have no idea who you are, do we, Eva?'

The baby gurgled, and I smiled before I could stop myself. Kerry's face softened.

'I'm Rose,' I said. 'Rose Barton.'

'So, tell me, Rose, how did you have the misfortune to find yourself on the wrong side of Roy Matthews?'

I answered her question with one of my own. 'Did you ever meet his daughter, India?'

She nodded. 'Nice girl. Very quiet. She used to stay with her dad a couple of nights a week.'

'She killed herself in July. Matthews blames me for her death.'

Kerry was silent as I recounted how India had been on the phone to Sisterline shortly before she died, and that her father had wrongly assumed I'd taken the call. How he'd slashed my tyre and vandalised the office. How he'd worked out where I lived and had trashed my house and poisoned my cat.

'And you're worried he's going to turn up on *your* doorstep with a baseball bat?' she said bluntly.

It was my turn to nod.

'Are you hoping I'm going to tell you his bark's worse than his bite? Because if you are, you're going to be disappointed. The man's a complete psycho.'

I licked my lips. 'According to the report I read online, he never actually hit you. Perhaps he was just trying to intimidate you?'

Kerry stood, scooped Eva out of her chair, and hugged her tightly. 'Only because he didn't have the chance. He knew the police were on their way. Otherwise I don't know what would have happened.'

Eva grabbed a fistful of her mother's hair with a gleeful cry. Kerry smiled, but when she spoke again, her tone was serious. 'I used to hear him lose his temper with India sometimes.'

'India?'

'When he'd been drinking.'

'And was that often?'

'Often enough.'

'D'you think he was ever violent towards her?'

Kerry untangled her hair from Eva's grip and planted a kiss on the baby's palm. 'Probably.' She glanced at me. 'India had a bruise on her cheek one time. When I asked her about it, she claimed she'd walked into a door. I remember thinking, yeah, right.'

'You didn't think to call the police, alert social services?'

'Of course I thought about it! But I had no evidence, just a hunch. It would have been my word against his. And India would have denied it.'

'Yet you reported him to the council for playing his music too loudly.'

'Yeah, well, I knew I could build a case against him for that. It was my best chance of getting him kicked out of the house.'

'And it worked,' I said. 'You don't have to worry about him any more.'

'Maybe. But it doesn't stop me from constantly looking over my shoulder. As I said, he's not right in the head. I'm not surprised poor India topped herself. I'd do the same if he was my dad.'

If I thought a chat with Kerry might allay some of my fears about Roy Matthews, I was wrong. If anything, her revelations ramped up my paranoia, and my heart was thudding wildly as I drove along the A2 towards Faversham. Kerry had called Matthews a psycho. Obviously, she wasn't a trained psychiatrist, and it wasn't a clinical diagnosis. However, her meaning was clear. The man was both unhinged and dangerous.

But I'd learned something useful. Roy Matthews might have been physically abusing his daughter. My lips curled as I remembered the sickly comment he'd posted on her Facebook page. *You broke my heart the day you left us. You were, you are, my everything. Sleep tight, baby girl.*

Duplicitous bastard.

I wondered what to do with my newfound knowledge. The inquest into India's death was just over a week away. What if the phone call with her father was the tipping point, and his words had pushed her over the edge, not Rhona's? Putting my own antipathy towards Rhona to one side, I had to admit it was more likely. Rhona was tactless and insensitive, but I couldn't think of a single scenario in which she might encourage someone to take their own life. Whereas if India had just had a massive falling out with her dad…

I had pulled up in a long line of traffic at some temporary traffic lights when my phone rang. It was Eloise.

'Are you all right?' I demanded, another spike of adrenalin making my heart pound even faster.

'Of course. Why wouldn't I be?'

'Because some nutter broke into the house yesterday

and trashed the place,' I said. *And took my father's air rifle from the shed and hid it under my bed.* But I didn't say this, because in the cold light of day I wasn't even sure if they had, or if I'd put it there myself and just forgotten because I was so damn tired.

'Rose, did you hear me?' Eloise's voice crackled out of the phone.

'Sorry, no, I lost you there for a moment. What did you say?'

'I'll make meatballs for tea if you can pick up some mince and a tin of chopped tomatoes.'

'Of course.'

'Have you remembered to feed Mary's fish?' she asked.

Shit. I'd been so preoccupied with Roy Matthews that I'd clean forgotten about Theo. 'I'll pop by on my way home,' I said. The traffic lights turned green and the cars in front of me began inching forwards. 'Listen, I've got to go,' I said. 'I'll see you later.'

Theo started on me the minute I pushed the door of the pillbox open.

'I have evidence if you don't believe me.'

'Evidence of what?' I said, dropping a Sainsbury's carrier bag on the ground.

'That Eloise is batshit crazy.' He shuffled over to the bag on his bottom, peered into it and pulled out a quiche. While he busied himself ripping open the packaging and breaking off a handful, I picked up the bucket and took it outside to empty it, careful to slide the bolts across the door while I was gone.

'My phone, do you have it?' he asked on my return.

'No.'

'Merde. Does Eloise have it?'

'I guess so. Why?'

'I recorded the last fight we had, in case I ever went to the police. It shows her smashing a glass on the worktop and threatening me with it, all because I had not answered my phone when she called me.'

'Which is all very convenient, as I don't have your phone to prove it,' I said, shaking my head.

'She will have it. You just need to find it.'

'Even if I believed a word of the crap that comes out of your mouth, it would be pointless, because she'd have deleted the footage.'

'You are wrong. She would not have been able to find it. I hid it.'

'Hid it?' I said, not bothering to hide my own disbelief.

'I moved it to a hidden album so it wouldn't appear in my library, and I turned off the hidden album, so it was completely invisible.'

'How very shrewd of you.'

He broke off another piece of quiche. 'Living with someone like Eloise makes you paranoid. So, you'll look for it?'

Suddenly, my vision blurred, and I staggered backwards. Faces pressed in on me, a hiss of accusations and entreaties. Theo, Roy Matthews, Rhona, Eddie, Eloise. Their wants and desires, threats and recriminations.

Between them, they were sucking me dry. Theo's assumption that I'd do his bidding was the final straw. I cradled my head in my hands as I tried to silence their voices, a parody of the agonised face in Munch's The Scream.

'What is it? What is wrong?' Theo's voice broke through my fugue and I turned on him.

'You!' I said, stabbing the air with my index finger. 'Why has it taken me this long to realise?' I shook my head, staggered at my stupidity. 'You're behind it all, aren't you?'

He stared uncomprehendingly at me.

'Don't play the innocent with me. I wasn't born yesterday,' I spat. 'You're the catalyst, the common denominator. It all went to hell the night you turned up on my doorstep. It's all your fault.'

'I do not know what you are talking about.'

'Shut up!'

Theo shrank back against the wall. Inexplicably, the sight enraged me further. 'Just shut the fuck up!' I yelled.

I'd spent days vacillating, but now my path was clear.

Theo had started it. Now I was going to finish it.

CHAPTER THIRTY-SIX

JUNE 1999

I didn't tell Juliet I'd seen Danny's inhaler. I kept the knowledge to myself, hugging it tightly to my chest until I worked out what to do with it. Because I had to do something. He'd broken her heart twice before and he would do it again if I didn't intervene. I was certain of it.

The fact that Juliet oozed happiness the entire weekend merely strengthened my resolve. The happier she was, the greater the fall when Danny inevitably strayed. Men like him never changed.

But what could I do? Juliet had never listened to my warnings in the past, and I was pretty sure she wasn't about to start now. Would Danny listen to me? I pictured him, tanned walnut-brown by the Melbourne sun, cold blue eyes hidden by aviator glasses, nodding and agreeing that, yes, of course he would piss off back to Australia because Juliet was better off without him.

Even though I suspected he'd rather cut off his own dick than listen to me, I figured it had to be worth a shot. And if it didn't work? Well, I'd have to think of something else.

I rang John the next day. If anyone knew which rock Danny was lurking under, he would.

'Rose,' he said. 'To what do I owe this pleasure?'

'Does there have to be a reason? Can't two old friends just enjoy a chat?'

He laughed. 'Put those hackles back down. I'm only kidding. How's it going?'

'Oh, you know, same old same old.'

John had recently spent his obscenely large annual bonus on a two-bedroom flat in a converted warehouse in Docklands with enormous windows overlooking the Thames and a swimming pool and gym in the basement. I'd tried to hide my envy when he'd shown me around. I still couldn't get my head around the fact that the computer nerd I'd met at uni was now a City whizz kid whilst I, the high achieving med school student, was living at home with my father, spending my days sorting through other people's grubby cast-offs in a charity shop. What the hell had gone wrong?

I dragged my attention back to the matter in hand. John was still of the view that Juliet's love life was none of my business, so I needed to be subtle.

'I've put my name down for a charity fun run.'

'You? Running?' A bark of laughter. 'I've heard it all now.'

'Very funny. It's a 10k, which I'm told is six miles. So, I'm looking for a personal trainer and I wondered if you knew anyone?'

There was a sigh on the other end of the line. 'You've heard Danny's back,' he said.

'Juliet may have mentioned it, yes. Is he staying at yours?'

Another pause. 'For now. He's looking for somewhere more permanent.'

I bet he is. 'Do you think he'd be interested?'

'In what?'

'Helping me train for my 10k?'

'He is looking for new clients, although it's a bit out of your way, isn't it?'

'It is.' I gave a self-conscious laugh. 'But if I'm going to make a show of myself, I'd rather do it in front of a friend than a stranger.'

'A friend?' John's voice rang with disbelief.

'OK, someone I know,' I said. 'But I'm happy to catch the train up a couple of times a week. Perhaps we could use the gym at your place? It has running machines, doesn't it? And weights and things?'

'Erm, it's a gym, Rose. Of course there are running machines and weights and things.'

'Excellent. Tell him I'll be at yours at eleven o'clock on Friday.'

I ended the call before John had the chance to reply.

On Friday morning I sat on the London-bound train, clutching a sports holdall on my lap and feeling self-conscious in a purple nylon tracksuit I'd found at the charity shop, paired with the Dunlop Green Flash trainers I'd worn for PE at school. As the train chugged towards Victoria, I rehearsed what I would say.

'If you truly loved Juliet, you would end it now, before you broke her heart. If you don't love her, you should end it now anyway, because leading her on would be cruel.'

It seemed straightforward enough to me, although I doubted Danny would see it that way.

As for Juliet, she was aware I was using Danny's services as a personal trainer, but she had no idea I knew they were back together. She greeted my suggestion that the four of us went for a drink for old times' sake with apathy bordering on indifference, and her careless duplicity was like a stab between my eyes.

I was panting by the time I climbed the stairs to John's flat just before eleven. I took a moment to catch my breath, then smoothed my hair and rang the bell.

'Fuck me, if it isn't Jimmy Savile himself,' Danny said, holding the door open. 'Nice shell suit, Rose.'

I smiled tightly and strode past him into the flat. He sat on one end of John's black leather sofa and beckoned me to do the same.

'I need to run through a few questions with you before we start, so I can find out how I can help you and what you're hoping to achieve from our sessions,' he said.

'My, aren't you the professional?' I mocked, sitting at the other end of the sofa.

'Yeah, well, I'm not the same person I was at university. I've done a bit of growing up since then.'

I studied him as he picked up a clipboard from the coffee table. He was wearing a white sleeveless sports vest, navy shorts, fluffy white socks and navy Reebok trainers. On his left wrist was the Tag Heuer watch I'd found under Juliet's bed. Not that I'd ever been in doubt it was his.

Danny was leaner than he used to be, more athlete than bodybuilder these days, and his skin was the colour of a Werther's Original. There was a smattering of stubble on his cheeks and laughter lines fanned out from his eyes. The years had rubbed off some of the cocky swagger and even I could see how women might find him attractive.

'Do you have any medical conditions or injuries I should be aware of?' he asked.

I shook my head.

'Are you taking any medication?'

'No,' I said, because my vitamins were none of his business.

My mind wandered as he quizzed me on my diet and sleep patterns, whether I smoked and if there was any family history of high cholesterol or heart disease.

'Why did you come back?' I blurted.

'My visa ran out,' he said, not looking up from his clipboard.

'It wasn't for Juliet?'

He looked at me then. 'Jules? No.'

'But you're back together,' I said. A statement, not a question.

He shrugged. 'So what if we are?'

'What are your long-term plans?' I said, leaning forwards, my elbows on my knees.

'You know me. I go with the flow. I don't have long-term plans.'

'But you and Juliet…'

'… are having a bit of fun. Is there anything wrong with that?' He smirked. 'You should try it some time.'

And that's when I knew for sure. He might have a bit more polish, a certain Aussie allure, but beneath that craggy exterior he hadn't changed a bit. Not one iota. He was still a self-serving bastard who would break Juliet's heart without a moment's thought.

Because a leopard never changed its spots.

I pulled the holdall closer to me, my fingers encircling the handle and squeezing hard.

'We should get back to the questions,' Danny said, tapping the clipboard with his pen. 'What are your short and long-term goals?'

I smiled coolly. 'I've only ever had one goal,' I said. 'And that's Juliet.'

CHAPTER THIRTY-SEVEN

There was a note from Eloise on the kitchen table, propped up against the fruit bowl. *Gone for a walk. Won't be long.* I let out the breath I hadn't even realised I'd been holding. I loved having Eloise to stay but projecting the best version of myself at all times was exhausting and it was a relief to drop the act, if only for an hour or so.

After unpacking the shopping, I headed upstairs, trying to hold on to the sense of resolve I'd felt in the pill-box. Letting myself into my mother's room, I made a beeline for the locked mirrored cabinet above the sink. I ran my hands along the top, feeling for the key, smiling with satisfaction as my fingers closed around it.

The key turned smoothly in the lock, and I peered inside. It was a veritable candy store of drugs that I'd been meaning to get rid of for years. Now I was glad I hadn't.

Paracetamol, co-codamol, ibuprofen. Methotrexate for my mother's rheumatoid arthritis and tramadol to blunt the constant pain she was in. Warfarin tablets to thin her blood and diuretics for her high blood pressure. All potential killers in the wrong hands.

Food for thought.

Downstairs, the back door slammed. I closed the medicine cabinet, slipped the key into my pocket and, feeling more positive than I had for days, went in search of my goddaughter.

I found Eloise in the front room, lighting the log burner. She was still wearing my coat and her cheeks were rosy from the cold. I felt a rush of affection for her and smiled.

'Nice walk?'

'Bracing.' She dusted off her hands and stood. 'I've been fantasising about tea and crumpets in front of the fire for the last half an hour.'

'Coming up,' I said, making for the door.

'No, you sit down,' she said. 'You do enough for me. Let me spoil you for a change.'

She returned a few minutes later with two mugs in one hand and a plate of buttered crumpets in the other. We munched away for a while, then I said, 'Is it me or does it smell in here?'

'Smell?'

'Something dead, like a shrew or mouse or something. Dinah's always bringing them in and leaving them to die.' I noticed Eloise's troubled expression and corrected myself. 'Sorry, I mean she used to. Perhaps she brought one in before she died. A last supper.'

'I can't smell anything.'

I sniffed again. It was definitely there: the unmistakable odour of decay. Pungent, rotting flesh, overpowering the smell of beeswax polish and smouldering logs. I sprang from the chair and peered under it. Nothing other than a couple of dust bunnies. I knelt beside the bookcase and squinted under that, too. More dust. No rodents, dead or otherwise.

'We're in trouble if it crawled behind the skirting,' I said. 'I'll have to take the whole bloody thing off.'

'It doesn't smell, Rose,' Eloise said firmly. 'Now why don't you drink your tea, have another crumpet, then go upstairs for a nap while I make dinner? You look knackered.'

The prospect of surrendering to a dreamless torpor for a couple of hours was appealing. 'I didn't get much sleep last night, what with the break in and everything,' I admitted.

'Then that's exactly what you're going to do. No arguments,' she said, waggling her finger at me, and I nodded meekly, while inside I glowed with happiness because, for the first time since I could remember, someone gave a damn about me.

And in that moment, I knew exactly what I had to do. And the thought of it didn't faze me at all, because I was doing it for the one person I loved. I was doing it for Eloise.

I came downstairs at seven, showered and rested and feeling better than I had for days.

'It smells delicious,' I said, peering into the saucepan on the hob. Meatballs bubbled away in a rich, glossy tomato sauce. My stomach rumbled.

'Did you manage to sleep?' Eloise asked. She was at the sink, up to her elbows in soap suds. I picked up a tea towel and began drying the dishes.

'I did,' I said, still surprised that I'd fallen asleep the moment my head touched the pillow. When I woke almost three hours later, I was furry of mouth and stiff of neck, but I felt human again.

'I've opened a bottle of red. I needed it for the sauce. I hope that's all right?' Eloise said.

'You don't need to ask.' I smiled at her. 'And we can drink the rest with dinner.'

We ate at the kitchen table. The meatballs were as delicious as they looked, and we polished off the lot. Replete, we retired to the front room, taking a second bottle of wine with us. We sat either side of the Scrabble board, the fire warming our cheeks and the red wine warming our bellies.

'Z,' I sighed, showing her my tile. 'You'd better kick off.'

We were quiet for a while as we picked our letters and played around with them, the click clack of the tiles on our racks as we switched and swapped them reminding me of the Saturday night games Juliet and I used to play. It was a companionable silence, and after a while I felt able to ask, 'What was care like for you, El?'

She took a while to answer, and I worried I'd overstepped the mark, but then she put her rack of letters down. 'You really want to know?'

I nodded.

'It was shit. Not all of it, but most of it. Some bits were more shit than others. Or should that be shittier, I don't know.'

'More shit, probably,' I said.

'More shit it is.' Eloise gave the ghost of a smile. 'The first foster home I had was all right, I suppose, apart from the fact that the couple were used to having toddlers and didn't know how to deal with an eleven-year-old girl who'd just lost her mum.' She went quiet again.

'How long were you there?' I prompted.

'A couple of months? I can't remember. It's all a bit of a blur, to be honest. The children's homes were the worst. I counted down the days until my eighteenth birthday. I mean, literally counted them down. I Blu-tacked a piece of paper on the wall by my pillow and marked every day off, like that bloke on the desert island.'

'Robinson Crusoe?'

'That's the one.'

'I'm sorry,' I said.

'What for?'

'That you had to grow up in care. Do you…' I broke off.

'Do I what?'

'Do you ever wonder what your life would have been like if social services had let you come and live with me?'

'Do you?' Eloise hit back.

I shuffled the letters on my rack around, then met her gaze. 'I didn't,' I said. 'But I do now.'

Later, when Eloise had beaten me by a creditable thirty-two points and the fire in the log burner was little more than an orange glow, she drained the last of her wine and said, 'Who d'you think's behind everything that's been happening to you: the dead girl's dad or the woman at work?'

The temperature in the room seemed to drop a few degrees, and I pulled my cardigan tighter around me. 'Oh,' I said with a self-conscious laugh. 'I was trying to forget about all that.'

'That's not an answer.'

'Roy Matthews, I suppose,' I said after a while. 'He has a stronger motive than Rhona, or should I say he *thinks* he does.'

'Want me to have a word with him?' Eloise asked.

I thought she was joking until I realised her expression was deadly serious.

'Thanks, but you're good. I can fight my own battles.'

She studied me for a minute or two, then smiled. 'I don't doubt it,' she said.

CHAPTER THIRTY-EIGHT

JUNE 1999

Danny frowned.

'John said you were training for a 10k.'

'Oh, *that*,' I said. 'I don't actually think I can be arsed.'

'So why are you here?'

I crossed my arms in front of my chest. 'Because I need to find out what your intentions are regarding Juliet.'

'My intentions regarding Juliet?' He spluttered with laughter. 'Have I fallen asleep and woken up in a Jane fucking Austen novel?'

'I won't stand by and let you break her heart again,' I said.

'I don't know what you're talking about. It's just a bit of fun. Juliet knows that.'

'Just a bit of fun?' A white hot rage coursed through

my body and I could feel my cotton T-shirt sticking to my back. I unzipped my tracksuit top, wrenched it off, and flung it on the sofa between us. 'My God, you really are more stupid than I gave you credit for. Juliet doesn't think it's a bit of fun. For some inexplicable reason, she thinks you're the love of her life.'

'So, you don't want a personal training session?' Danny said, puzzled.

'I'd rather eat my own entrails.'

His expression hardened. 'I turned down a one-to-one with a new client for this,' he said, slamming the clipboard on the coffee table with a crack that made me jump. 'John said you needed my help. I should have known it was all bullshit.'

I laced my hands together on my lap. My palms were damp with sweat. 'You can't keep treating Juliet like a piece of meat,' I said.

'Like it's any of your fucking business.'

'The thing you don't seem to understand is that Juliet is the most precious thing in the world to me. She is my life.'

'I always thought you had the hots for her. Fuckin' lezzer.' His mouth curled into a sneer. 'Perhaps it's time I showed you what you're missing.'

I looked him up and down and shook my head dismissively. 'It's OK, I'll give it a miss, thanks.'

A muscle in Danny's cheek twitched. 'You think you're so fucking clever.'

'At least I don't think with my dick.'

His hands curled into fists. 'How fucking dare you.'

I picked up my tracksuit top and folded it carefully. 'As delightful as it's been to see you, I must take my leave. I have a train to catch.'

It was as if he hadn't heard me. He was staring at me with a peculiar expression on his face, his hands still balled into fists by his side. I unzipped the holdall, pushed the tracksuit top inside and was about to stand when he lunged forwards, grabbed my shoulders and shoved me onto the sofa with a force that took my breath away. I twisted and turned, trying to wriggle out of his grip, but the more I struggled, the tighter his hold became.

'Get off me!' I shrieked, bucking and kicking beneath him.

'Shut the fuck up,' he snarled as he pinned me down with one forearm and clamped his other hand over my mouth. I threw my head from side to side, but again his grip tightened until my head was jammed against the arm of the sofa and my breaths were hard and fast.

He leered over me, his face inches from mine and his knee at my crotch.

'Wanna know how Juliet likes it, lezzer?' he whispered in my ear.

I shook my head, my eyes pleading *no*.

'You'd never guess looking at her, but she likes it rough.' Danny reached for the waistband of his shorts and laughed. 'The rougher the better.'

Pinned underneath him, I couldn't move. I tensed my muscles, willing my body to fight back, to claw and scratch until he let me go, but it was as if I was paralysed from the neck down. My stomach turned to liquid as the realisation hit me. Danny wasn't fooling around. He was about to rape me on the sofa in John's swanky apartment overlooking the Thames, and there was nothing I could do to stop him.

I turned my head, closed my eyes and retreated to a place even Danny Reeves couldn't reach.

A crushing weight on my chest.

Wheezy, rasping breaths hot against my neck.

A knee pushing my legs apart.

Wheezy breaths.

I forced my eyes open. Danny, still looming over me, wasn't just breathing heavily, he was *wheezing*. His vice-like hold loosened a fraction as he sneezed twice in quick succession. A flicker of uncertainty crossed his features, so fleeting I wondered if I'd imagined it. He sneezed again, spraying my face with tiny droplets that I longed to wipe away. I risked another look at his face. His eyes were dark and expressionless, and his mouth had fallen slightly open, the tip of his tongue protruding from his teeth like some obscene invertebrate on a David Attenborough wildlife documentary.

'Please, Danny,' I begged. 'Don't do this.'

'Shut up,' he snarled.

'Whatever I've done, I'm sorry.'

He opened his mouth to speak but was gripped by a sudden storm of coughing. As his body convulsed, I wriggled out from beneath him and jumped to my feet. His hand shot out to clasp my wrist, but I was too quick for him, ducking out of his reach and sprinting for the door.

Roaring in anger, he lunged at me again. But halfway across the room, he stopped, clawed at his throat, then sank onto the floor.

'Rose!'

I stopped in the doorway and turned back to him. 'What?'

'My inhaler,' he gasped.

I paused, even though every sinew of my body was telling me to grab my things and run from the flat as fast as my legs would carry me. 'You still get asthma?'

'Not... since... university,' he wheezed.

My mind whirred, running through the possibilities. What if he was faking it, feigning an asthma attack, so I stayed? Because John didn't have a goldfish, let alone a cat. Then I remembered coming down to breakfast and finding Smokey curled up in the laundry basket. My tracksuit must have been covered in his hair.

Reaching a decision, I stood with my hands on my hips.

'Where is it?'

'On top of the chest of drawers, spare room.' He was panting now, his breath coming in short, laboured gasps.

Nodding, I headed out of the room.

'Hurry!'

'All right, all right,' I muttered. I came to a halt in the hallway, trying to remember which door led where. I tried a couple, finding the airing cupboard and the bathroom. The third door led to John's bedroom. Ignoring the coughing from the lounge, I crossed the room and gazed out of the window to the Thames below as my heart rate returned to normal. Tugboats, river taxis and the occasional speedboat cut through the brown ribbon of water, beyond which stood the uncompromising London skyline.

'Rose!' Danny puffed from the lounge.

'I'm coming!' I shouted, pushing open the fourth and final door. The air was stale, and the bed unmade. Dirty coffee cups littered the bedside table and a chair in the corner of the room was hidden under a pile of clothes. Propped up against the wall was one of those enormous rucksacks people used for gap years. Resisting the urge to have a poke through it, I turned my attention to the chest of drawers, my eyes travelling over the clutter, looking for the blue inhaler. I found it tucked between a black leather wallet and a silver keyring. The keyring was engraved with a centaur, bow drawn. Sagittarius, the sign of the zodiac that represented optimism, freedom and energy, if you believed all that crap. Juliet's star sign. I brushed the inhaler to one side and picked up the keyring. Two keys dangled from it: a polished brass Chubb key and a chrome Yale key. The spare set for Juliet's house.

A crash from the lounge made me drop the keys on the chest of drawers. I grabbed the inhaler and headed towards the noise.

Danny was writhing on the floor, a hand pressed against his chest as he fought to open his airways. He'd upended the coffee table, sending his clipboard, an asparagus fern and the television remote control flying.

I stood in the doorway and watched him, my fingers

curled around the plastic inhaler. I'd always known Danny was a chancer, but today I'd seen another side to him, a side that was pure evil. I trembled as I remembered his hot breath, his crushing weight. What would have happened if Smokey had spent the night in his own bed, and not in the laundry basket? Would Danny have carried out his threat to "show me what I was missing"?

'Rose,' Danny said again. Each exhalation whistled as he forced his lungs to work. I gained no pleasure from seeing him suffer. But he needed to be taught a lesson.

'Is this what you want?' I said loudly, so he'd hear me over the rasp of his own breathing.

I dangled the inhaler between my thumb and forefinger. He nodded, his head bobbing furiously, and reached out a trembling hand, panting, 'Give… it… to… me.'

I narrowed my eyes. 'What's the magic word, arsehole?'

His head jerked back, as if I'd slapped him. 'P… please. Give… it… to… me… please.'

I took a couple of steps forwards, my arm outstretched, my fingers poised to release the inhaler as if I was a human claw crane at an amusement arcade.

'B… bitch,' Danny panted, lunging for my ankles.

Something inside me snapped, and I stepped neatly out of his way. 'I should never have saved you the last time,' I said, pocketing the inhaler. 'You despicable piece of shit.'

His breathing was growing fainter, his bronchial tubes narrowing as the muscles around his inflamed airways contracted. He crumpled to the floor, his eyes bulging, and his teeth bared in a rictus grin.

There was still time to save him. All I had to do was push the inhaler's mouthpiece between his blue-tinged lips and press the top.

So much power resting in my hands. I thought of all the reasons why I should save him. It didn't take long. Then I thought of all the reasons why I shouldn't.

I stepped over him to the window and watched the tugboats and the river taxis and the speedboats slicing through the water, each leaving a rippled wake behind it like a memory.

CHAPTER THIRTY-NINE

On Monday morning, I dressed carefully, wanting to make a good impression on my first day as Sisterline's new chief executive. Eddie had arranged an interview with the local paper, and as I put the finishing touches to my makeup and pinned a brooch to the collar of my suit jacket, I rehearsed what I would say.

'It's the first sign of madness, you know,' Eloise said, appearing in the doorway and making me jump like a scalded cat.

'What is?'

'Talking to yourself.' She peered at me. 'Are you all right? You look a bit stressy.'

'Do I?' I stared at myself in the mirror. Apart from larger than usual pouches under my eyes, I looked the same as I always did: pale, freckly and every one of my fifty-one years. 'I suppose I'm a bit nervous, it being my first day and everything. And I didn't sleep very well again last night.'

In fact, I'd barely slept a wink since the nap I'd taken on Friday afternoon. I was hollow-eyed with exhaustion, yet nervous energy zipped through me, making my heart race and my hands tremble.

'You'll kill it.' Eloise said.

Stiffening, I said, 'Kill what?'

'The job, of course. What else?'

I breathed in deeply, then frowned. 'I can smell that bloody shrew up here now.' I looked around wildly, then fell to the floor and checked under the dressing table. 'Where the hell can it be?'

'Oh Rose, there is no shrew. It's all in your head.'

'Just because I couldn't find it yesterday doesn't mean it's not here.' The smell of decay had grown stronger as the weekend went by, and I'd spent the previous afternoon with a crowbar, prising off the skirting boards in the library in search of the little blighter. When I'd started on the skirting in the hallway, Eloise had taken the crowbar from me and guided me into the front room, where she'd sat me down with a cup of tea and a couple of chocolate digestives in front of Countryfile. But if she'd hoped the craggy John Craven would take my mind off the shrew's rotting corpse, she was mistaken. I'd just waited until she'd gone to bed, then jemmied them off. But I hadn't found the dead shrew.

I realised Eloise was staring at me as if I had a blob of raspberry jam on my chin.

'What's wrong?' I said, rubbing at my face with my sleeve.

'I was saying, hadn't you better get going? You don't want to be late on your first day.'

I checked my watch and groaned. 'Shit. *Shit.*' I pulled on my jacket and slid my feet into my shoes. 'I'll see you tonight.'

Eloise handed me my handbag and smiled. 'Knock 'em dead,' she said.

The reporter from the *Faversham News* was already in Eddie's office when I arrived, hot and bothered and ten minutes late. Eddie beckoned me to join them and I held out my hand and said, 'I'm so sorry. Car trouble.'

'No problem at all,' the reporter said. 'Nice to meet you.' His handshake was firm and assured, even though he looked barely old enough to shave. He surreptitiously wiped his hand on his trousers before reaching for his notebook.

'Gosh, it's warm in here,' I said brightly. 'Mind if I open a window?'

The other two murmured their assent and when I'd opened the window as far as it would go, I took the empty chair, cocked my head, laced my hands in my lap and, with a smile, said, 'Let the interrogation commence!'

A look of bemusement flickered across the young man's face, but he quickly rallied. 'Interrogation, yes. Funny.' He cleared his throat. 'Eddie's been telling me you have ambitious plans for Sisterline. What's your first major project going to be?'

My mind went blank. What *was* my first major project? 'That's a great question,' I said, frantically searching my memory for the answer and finding nothing. As the silence stretched uncomfortably between us, Eddie jumped to my rescue.

'Rose has already been talking about collaborative opportunities, such as working with local secondary schools and making the most of social media to spread our message,' she said.

'That's right. Social media and collaboration,' I agreed, tugging at the neck of my blouse. Despite the blast of cold air blowing in through the open window, my palms were still clammy, and I could feel a trickle of sweat sliding down my spine.

The reporter jotted something in his notebook. 'And what made you want to work for Sisterline in particular? Was it because you know someone who committed suicide?'

My eyes widened at his cheek and my first reaction was to tell him it was none of his bloody business. I stole a look at Eddie. Perhaps she'd mentioned I'd lost a friend while they were waiting for me to arrive.

'You shouldn't say "commit suicide",' I said. 'It infers suicide is a crime and suicidal thoughts are a sin.'

He looked flustered. 'Sorry, I didn't mean to…'

'It's not a problem,' Eddie interjected. 'It's just that we've been campaigning for the media to stop using the phrase for a couple of years now. Unfortunately, the message is taking a while to filter through. We prefer "die by suicide" instead.'

'Got you.' He turned back to me. 'So, I was wondering if one of your loved ones died by suicide and that's why you wanted to work for Sisterline?'

'I did have a friend, a friend who…' I licked my lips and tried to ignore the sensation of intense heat that was rushing through my body from my feet to the top of my head in waves, leaving me drenched in sweat. I could feel beads of perspiration on my forehead and a red rash on my chest. It was like I was on fire, and as I dropped my gaze, I quite expected to see flames licking around my ankles. But of course there weren't any.

'Rose, are you all right?' Eddie asked.

I brushed her concern away with a wave of my hand. 'You're the second person to ask me that today. I'm absolutely fine. In fine fettle, you might say. Hunky dory, in fact. Just a bit hot.' I fanned myself with my hand. 'Is it me or is it like a furnace in here?'

I looked from Eddie to the reporter and back again. Both were wearing the same slightly baffled expression.

'I suppose now you come to mention it, I do feel as though I might be coming down with something,' I said, touching my temple. 'I don't suppose you could email me your questions instead? I can have the answers back to you by end of play today.'

The reporter nodded a little too vigorously. 'That would be great. I'll just take a quick picture of you at your desk, then I'll leave you in peace.'

'What was all that about?' Eddie asked, as we watched him leave a few minutes later.

'A hot flush, I think. And a total brain fog. Sorry, Eddie. I'll make sure he has everything he needs.'

She patted my arm. 'No need to apologise. But are you sure that's all it is? You seem a bit on edge.'

'You're the second person today to tell me that, too.' I gave Eddie a quick smile. Her eyes were full of concern and I longed to unburden myself to her. But how could I tell her that the previous evening I'd crept into my mother's room, ransacked her medicine cabinet, ripped pills from their blister packs and crushed them with a pestle and mortar until they resembled chalk dust, stirring the powder into a tub of organic lemon curd yoghurt I'd bought from the supermarket because I'd read online that lemon masked the bitterness of the pills? How could I tell her I was planning to feed the yoghurt to the man I was keeping prisoner in a concrete bunker in the middle of my woods? How could I tell her that?

I couldn't.

So, I summoned another smile. 'Don't worry, I'm fine,' I said.

CHAPTER FORTY

JULY 1999

Danny's funeral was a surprisingly touching affair. Grief hung heavily over the red-bricked crematorium as the mourners shuffled in. Misery was carved into the faces of Danny's parents, because to lose a child was unthinkable. It was the wrong order of things. His friends were red-eyed and silent, still reeling in shock. Death was never easy, but the sudden death of a young man in his prime was even harder to stomach, because it was a stark reminder that the line between life and death was perishingly thin.

And as for Juliet... well, Juliet was an enigma. I'd expected her to be a sobbing, snotty mess, but she was pale-faced and composed. Almost tranquil. I could only suppose she was in denial and that any minute the grief would hit her like a steamroller, and she would fall to pieces.

As we traipsed into the crematorium and took our places behind Danny's parents, I felt the heat of eyeballs on my back. Although my eyes were trained on the coffin, I knew people were staring at me, some curious, some sympathetic, and I knew what they were thinking. *Is that her, the woman Danny was training when he died? The one who couldn't save him?*

When the paramedics had stormed through John's front door, the flat was hazy with steam. After I'd checked Danny's pulse, I'd set the stage carefully, stowing his inhaler in the bottom of my holdall, switching on the kettle and heating pans of water on the hob before I phoned 999. I even made Danny a coffee, which had grown cold by the time the ambulance arrived.

'He had an asthma attack,' I sobbed, as the paramedics hurried into the lounge. 'It happened so quickly. I tried everything I could think of,' I added, waving an arm at the hob. 'But he collapsed, and I think he's... I think he's gone.'

One of the paramedics guided me to the sofa while the other checked Danny's vital signs. He looked up at his colleague and shook his head. I clamped my hands over my face and imagined Smokey being hit by a car, his lifeless body flung onto the verge like a piece of rubbish. As the tears came, I buried my head in my hands, my shoulders shaking.

It wasn't long before two police officers turned up, closely followed by a doctor. While the doctor bent over

Danny's prone body and spoke quietly to one of the officers, the second led me onto John's narrow balcony, shot me a sympathetic look, and flipped open her notebook.

'Can you tell me what happened?'

'Danny's a personal trainer,' I said. 'He was helping to train me for a charity run. We've been friends for years, you see. Since university, in fact. Anyway, we were just sitting on the sofa talking when he started wheezing. The next thing I know he's having a full-on asthma attack.'

'Did you know he suffered from asthma?'

I nodded. 'He had an attack in front of me when we were at uni. I managed to get him through it.' I gazed at the officer's polished boots and lowered my voice to little more than a whisper. 'I couldn't save him this time.'

'Did he have an inhaler?' she asked.

'He always used to, but this is the first time I've seen him for years. I don't know if he still did.'

'Did you look for one when the asthma attack came on?'

'Everywhere. The bathroom, his bedroom. I couldn't find one anywhere.'

She wrote something in her notebook. 'Have you any idea what triggered the attack?'

I shook my head. 'Sorry.'

'No matter.' She closed her notebook and smiled at me. 'Apologies for all the questions, but we have to file a report to the coroner for all sudden or unexpected deaths.'

'Of course. What happens next?'

'We'll contact Danny's next of kin and arrange for his body to be taken to the local mortuary. The coroner may ask for a post mortem examination to confirm the cause of death.'

'But it was his asthma, surely?'

'It seems likely on the face of it, but let's not count our chickens.'

Even though I knew that asthma was the only conceivable cause of death, a shiver of unease still ran through me.

'Three people die from asthma in the UK every day,' I blurted.

Surprise flickered across the police officer's features.

I gave a self-conscious shrug. 'It's the kind of useless fact you pick up at med school.'

She raised an eyebrow. 'You didn't say you were a doctor.'

'I'm not. I had to leave at the end of my third year to look after my parents. But I had a particular interest in chronic lung disease because my mother had emphysema.' The lies were tripping off my tongue. Was she buying it, or did she think I'd had a hand in Danny's death? I watched her face carefully, but it was impossible to tell.

And then she patted my knee awkwardly.

'So, if anyone could have saved Danny's life, it was you.'

I smiled, relief coursing through me. 'I guess you're right,' I said.

The wake took place in a pub a short drive from the

crematorium. Juliet and I found a table in the corner while John went to the bar for drinks: a large red wine for me and an orange juice for Juliet.

I took her hand and squeezed it. 'Are you OK?'

She sucked in a breath, then let it out slowly. 'I will be.'

After the private ambulance had arrived to take Danny's body to the mortuary, John and I had gone straight round to Juliet's to break the news. We sat on either side of her until her tears ran dry. When John disappeared into the kitchen to make us tea, Juliet turned to me and said, 'I should have told you, Rose. We were back together.'

'It's OK, I know. Danny told me.'

'He'd changed.'

If you say so.

'He loved me.' There was a pleading tone to her voice, as if she was trying to convince herself as much as me.

I hesitated for a moment, then nodded and said, 'He did.'

Her tear-stained eyes lit up. 'He said that? To you?'

'He told me that letting you down was the biggest regret of his life. That's why he came back from Australia. He came back for you.'

Juliet's gaze never left my face as she hung onto my every word and I warmed to my theme. 'That's what he said. He wanted kids, marriage, the lot. That's why this is all so fucked up.' I shook my head sorrowfully. 'What a waste.'

Now, sitting opposite Juliet in the pub, a sticky-topped

table wedged between us, I had a sudden sense there was something she wasn't telling me.

'What's the matter?' I asked.

'Nothing.'

'You've spent the last five minutes ripping that beermat to shreds. What did it ever do to you?' I joked.

She sighed. 'I guess you're going to find out sooner or later.' There was a pause. 'I'm pregnant.'

The beer-stained paisley carpet shifted under my feet. '*What?*'

'I thought I was late because of the shock, but I did a test this morning.'

'Christ.' I was silent as the bombshell sank in. 'Is it Danny's?'

Her eyes flashed. 'Of course it's Danny's!'

'Sorry,' I said, holding my hands up, palms facing her. 'Stupid thing to say. It's just a lot to take in.'

'For me, too,' she admitted. She smiled and her hand crept down, cupping her stomach protectively. 'But I'm kind of getting used to the idea.'

I forced a smile, but inside I felt disappointment crushing the air out of my lungs. With Danny out of the picture, I'd assumed I'd be promoted to Most Important Person in Juliet's life. But I'd never be able to compete with his baby. A mother's love was unconditional, enduring, the strongest love of all. Unless you happened to be my mother, of course. But she'd been the exception to the rule.

'How far along are you?' I asked.

'Only eight weeks. I wasn't going to tell anyone until after the first scan.'

No wonder she'd seemed composed at the funeral. As Danny's coffin disappeared behind the curtains, Juliet knew she had his genes living on, his cells multiplying inside her. I thought back to obstetrics lectures at med school. By eight weeks, the fetus was the size of a kidney bean. Its facial features were becoming more defined and the nerve cells in its brain were branching out to form early neural pathways. Its legs were forming, and its hands were developing ridges where its fingers would be. It looked less like an alien and more like a human, albeit a tiny, non-functioning one.

'You're going through with it?'

Her head snapped back. 'Of course I'm going through with it!'

'It's a big ask, bringing up a kid on your own. How will you cope?'

She narrowed her eyes. 'Sometimes I think you think I'm totally incompetent. You're forgetting I run a house and have a stressful job.'

I hooted. 'A house your parents bought and a job that basically involves you sitting behind a desk in a big white box looking pretty.'

'Well, at least I have a proper job,' she retorted. 'At least I finished my degree. And at least I stand on my own two feet, unlike you. Almost thirty and still living at home. Tell me, Rose, because I'd love to know, who's the incompetent one here?'

'What if you meet someone else? They won't want to

take on Danny's bastard!' I cried. I was clutching at straws now, but I had to make her see she was making the biggest mistake of her life. 'Twenty-nine is nothing. You've plenty of time to meet someone and have a family. A *proper* family.'

'Don't you get it? I'll have a family. Just me and the baby. A little unit of two. That's all I need.'

'But what about *me*?' The words slipped out, unstoppered.

She shook her head. 'You can't see it, can you, Rose? You're a friend, nothing more. Someone to have a laugh with once in a while. But I don't need you in my life. I never have. Not like you seem to need me.' She must have seen the shock on my face because she said, 'If this is news to you, I'm sorry. But you have a distorted view of our friendship. You've always given it far more weight than I ever have. In fact, I've been meaning to say for a while that I think you should stop coming up to London. You need to build your own life, not leech off mine. Do you understand?'

She said this slowly and with enunciation, like she was speaking to a particularly stupid toddler. As I nodded, a tear leaked out of the corner of my eye.

'But we can still see each other every now and then? I can come and see the baby when it's born?'

'Danny's bastard?' She laughed mirthlessly. 'Christ, you're a human fucking Terminator. No matter how many times I shoot you down, you never give up.'

'Please, Juliet.'

She shook her head. 'I'll think about it.' Her face softened, and she pulled a tissue from her pocket and gave it to me. 'But seriously, you need to back the fuck off and give me some space. Understood?'

I nodded miserably. And I did. I gave Juliet and her pregnancy space while I threw my energies into charity work. When the baby was born seven months later, Juliet emailed me a photo taken on the maternity ward, her sweaty fringe plastered to her beaming, shiny face and a grizzly-looking scrap of a thing with a red, scrunched-up face and a nest of black hair cradled in her arms. I studied the baby's face, curious to see which parent it took after, but it could have been left on the steps of a fire station for all it looked like either of them.

Juliet called the baby Eloise after her favourite song by The Damned. I kept my distance and, as a reward for good behaviour, she asked me to be the child's godmother.

I saw Eloise for the first time the day she was christened. When Juliet gave her to me to hold, Eloise took one look at me and her face puckered and reddened and she started to wail, arms and legs pumping violently. It was with relief that I handed her back to her mother.

CHAPTER FORTY-ONE

India Matthews' inquest was held at Archbishop's Palace in Maidstone, an impressive fourteenth century building on the banks of the River Medway that was also, incongruously, used as a wedding venue. The coroner, Josephine Berisford, had steel-grey corkscrew curls that she'd coaxed into a loose chignon and a keen intellect beneath her disarming manner.

'The purpose of this inquest is to determine who the deceased was, when they died, where they died and how they came by their death,' she said, her gaze sweeping the room. 'It is an inquiry, *not* a trial.' She directed her comment at India's father, Roy, whose jaw was clenched so tightly I could see a vein pulsing in his neck. 'That is to say,' she continued, a smile taking the sting out of her words, 'it is a fact-finding, not a fault-finding hearing.'

The words rolled off her tongue so easily, I wondered just how many inquests she had presided over as she sought to answer the questions a sudden death posed.

Hundreds, probably. And every single one told a story: a story about a life, a death, and the family and friends left behind.

India's story began with the pathologist's report, and I watched with interest as the pathologist took to the stand. Although I had found dissecting Buxom Beryl at med school fascinating, pathology wasn't an area of medicine I'd ever been interested in pursuing. What was the point of being a doctor if not to save lives? Spending my days carving open the dead to reveal their secrets held no appeal.

As he ran through India's injuries in an almost-bored monotone, I sneaked another look at Roy Matthews and the rest of India's family. Sitting to Matthews' left was a hand-wringing, grey-faced woman I assumed was India's mother. Her bloodshot eyes were glued to the pathologist as he droned on about pulmonary contusions and subcutaneous haematomas. I don't suppose she understood a word of it, but you didn't need to be medically trained to realise that being hit by a fast-moving train would cause catastrophic trauma.

Sitting on her far side was a white-haired man in his late seventies who had a pale blue handkerchief balled in his fist and knuckles swollen with arthritis. He must be India's grandfather. As I watched, he stuffed the handkerchief in his pocket, leaned over and took one of his daughter's hands. It was such a small but poignant gesture that my eyes filled with tears. He looked up at me as if he'd felt my gaze on his skin and I looked away, flustered, but not before a look of loathing hardened his features and, with a jolt, I realised he also blamed me for his granddaughter's death.

My eyes slid over the motley collection of people who made up the rest of the Matthews family contingent. A teenaged boy with angular features and unwashed hair; a jowly woman in her sixties with the same piggy eyes as Roy Matthews; a harassed-looking woman trying, unsuccessfully, to quieten the snotty-faced toddler on her lap; a blonde girl around India's age whose face was swollen with crying.

Did they all think I was to blame for India's death? That it was me who India was speaking with in the precious minutes before she died? I willed the pathologist to get a move on, because the sooner Rhona took to the witness stand, the sooner everyone would realise I was not culpable. Not of India's death, anyway.

'... and so I conclude that the cause of death was multiple injuries consistent with being hit by a train,' the pathologist said.

'No shit, Sherlock,' I muttered under my breath, earning a disapproving look from Rhona who was sitting to my right.

The coroner plucked an A4 sheet from the sheaf of papers on her desk and slid a pair of glasses onto her nose.

'Next, I will read the statement from Greg Thornhill,' she said.

Greg Thornhill, it transpired, was the train driver unlucky enough to be at the controls of the 9.20am Ramsgate to Faversham service the morning India died. Visibility had been good that day and as he approached the level crossing at Graveney he'd seen a woman crouching on the embankment. He sounded the horn but instead of backing away, the woman stood and casually walked onto the line towards the train.

He applied the emergency brakes and repeatedly sounded the horn, but it was impossible to stop the train in time. The last thing he reported seeing was the woman staring at him with her hands over her ears.

The engine stopped "a few seconds on" and he stayed in his cab until the emergency services arrived.

'That concludes the evidence of Greg Thornhill,' Josephine Berisford said. She placed the statement on her pile of papers and glanced up at Eddie, Rhona and me.

'And now I would like to call Miss Rhona Richards,' she said.

There were audible gasps as Rhona rose stiffly to her feet and shuffled over to the witness stand to take the oath. India's family looked from one to another in confusion and then, as realisation dawned, turned angry gazes on Roy Matthews. But he didn't notice. He was too busy staring at Rhona in bewilderment. As she took the bible in her right hand and confirmed the evidence she was giving would be the truth, the whole truth, and nothing but the truth, I willed him to look at me. Finally, he did, and I jutted my chin out and locked eyes with him until his gaze fell to the floor.

With something akin to jubilation, I turned my attention back to Rhona.

'You were one of the last people to speak to India on

the day she died,' Josephine Berisford was saying. 'Please take us through what happened.'

'I'd just started my shift at Sisterline when I took the call from India. She sounded distressed, and when I asked her if she wanted to talk about why she'd called, she told me she'd had an argument with her father. He'd lost his temper when she'd told him she was moving into a flat with her best friend and he'd hung up on her.'

At this, the blonde girl with the puffy face broke into a storm of noisy sobs. A court usher scurried over with a glass of water and, once the sobs had subsided, the coroner said, 'Did India elaborate on the state of her relationship with her father?'

'She told me she'd spent her whole life trying to keep her father happy,' Rhona said. 'She said he was fine when he had his own way, but he flew into a rage if she ever disagreed with him. She said she'd been plucking up the courage to tell him she was leaving home for weeks but had kept putting it off because she knew he'd take the news badly.

'I asked India if she was having any suicidal thoughts and she said no, she just wanted someone to talk to. I gave her some coping strategies and signposted her to a couple of organisations I thought might help her. She thanked me and hung up.'

'How long did the call last, approximately?'

'About ten minutes.'

Josephine Berisford nodded. 'I have read the transcript. As someone who must have spoken to many distressed and suicidal people while manning the phones at Sisterline, was it your opinion that India was at risk of self-harm?'

Rhona shook her head. 'She was upset, but calm. She told me she was looking forward to moving in with her friend and having her own independence. I had the impression it wasn't the first time her father had upset her, and it probably wouldn't be the last. I classed her as low risk.'

'Thank you,' the coroner said. She smiled at India's family. 'Any questions?'

If I'd expected Roy Matthews to give Rhona both barrels, I was wrong. Slumped in his seat like the stuffing had been knocked out of him, he didn't even lift his head. When no one else spoke, the coroner thanked Rhona and she stepped down from the stand and returned to her seat.

'In that case, I ask Roy Matthews to take the stand,' the coroner said.

CHAPTER FORTY-TWO

The usher accompanied Roy Matthews to the witness box, handed him the bible and a card and he mumbled the oath, his chin pressed against his barrel-like chest.

'I'm afraid I'm going to have to ask you to speak up, Mr Matthews,' Josephine Berisford said. 'Please read from your statement if it's easier.'

He gave her a baleful look, fished a pair of spectacles from his pocket and put them on with fumbling fingers. 'I am Roy Matthews, father of India Matthews...'

He spoke of a happy child who began to suffer from periods of anxiety following her parents' divorce. How India used to stay with him a couple of nights a week until she was sixteen, after which she lived full time with her mother so she could see her friends.

And because you were inside doing time for assaulting poor Kerry Davis, I thought, glaring at him.

'Could you please take us through the events of the

morning of Friday, July thirtieth?' the coroner asked, picking up her pen.

'India phoned me just after eight. She said she had some news. I said I had some news, too, and told her I'd put down a deposit on a two-bedroom place in Minster, down the road from her mum's, so she could start splitting her time between the two of us again. Then she dropped her bombshell.'

'Her bombshell?'

'She told me she was moving in with her mate Kelsey, that she was sorry, but it was all sorted, like. I told her I'd put down a grand's deposit, so she'd have to change her plans, but she refused. She said she was going to do what she wanted for a change. Things got a bit heated, and she hung up on me.'

'India hung up on *you*?' Josephine Berisford queried, flipping through her notes. 'Only according to Miss Richards' evidence, India said you ended the call. Please think carefully about your answer and remember you are under oath.'

He rubbed his face. 'I dunno. It may have been me who hung up first. I was sore she hadn't told me she was moving in with Kels. I don't like her keeping things from me.'

'Did you speak to India again that morning?' the coroner asked.

He looked up at the ceiling briefly, then nodded and mumbled something into his chest.

'I'm sorry, but you're going to have to speak up,' Josephine Berisford said again.

'I did,' he said.

The room was so quiet I could hear Rhona's shallow breathing next to me. I wriggled my toes in anticipation. This was better than any television crime drama.

'And when did you speak to India again?' the coroner asked.

'Just before ten o'clock.'

'You're certain of the time?'

He nodded. 'I was on my tea break. She phoned to apologise, to say that she could still come and stay with me in the new place now and then.' He lifted anguished eyes to his family. 'I saw red. I told her it wasn't enough. She'd lied to me, see? She'd broken my trust.' He gulped and lowered his gaze. 'So, I told her she was dead to me.'

'And what happened then?'

Beads of perspiration had broken out across his forehead. 'I heard a thud, like she'd dropped the phone, then a horn blasting over and over. A whooshing noise, then... nothing.'

India's mother jumped to her feet, her face contorted. 'You said she was on the phone to them when she died!' she shrieked, pointing at us. Rhona shrank back in her seat. 'But she was on the phone to *you*. I might have known. You're the reason she killed herself. You!'

'Mrs Matthews, please,' Josephine Berisford said, nodding to the usher who magicked another glass of water from nowhere. India's mother crumpled back into her chair, a shell of a woman. India's grandfather put his arm around her shoulder and pulled her to him as she sobbed.

'I know it's my fault,' Roy Matthews said, directing his

words at his ex-wife. 'I wish I could turn back the clock. I wish I hadn't lost my temper with her. That whooshing sound...' He clamped his hands over his ears and shook his head from side to side. 'I hear that fucking sound every second of every fucking day and I will for the rest of my life.'

The coroner cleared her throat, dragging everyone's attention back to her. 'I understand this is a distressing time, Mr Matthews, but can I please ask that you moderate your language. And remember, we are here to establish the facts of India's death, not to lay blame at anyone's door. We'll take a ten-minute comfort break before we hear from my officer.' With that, she pushed her chair back and left the room.

Telling Eddie and Rhona I was popping out for some fresh air, I headed through the main doors onto the circular driveway at the front of the building. I was about to call Eloise to tell her I would be home earlier than expected when I felt a heavy hand on my shoulder. My breath caught in my throat as I spun on my heels.

'Get your hands off me,' I cried.

Roy Matthews backed away, his palms raised in surrender.

'Sorry, I didn't mean to frighten you.'

'Then what *did* you mean to do?'

He rotated his hands slowly and stared at them as if he'd never seen them before. 'I wanted to apologise,' he said. 'I was wrong to blame you for what happened.'

'Too right you were. It was Rhona who took India's call, not me.'

'I realise that now. But that day in the car park, I saw you go into the Sisterline offices. I thought you must be the one who turned India against me.'

'No one turned India against you, Mr Matthews. Rhona was there when she needed support. She helped her.'

'I know.' His body started to convulse, and for one awkward moment I feared he was about to have a seizure and I might actually have to help him, but then a tear slid down his face, and another, and he broke into noisy sobs.

'I'm sorry,' he blurted. 'I was hurting so bad inside that I lashed out.'

'It was one thing slashing my tyre and threatening me in the car park but sending lilies to my house was something else. My cat died because of you.'

His faced creased with confusion. 'Your cat?'

'She was poisoned by the lilies you left on my doorstep.'

He shook his head. 'I didn't leave any lilies. I don't even know where you live.'

'That's not what your note said.'

'I just said that to frighten you.'

'I know you're lying. You trashed my house.'

His eyebrows shot up to his non-existent hair line. 'I didn't!'

'My goddaughter saw you,' I said, trying to think. Eloise heard our intruder as he'd wreaked havoc downstairs, but had she actually seen him? I couldn't remember.

'Honestly, it wasn't me. I don't know where you live.'

'Either you were lying then or you're lying now. Whichever way you look at it, I can't trust a word you say. You deserve to have India's death on your conscience, you unpleasant excuse for a man.'

I left him gaping at me like a fish out of water and marched back inside.

I was still shaking with anger as I retook my seat in the courtroom. I didn't feel a shred of sympathy for Roy Matthews. Men like him used their anger issues as an excuse for frankly diabolical behaviour. They were pathetic. And how dare he deny killing Dinah? He made me sick.

Josephine Berisford's eyes roved the room until she had everyone's attention.

'India Matthews did not appear to be suicidal when she phoned Sisterline on the morning of her death, and I would like to pay tribute to the charity and its staff and volunteers who do such sterling work in helping people when they are at their most vulnerable.' She smiled at Rhona and I groaned inwardly. The bloody woman would be insufferable.

'However, this was before India's final conversation with her father, in which harsh words were exchanged,' the coroner continued.

'The train driver took all action possible by applying the brakes. There was absolutely nothing he could have done to avoid striking India and my sympathies are with him.

'Based on the evidence, I am satisfied on the balance of probabilities that this was a deliberate act on India's part and so I am recording a verdict of suicide. My deepest condolences to India's family and my heartfelt thanks to everyone who has given evidence today.'

The Matthews contingent came together and embraced, tears running down their cheeks. All except Roy Matthews, who was sidling towards the door with a woebegone look on his face. Keen to avoid another confrontation with him, I said goodbye to Eddie and Rhona and hurried from the room. We could have a de-brief in the morning. Right now, I just wanted to get home.

I needed all my powers of concentration to navigate Maidstone's complicated one-way system, but once I was on the motorway, I replayed the conversation with Matthews in my head. He'd admitted he left the note in which he professed to know where I lived, yet he'd also claimed that was a lie designed to intimidate me and he'd seemed genuinely baffled when I'd blamed him for leaving the lilies and trashing the house.

Could I trust the words of a liar and a bully?

One thing was sure: either he was lying then, or he was lying now. The flip side of that, of course, was that one of his assertions was true.

But which one?

And if he hadn't left the lilies and trashed the house, who had?

My scrambled thoughts began to untangle as the Land Rover ate up the miles. For too long, my mind had been a mess, a jumble of suspicions and paranoia, one feeding off the other. I hadn't been able to sleep, I could barely eat, and the smell of death had followed me everywhere.

Sitting through India's inquest, I'd been quietly impressed at how the coroner had listened to the evidence, analysed the facts and reached a logical conclusion. Her calm, reasoned approach had caused a shift in my thinking and, slowly, the rational, methodical side of my brain reasserted itself.

As my mind cleared, I realised I had been deluding myself for days.

I'd thought that where Theo was concerned, I had a choice.

But I was wrong. There had only ever been one course of action. And the sooner I set that course in motion, the better.

I stepped on the accelerator, and the Land Rover lurched towards home.

CHAPTER FORTY-THREE

SEPTEMBER 2007

Juliet was as good as her word and kept me at arm's length. We spoke on the phone every few weeks and I dutifully sent my goddaughter a card with a ten-pound note tucked inside every year for her birthday. When I offered to go up to London for Eloise's fourth birthday and deliver her card in person, Juliet politely but firmly declined.

'If I open the door even a crack, you'll push it open and then you'll be here every weekend, making yourself at home. You always do. You can't help yourself,' she said.

'I won't,' I promised. But she stood her ground, so I bought a stamp and put the card in the post.

I didn't hold it against Juliet because I wanted her to

be happy. And if that meant limiting my contact with her to a couple of phone calls a month, then so be it.

And she was. Happy, I mean. She seemed to find motherhood effortless, and her voice was filled with warmth when she relayed Eloise's latest achievements, whether it was learning to tell the time or playing a solo at recorder club. Her boss at the gallery agreed she could cut her hours to three mornings a week when Eloise was born. It wasn't enough to live on, but her parents helped financially, and when they died, six months after each other when Eloise was five, Juliet lived off her inheritance.

One time I phoned her I was surprised to hear a faint slur to her words, even though it was barely six o'clock on a Sunday evening.

'Have you been drinking?' I asked.

She giggled. 'One of the mums was making margaritas at the party Eloise went to this afternoon. I may have had a couple.'

'And the rest,' I said archly, and Juliet laughed harder.

'Oh, Rose, don't ever change, will you? Keep saying it as it is. It's so refreshing. The mums here can be a bit… oh, I don't know. A bit two-faced, you know? Perfectly pleasant to your face and then bitching about you behind your back.'

A warm flush was spreading through my body, from the top of my head to the tips of my toes, as I savoured her words. *Don't ever change, Rose.*

'I can't imagine anyone bitching about you,' I said. I wasn't trying to flatter her. I genuinely couldn't think of a single reason anyone might have something nasty to say.

'Oh, it's the whole single mum vibe. I'm an anomaly among the Smug Marrieds, their two point four children and their bloody labradors and four by fours. The women think I'm on my own, therefore I must be after their husbands. The husbands think I'm fair game.' There was a pause, a chink of glass and the sound of swallowing. Juliet cleared her throat. 'Sometimes I just wish Danny was here, you know?'

I gripped the handset tightly. 'I know. But you're doing so well. And you have Eloise. Any more head teacher awards?'

'It's the summer holidays, Rose.'

'Oh yes, silly me. How's ballet?'

'She's moved onto tap, now. Says she likes the noise it makes.' Juliet's voice was indulgent. 'She reminds me so much of her father. She has the same single-mindedness, the same determination. If she sets herself a goal, she'll do whatever it takes to reach it. Sometimes I look at her and it's like I'm seeing him.' She laughed. 'Well, a small, female version of him, anyway. Does that sound weird?'

'Not at all.'

Juliet mellowed towards me after that, and our phone calls were longer, more intimate. I didn't suggest visiting her in London, not just because I was busy with my charity work, but because I knew I would have to share her with Eloise, and I didn't want to. So, we kept it to late-night phone calls when we drank wine and put the world to rights, and it was almost like old times.

And then my father died, and everything changed again.

'I'm coming to the funeral,' Juliet announced.

I protested weakly, but she cut across me.

'It's the least I can do. I know how close you were to him. I'll have to bring El, but that's all right, isn't it? We can share a bed. Where is it you live again? Eastchurch?'

'Eastling, just outside Faversham. Don't go to Eastchurch, it's on the Isle of Sheppey.' It was dispiriting that I knew every detail about Juliet's life, yet she didn't even know where I lived.

She turned up at the house an hour before the service was due to begin with a small, solemn-faced girl in tow. Wrapping me in her arms and holding me tightly, she whispered, 'I'm so sorry,' in my ear.

I nodded and pulled away. Sniffed and dabbed my eyes with the corner of my sleeve.

She placed her hands on her hips. 'Aren't you going to say hello?'

'Oh, sorry, yes, of course. Hello Eloise, I'm Rose, your godmother. The last time I saw you, you were in nappies. Remarkable where the time goes.'

Juliet laughed, pushing her daughter towards me. 'I was talking to Eloise,' she said. 'El, say hello to your Auntie Rose. There's a good girl.'

The child murmured a greeting, her gaze firmly on the ground at our feet.

'Don't I get a curtsy?' I asked, arching an eyebrow.

Eloise's mouth fell open, and she shot a worried look at her mother. Juliet laughed again.

'Your Auntie Rose is teasing you, Eloise. She has a strange sense of humour. You'll soon learn not to take everything she says at face value.'

I picked up Juliet's overnight bag. 'I've put you both in the spare room. I hope that's all right.'

'It'll be perfect, I'm sure.' Juliet gazed at the cottage, at the flaky paintwork and the rotten windows, the crumbling pointing and the Virginia creeper that encased the brickwork like a verdant coat of armour. It was a world apart from her pretty mews house in Marylebone.

'Sorry about the state of the place,' I said, marching towards the back door. 'I'm afraid it's not been a priority these last few years, what with my mother's illness and everything.'

'Don't apologise. It's charming,' she said, following me into the kitchen and dropping her handbag on the table.

'That's one word for it,' I said. 'Ramshackle is another, and it's rather more accurate. If you'll follow me.'

Once I'd settled Juliet and Eloise in the spare bedroom, I headed for my room, wrenched open my wardrobe door and reached for my black funeral dress. The rayon fabric felt coarse against my mottled skin. I hugged myself, rubbing warmth into my arms, and paced over to the window. The sky was a sullen grey apart from a single ray of light as the sun tried heroically to pierce the thick rain clouds.

A sob caught the back of my throat, and I pressed my forehead against the glass. A black limousine was nosing its way up the drive towards the house. I wiped my clammy hands on my dress, slipped on a pair of plain black court shoes, and stepped onto the landing.

The funeral passed in a blur of readings and hymns. I sat with my head bowed, Juliet to my right, Eloise one along. She was a serious little girl with dark-blonde hair and hazel eyes a couple of shades darker than her mother's. I'd tried to engage her in conversation as we'd waited for the service to begin but had little joy.

'She's a bit shy,' Juliet had mouthed over the top of Eloise's head. 'Just leave her - she'll soon come around.'

Back at the house, Juliet walked round with the trays of sandwiches I'd ordered from the pub and charmed the incontinence pants off the old boys my father used to work with at the Post Office while I made endless cups of tea and smiled politely through anecdotes I'd heard a dozen times before. When the last mourner had left and Juliet had put Eloise to bed, I fetched a bottle from the sideboard and placed it on the coffee table with two tumblers.

'What's that?' Juliet asked.

'Dad's Laphroaig. I'd like to drink a toast to him.' I poured two generous measures and handed Juliet a glass. I watched her face as she took a sip.

She grimaced. 'Christ, it tastes like TCP.'

I laughed, some of the tension leaving my shoulders. 'It's one of Scotland's finest single malts, I'll have you know.'

'You're telling me people drink this stuff for pleasure?'

'It's Prince Charles's favourite whisky,' I told her. 'Have another sip. It'll grow on you, I promise.'

After we'd had a couple of glasses, Juliet decided she liked it after all. After another couple, the room's edges had blurred and softened. By the time we were halfway through the bottle, we were both slurring our words, and when I stood to throw another log on the fire, the room span, and I had to grab the arm of the chair to steady myself.

'Whoa!' I said, sitting down with a thump.

Juliet's giggle turned into a hiccough. 'Haven't been this pissed since university.'

I topped up her tumbler with exaggerated care. 'To university!' I slurred, clinking my glass against hers.

She nodded, her expression suddenly serious. 'Yes, Rosie. And to absent friends.' A tear trickled down her cheek.

'Don't get maudlin,' I said. 'You'll set me off.'

We drank in silence for a while, lost in our thoughts. Then Juliet clutched her chest just below her breastbone.

'Wha's the matter?'

'It hurts, right here,' she said.

I nodded sagely. 'Heartburn. It'll be the whisky. That's my official diagnosis.'

Juliet squinted at me myopically. 'Do you have anything for it, Doctor Rose?'

'There's some Gaviscon in my room.' I slapped my hands on the arms of the chair. 'I'll find it.'

But Juliet was already on her feet. 'I'll go. Tell me where it is.'

'Bottom drawer, bedside table.' I, too, could feel a burning sensation in the middle of my chest. 'Bring the packet, will you?'

She saluted me and stumbled into the hallway. I pulled myself to my feet and walked unsteadily around the room, stacking the last few teacups and saucers on a tray and carrying it into the kitchen.

I'd reached the bottom of the stairs when Juliet shouted my name.

I stopped in my tracks. She was halfway down the stairs, her raised fist held in front of her as if she was about to show me a magic trick.

'Did you find them?'

She shook her head. Kept shaking it. It was unnerving, and I took an involuntary step backwards.

'What's the matter?' My voice was thin, reedy.

'This is the matter,' she said. She sounded stone cold sober. I watched in horrified fascination as she turned her wrist and uncurled her fingers one by one. 'I found it in your bedside drawer.'

A sharp intake of breath. Mine. And the tray slipped out of my fingers and crashed to the floor, the delicate porcelain cups and saucers shattering into a thousand pieces on the flagstones.

My hand crept to my throat, the heartburn forgotten.

'Juliet -'

'What the *fuck* is this doing in your bedroom?' she demanded.

CHAPTER FORTY-FOUR

It was almost six o'clock before I arrived home. I felt bone-tired. Disconnected. Numb to the core, as if an anaesthetic had been injected into my veins to stop my nerves from passing signals to my brain, to stop me feeling anything.

Wearily, I let myself in the back door and plonked my bag and keys on the kitchen table. I shuffled into the hallway and sniffed. The smell of death had gone.

'Eloise?' I called up the stairs, even though a sixth sense told me she wasn't in. The house felt too still, the air so dense it was almost solid. I was alone. I closed my eyes briefly, then trudged back into the kitchen, filled the kettle, dropped a teabag into a mug and found a packet of bourbons in the cupboard. I carried the tea and biscuits into the front room and turned on the television, not because I wanted to watch a programme about a deeply tanned couple from Newcastle who were desperate to relocate to Spain's Costa del Sol but because the soft buzz of their Geordie accents was soothing.

I drank the tea and ate six biscuits, and still there was no sign of Eloise. I pulled my phone out of my pocket and called her, but it went straight to voicemail.

'Hello Eloise, it's Rose. Just checking you're all right, only I'm home and you're not here.' Christ, that sounded creepy. I cleared my throat and tried to sound jovial. 'Anyway, I thought I'd make a start on supper and wondered what you fancied. Perhaps you can call me when you get a chance?'

As I tossed the phone onto the sofa, a thought popped into my head. Would she have left without telling me? I dragged myself upstairs, pausing on the landing. Her door was shut, but there was nothing unusual about that. She always left it closed, no doubt a legacy from a childhood spent in care. Would she have left her door open if I'd agreed to take her in when Juliet died? Was the door a metaphor for her heart? And if so, had I damaged her beyond repair when I'd told that silly social services woman I didn't have the bandwidth to take her in?

I'd pretended I was too busy, but the real reason I'd turned Eloise away was because I thought I was incapable of love. I had loved once, of course, and look where that got me.

But I'd been wrong. I knew that now.

'Eloise?' I called, knocking softly on the door. 'El?'

There was no answer, so I turned the handle and pushed the door open, taking in the unmade bed, her holdall in the corner and her clothes draped over the chair. She was like her mother in more ways than she knew.

I was about to leave when I saw the corner of an envelope poking out from a zipped side pocket on the holdall. Something about the loopy handwriting scrawled across it stopped me in my tracks. Without thinking, I crossed the room, unzipped the pocket and pulled it out to see if I was right.

I was. It was Juliet's handwriting. An envelope, addressed to Eloise and dated the eighth of June 2011, two weeks before Juliet died.

My head swam alarmingly, and I perched on the edge of the bed until the dizziness passed. I knew I shouldn't read it, but I was greedy for an insight into their relationship, to step into Juliet's shoes even if just for a moment so I could learn how to navigate this strange new landscape I found myself in, so I could learn how to be a mother and right the wrongs of the past. I pulled the letter out before I could talk myself out of it.

June 2011

My darling, darling Eloise,

If you are reading this letter, it means that I am no longer here, and for that I apologise with all my heart. I tried so hard, baby girl, you have to believe how much I tried, but I just couldn't do it on my own any more.

If you are reading this letter, you are also celebrating your twenty-first birthday. Many happy returns, my darling. I hope life has been kind to you and you have turned into the beautiful, bright, brave girl you were destined to be.

It's Friday evening and you are sitting at the kitchen table finishing your English homework as I write. It is what artists call the golden hour, and a shaft of sunlight is playing on your hair, turning it flaxen. The tip of your tongue is poking out of your mouth and your forehead is creased like a frown as you concentrate. You look so achingly like your father that sometimes I can't bear to look at you at all, because it hurts too much.

I know you will have questions, and I will do my best to answer them. But I hope you understand that there are some questions I have no answer for, only suspicions. I have drawn my own conclusions but be warned - my standard of proof has been a balance of probabilities rather than the rigid "beyond reasonable doubt" of a criminal court. You must make up your own mind.

I will put myself in your shoes for a moment. Your beloved pair of Heelys, in fact! Do you remember the day we bought them? We caught the bus into Kensington and you free-wheeled home again in your new shoes, proud as punch. That was a happy day. There were so many happy days.

But I mustn't get sidetracked. I have too much to tell you. And I want to begin with your father. I knew he was The One the moment I met him. Some people thought he was cocky and feckless, but that's not how I saw him. I admired his confidence. It was something I recognised in myself. He had a beautiful soul beneath that Jack the Lad persona. He had an eye for a pretty face, yet he was insanely jealous if another man looked at me. He was physically strong, yet his asthma made him weak. He was a paradox, and I loved that about him.

You already know that your father died from an asthma

attack when I was pregnant with you. What I never told you is that it wasn't his first serious attack. The first happened when we were still at university. Your godmother, Rose, saved his life.

Do you remember Rose? She lives in Kent, in a funny little house in the middle of the woods.

Rose was training to become a doctor when we were at university. She knew exactly what to do when your father was struggling to breathe.

He always carried an inhaler with him after that. Always. Until the day he died.

By a strange quirk of fate, Rose was with him that day, too. I never told you that, did I? She did everything in her power to save him – or, at least that's what she told us. And I believed her, because I had no reason not to.

But in my darkest moments after his death, my doubts multiplied like cancerous cells. I couldn't stop wondering what had sparked his asthma attack and why Rose, with all her medical knowledge, couldn't save him. Most of all I wondered why his inhaler was never found.

I never asked her. Perhaps I didn't want to know the truth. But the truth found me in the end.

We were staying at Rose's house for her father's funeral. I'd only gone out of a sense of duty. You were asleep upstairs and Rose and I were sitting by the fire in her fusty front room, drinking her father's whisky, and it had given me heartburn. When I went looking for some anti-acids, I found an inhaler. Not any inhaler. It was your father's, hidden in a drawer by her bed. I knew it was his because of the expiry date. Rose had taken it. There was no other explanation. Which meant she stood by and watched him die.

If it hadn't been for Rose, you'd have grown up with a father. A mother, too, because I'm sorry, El, but I just can't carry on without him. My heart has been shattered into a million tiny pieces, and it can never be put back together.

If you are reading this letter, it is because I have exercised my right to exit this world.

Whether or not I am of sound mind is for others to decide. All I know is that my life, even with you in it, my sweet girl, is not worth living.

As I plan my end, you are just at your beginning, and I hope with what is left of my shattered heart that you are happy. Know that I will be happy, too, once I am reunited with your father. My darling Danny.

Reading this letter back, I fear I may have posed more questions than I have answered. I am sorry for that. And I am sorry I didn't have the strength to seek justice for your dad.

I am giving you this information. What you do with it is entirely up to you.

Always and forever,

Mum xx

CHAPTER FORTY-FIVE

SEPTEMBER 2007

I stared in horror at the blue plastic inhaler in Juliet's hand, wondering how the hell I was going to dig myself out of this hole.

When I'd shoved the inhaler in my drawer for safe-keeping, I'd intended to throw it away as soon as things had settled down. But as the months turned into years and the memories of that day faded, I'd forgotten all about it. Until now.

I took a deep breath. 'It was my father's.'

'Don't lie to me.' Juliet came down the stairs and I shrank against the wall. 'The expiry date's the same year Danny died. It's his, isn't it?'

'I -'

'You told the police you couldn't find it. You were

lying, weren't you?' She brandished the inhaler in my face. 'You... you killed him!'

I ran a tongue over my lips. 'I didn't. He had an asthma attack.'

'Semantics. You let him die. You could have saved him. You knew what to do. For Christ's sake, you even found his inhaler, didn't you?' She stared at me with repulsion. 'You sat beside him and watched him die. Why, Rose, why?'

'Because he treated you like a piece of meat,' I said, unable to stop myself.

'He loved me! He wanted kids, marriage, the lot. You said so!'

'I was lying. I said it to make you feel better. He didn't come back for you. He came back because his visa ran out. As far as he was concerned, you were a bit of fun. He had no intention of sticking around.'

'You don't know that!'

'Juliet,' I said, reaching towards her. She recoiled from my touch and her face contorted with anger.

'Get your hands off me!'

'He wasn't good enough for you.' *And he tried to rape me*. But the words died on my lips. What was the point? She wouldn't believe me.

Juliet turned and headed back up the stairs, still shaking her head. Halfway up, she stopped. Turned around. 'You had no right. No fucking right.'

'I'm sorry,' I cried.

But she was already clomping across the landing to the spare bedroom.

I hovered by the front door as Juliet crashed and banged about upstairs. A few minutes later, she appeared, her case in one hand and her phone in the other.

'You're not going?' I said, my hand fluttering to my throat.

'I can't stay under the same roof as you a minute longer. You're poisonous.' She threw the suitcase on the floor. 'I've called a taxi.'

'You've missed the last train.'

She shrugged. 'So, we'll sleep at the station.' She turned on her heels and marched back upstairs. This time I heard her rousing Eloise, and moments later the child appeared at the top of the stairs dressed in leggings and a hooded top, her bewildered face sleep-creased and her hair dishevelled.

'Would you like a snack to take with you?' I asked, scuttling into the kitchen. Finding some clingfilm-wrapped sandwiches left over from the wake, I darted back and offered them to Juliet. For a moment, I thought she was going to bat them out of my hand and onto the floor, but then she snatched them and handed them to Eloise before barging past me and tugging at the front door.

'Wait outside,' she instructed her daughter. Eloise's eyes widened, but she did as she was told. Juliet fetched her handbag from the kitchen and picked up her case.

'I never, ever want to see or speak to you again,' she said, her voice quivering with rage. 'Understood?'

'But -'

'No buts. I want you out of my life.'

'Juliet,' I said urgently, as she disappeared into the darkness. 'You're not going to report me to the police, are you?'

She paused, one hand on the jamb. Her expression, illuminated by the security light, was impossible to read. 'I don't know yet,' she said finally. She cocked her head as the sound of a car filtered through the trees. The taxi slowed and turned into the driveway, the tyres loud as they crunched on the gravel. I fought the urge to flag the driver down, to tell him it was a mistake, that we had no need for him because Juliet wasn't going anywhere. Instead, I stayed where I was, watching her warily.

'Telling the police won't bring Danny back,' I pleaded.

She narrowed her eyes. 'You need to pay for what you've done.'

'I've said I'm sorry.'

'You think you can erase everything with an apology?' She shook her head in disbelief. 'You're sicker than I thought.'

The taxi pulled up outside the house and the driver wound down the passenger window. 'Taxi for Mrs Cavendish?' he said.

Juliet nodded, opened the back door and bundled first Eloise and then the case onto the back seat. While Eloise was occupied fixing her seatbelt, Juliet turned back to me, her face so close to mine I could smell the whisky on her breath. 'I'm not sure I need to tell the police,' she whispered. 'Because I have a feeling you'll pay one way or another. You reap what you sow, Rose. There'll come a day when you'll have reason to regret what you did, you mark my words.'

With that, she climbed into the taxi and slammed the door in my face.

My legs buckled, and I crumpled to the ground, my head in my hands, as the thrum of the engine faded away.

In the weeks that followed, I waited for a knock at the door. A solemn-faced detective on the doorstep. A polite but firm, 'Good afternoon, Miss Barton. We wondered if you would accompany us to the station?' A hand pushing my head down and propelling me into the back of a police car. The same detective reading my rights. A brightly lit interview room with polystyrene cups of tea and a barrage of questions. A charge. Not murder, that would never stick, but manslaughter. Crown court, a bewigged judge glaring at me from over half-moon glasses. Twelve good men and women in the jury box. A verdict. 'We find the defendant guilty, m'lud'. A prison sentence. Jarring headlines, public humiliation. Time inside. Butch women with an eye for fresh meat. 'Whatever you do, don't drop the soap, Rose.'

My arrest and subsequent incarceration seemed as inevitable as the thaw that followed snow, yet no one knocked on the door, no one stood on the doorstep with a police radio in their hands inviting me back to the nick. Months passed, and I realised Juliet couldn't have told the police I'd lied about Danny's inhaler. Was she protecting me, or Eloise? I couldn't ask her, because she never spoke to me again. And did it matter who she was protecting? What mattered was that she spared me.

The conversations I had with her in the days before she jumped from the cliffs at Dover were in my head, figments of my imagination. Admittedly, they were based on information I gleaned from her inquest, but I invented details to fill in the gaps.

Eloise's call was real enough. She must have remembered I was her godmother and found my number among her mother's personal effects. Did she recall the fateful trip to Kent for my father's funeral? Did she understand what had happened?

Is that why she was here?

CHAPTER FORTY-SIX

The letter slipped from my trembling fingers and fluttered to the floor. A feeling of dread gripped my heart and squeezed it so tightly I struggled to breathe. Eloise knew I'd been with her father when he died. She knew her mother had found his inhaler here, in this house. Juliet hadn't said outright that I'd killed Danny, but you didn't need to be Einstein to join the dots. And Juliet had all but admitted she planned to end her life because she couldn't live without him. She had told her daughter it was my fault she'd lost both her parents.

My fault.

A sound downstairs made me jump, and I grabbed Juliet's letter, folded it and was about to slip it back into the side pocket of the holdall when I saw the tip of a second envelope. I cocked my head, listening, but the house was quiet again. It must have been Dinah's cat flap banging in the wind. Grabbing the envelope, I pulled out the folded sheet of paper inside.

The letter was typed and dated six weeks ago. I glanced at the address in the top left-hand corner. Kent Social Services.

Dear Ms Cavendish,

Regarding your recent subject access request under the General Data Protection Regulations 2018 for copies of your social care records between 01/01/2008 and 31/12/2010…

My blood ran cold. Eloise had made an application to see her records. Records that would reveal I had refused to take her in after Juliet died. Records that would show she had spent her childhood in care because I was "too busy".

My eyes glazing with tears, I continued reading. Words leapt out at me. *No named guardian… a preference to live with her godmother… Ms Barton felt she didn't have the bandwidth… not in Eloise's best interests… gave her a chance to change her mind… family court hearing… care order…*

'What are you doing?' said a cold voice.

Eloise stood in the doorway, her lips pressed together and her arms folded across her chest.

I forced myself to smile. 'I was about to change your bed linen.'

We both gazed at the letters in my hand.

'Don't lie to me, Rose.'

'They'd fallen out of your bag. I was putting them back.'

She was across the room in a flash and plucked them from my hands.

'So, you know why I'm here.'

'Because you wanted the truth?'

She gave a bark of laughter. Empathy wasn't one of my strong suits, but even I could feel the hostility coming off her in waves.

'I've known the truth since my twenty-first birthday. I was summoned to a solicitor's office and handed a letter from my mum.' She watched me carefully, then nodded to herself. 'Yes, I found out you murdered my parents the day I turned twenty-one.'

'I didn't murder them,' I said, my voice hoarse. 'No one could have saved Danny. And I hadn't seen your mum for three years when she died. How can you blame me for that?'

'Because you're lying,' Eloise said. She leaned over me, her face inches from mine. 'In fact, it wouldn't surprise me if you triggered his asthma attack on purpose.'

'I didn't, I promise,' I stuttered.

'But you could have saved him.'

'He tried to rape me.'

Her eyes blazed. 'How dare you say that about my dad, you evil *bitch*!'

I wrapped my arms around my head and waited for the blows to fall, but when they didn't, I sneaked a look at Eloise. She'd moved to the window and was staring out at the woods.

'What do you want from me?' I whispered.

'You stood beside me at my mother's graveside and

you told me social services wouldn't let me live with you. But it was a lie, wasn't it? You couldn't be bothered to have me.'

'That's not true,' I said, desperation seeping into my voice.

'Then why didn't you let me come and live with you? You were all I had!'

'I was frightened I didn't have enough love for you. I thought you'd be better off with a foster family.'

'Better off?' Eloise laughed without mirth. 'This isn't a fucking fairytale. Life in care sucks.' She rubbed her arms, as if staving off the cold.

'I'm sorry,' I said.

'Sorry for what? Killing my parents, lying to me or for being found out?'

'For everything. I wish I could turn back the clock.' I hesitated. 'But you should know your father was no angel, Eloise. He cheated on your mother time and again. She was the only one who couldn't see him for what he was, a two-timing bastard.'

Eloise lunged forwards, grabbing the neck of my jumper in her fist and twisting it until it constricted my airway. 'How dare you! My mum was a far better judge of character than you'll ever be.'

'What d'you mean?' I gasped.

Her mouth curved into a lop-sided smile as she let me go. 'You let me in, didn't you?'

CHAPTER FORTY-SEVEN

Something inside me snapped. I pushed her away and scrambled to my feet. 'You can talk,' I shouted. 'You're no better than me. We've both taken a life. You killed Theo to protect yourself. I let Danny die to protect Juliet. Neither of us wanted to do it, but we had no choice. We're in this together, Eloise, watching each other's backs. Thelma and Louise.'

Her cackle of laughter was unnerving. I watched, frozen, as she began tossing her belongings into her holdall.

'What are you doing?'

'I'm leaving this shithole. I'm off to the Caribbean. The Dominican Republic, to be exact. I reckon I deserve a little break. I've transferred a couple of grand from your account to mine. Well, I say a couple of grand. More like ten. Hope that's OK?' she said, smiling sweetly.

I gaped. 'You've what?'

'Perhaps that'll teach you not to leave all your logins

and passwords in a notebook next to your computer,' she said. 'Honestly, Rose, you're very trusting for someone so devious. Anyone would think you're slowly losing your mind.' She looked sidelong at me and grinned. 'I found your prescription for amitriptyline. Vitamins, my arse.' She snorted. 'Christ, it's no wonder you're on edge going cold turkey from those. You were on the maximum dose.'

A long-ago conversation I'd had with John's doctor filtered through my cluttered mind. He'd listed the possible side effects of amitriptyline, which included constipation, nausea and a dry mouth. He'd also told me to come off them gradually, but why? Searching my memory, I pictured myself sitting in his consulting room, a yellow sharps bin on his desk and an anatomical skeleton in the corner staring at me from horror movie eye sockets. Slowly, I remembered. The withdrawal effects could cause anything from an irregular heartbeat and flu-like symptoms to insomnia and mania. How could I have forgotten that? Despite everything, a feeling of relief washed over me. The smell of death, the sleeplessness and the paranoia were withdrawal symptoms. I wasn't losing my mind, after all.

'Is that why you came here, to rob me?' I asked Eloise.

She shook her head, a brittle, puppet-like jerk.

'Then why?'

'I want you to suffer like I've suffered. You're going to pay for my parents' deaths by paying for Theo's.'

'What?'

'I couldn't be sure the police would have enough

evidence to convict you of my dad's death, so I had to think of another way to make you pay.'

I stared blankly at her.

'Come on, Rose, think about it. There's a dead body buried in your garden. One call to the police is all it'll take, and you'll be arrested and charged with Theo's murder.'

'But you brought him here!'

'Prove it,' she shot back. 'No one has seen me since I arrived. I've made sure of that. And you kindly destroyed my car and all traces of Theo's DNA for me.'

I realised with a frisson of unease that it was true. Eloise had arrived under cover of darkness and the only times she'd been out of the house was to go for walks dressed in my knee-length waterproof jacket, my scarf wound around her neck and my bucket hat pulled low over her face. From a distance, no one would have known it wasn't me. The only caller we'd had was the PCSO and Eloise had been upstairs.

She disappeared into the bathroom, returning moments later with her wash bag, which she squashed into the holdall.

'But it's been a blast,' she said, reaching for my copy of *Alice in Wonderland*.

I blinked. 'A blast?'

'Like when we had the visit from our "intruder".' She sketched air quotes and giggled. 'Your face was a picture.'

I couldn't see what was so funny. Eloise had been virtually incoherent with fear. 'I saw Roy Matthews at the inquest this morning. He denies even knowing where I live,' I said.

'The road rage guy? Well, he's probably right.'

'But if it wasn't him, who trashed the house?'

She wound a strand of hair around her little finger and smiled coyly. 'Can't you guess?'

'*You?*'

'Lighten up, Auntie Rose,' Eloise mocked. 'It was just a bit of fun. I don't even know why I did it, to be honest. Boredom, probably. It's so fucking *boring* here, I don't know how you stand it.'

Pieces were clicking into place as I recalled Roy Matthews' apology. He'd been telling the truth, after all. My head started spinning as I remembered he'd denied sending the lilies, too.

'*You* left the flowers. You killed Dinah!'

Eloise raked her fingers through her hair. 'I thought they would freak you out,' she said eventually. 'But I didn't mean to kill Dinah. I loved her.' Her voice caught. 'She reminded me of me. Imperfectly perfect. How the fuck was I supposed to know lilies are poisonous to cats?'

I sank down on the bed and covered my face with my hands. It was too much to take in. Eloise had played a blinder, stitching me up for a murder I hadn't committed as revenge for one she believed I had. I had to hand it to her. She'd thought of everything. Almost everything, anyway.

'When were you planning on calling the police?' I asked, dully.

'When I'm in departures, I think,' she said, zipping her

holdall closed. 'I don't want anything to wreck my little break. I would offer to come and visit you in prison, but I'll be too busy sipping cocktails on the beach. Sorry. Oh, and you don't mind if I borrow the Land Rover, do you? I'll leave it in the station car park with the keys in it. Hopefully no one'll pinch it.' She picked up the holdall and turned to go.

'Wait!' I said. 'What about Theo?'

She narrowed her eyes. 'What about him?'

'The argument you had the night you came here. Did it happen like you said? That cut,' I said, my hand creeping up to my collarbone. 'Did he really do that to you?'

Eloise peeled with laughter. 'Theo was as soft as shit. He would never have laid a finger on me. Wouldn't have dared.'

'You made it all up?'

'Yep.' Eloise smirked. 'I did all the chasing. I wanted him the moment I saw him. He was beautiful. And that accent! Makes me horny thinking about it.' She paused. 'I just had to convince him he wanted me, too.'

'Theo was never possessive and controlling, was he? It was the other way around. It was you!'

Eloise was the one with no regard for others, who was charismatic and impulsive, who lied and lacked empathy, who showed no remorse. Who quickly bored of things - and people. Just like her father. The apple never fell far from the tree.

'He was beginning to irritate me.' She shrugged unapologetically and swung the holdall over her shoulder.

'Are we done here? Because I'm going to miss my train if I'm not careful.'

'The police will never believe you. And for all you know I could have recorded this entire conversation on my phone.'

She pulled my elderly iPhone out of her back pocket and dangled it from her thumb and forefinger. 'You left it on the sofa. Rookie mistake.'

I went to swipe it out of her grasp, but she snatched her hand back.

'Eloise!' I said, desperation creeping into my voice. 'I'm sorry about Danny, and I'm sorry I didn't take you in after your mother died. But I can make amends.'

A glimmer of something - indecision? - swept across her face and I seized it with both hands. 'Stay here with me, El. We'll get a rescue kitten. Two, if you like! I'll help you find a job and I'll buy you a car so you can be independent. We can work it out. We'll find a way.'

She wavered for a second, then her features hardened. 'Maybe I could have forgiven you for killing my parents. You're right, it's surprisingly easy to take a life. But I will never, ever forgive you for turning your back on me. Nothing you do can ever make amends for abandoning me when I needed you most. All those lies, Rose. Lies and empty promises. Well, it's payback time.'

She marched out of the room and down the stairs. I scurried after her, watching over the top of the banisters as she pulled on her boots and coat. My fingers twitched as she wound my scarf around her neck. Could I make it downstairs in time? I imagined pulling the scarf tighter and tighter until her eyes bulged and she lost consciousness. As if she'd read my mind, she looked up and scowled at me.

'I wouldn't if I were you.' She turned and checked her reflection in the crackled mirror above the console table. Our eyes met briefly, and she said, 'You can't stop me. I've thought of everything.'

She swept through the kitchen, picking up the keys to the Land Rover on her way to the back door. I crept down the stairs and watched through the window as she tossed her holdall into the passenger footwell and jumped into the driver's seat. The engine growled into life, thick black smoke billowing from the exhaust. The gears crunched as Eloise threw the Land Rover into reverse, almost colliding with the coal bunker.

I replayed her words as she accelerated away. *You can't stop me. I've thought of everything.*

'Not quite everything,' I said, allowing myself a small smile.

CHAPTER FORTY-EIGHT

I packed an overnight bag, just in case. Then I sat in the front room and waited.

The knock at the door came just before nine o'clock. I tramped into the hallway. A man stood on the doorstep, a warrant card in his hand.

'Mrs Barton?' he said with a pleasant smile.

'Miss Barton,' I said, my gaze sliding over his shoulder. Parked next to a black saloon was a police van from which several officers in black jumpsuits were emerging. As I watched, a patrol car swung into the driveway and pulled up behind the van.

'I assume you're not here because I've broken the speed limit?' I said.

'DI Paul Barrett,' the man said, ignoring me. 'Can I come in?'

Huffing, I stood aside to let him pass, directing him along the hallway and into the front room.

'Please, take a seat,' he said, gesturing at the armchair

as if he owned the bloody place.

I bit back a retort and said instead, 'I know why you're here. It's my goddaughter, isn't it? Did she tell you her boyfriend's body is buried in my garden, by any chance?'

'What makes you say that?' he said, pulling a notebook and pen from the pocket of his jacket and perching on the sofa.

'I feel terribly disloyal saying this, but I'm afraid she's delusional.'

'Miss Cavendish claims you killed her partner, Theo Lombard, with a blow to the head on the night of Saturday, November the sixth, and buried him in a sinkhole in your back garden.' DI Barrett gave me a sideways glance. 'She also alleges you killed her father, Daniel Reeves, at the flat of your mutual friend John Worthington in 1996.'

'Danny Reeves died of an asthma attack,' I said coolly. 'I tried to save him, not kill him. You'll find it all in the coroner's report.'

He made a non-committal noise and switched tack. 'According to Miss Cavendish, she and Theo Lombard drove to Eastling to see you on the evening of November the sixth. Miss Cavendish wanted to tell you in person that Mr Lombard had proposed to her.'

I barked with laughter.

The detective frowned. 'Something amusing you?'

'Theo never proposed to Eloise,' I said. 'He was terrified of her. She threw acid over his car the first time he tried to end their relationship. He lived in fear it would be his face next.'

'You've spoken to him?'

'I have, actually.'

'Where is he?'

I glanced at my watch. 'Right now, he's on his way to France on the Eurostar. His train's due into the Gare du Nord at twenty past eleven. It's the main train station in Paris,' I added.

'I know where the Gare du Nord is, thank you.'

'He doesn't have his phone with him. But I have his parents' details.' I crossed the room to the bureau and found the scrap of paper on which I'd scrawled the Lombards' number. 'There's no point calling them yet. They don't know he's on his way home.'

The DI took the number, stared at it for a second, then folded it and slipped it into the inside pocket of his jacket. I could see what he was thinking as clearly as if a thought bubble was suspended over his dome-shaped head. He didn't believe me, and he wouldn't until his French counterparts had visited the Lombard residence and confirmed Theo was safe and well.

It was fair enough.

He flipped through his notebook. 'Miss Cavendish said you took the news of their engagement badly. She was of the impression that you were jealous. That you didn't want to share her with anyone else. And when Mr Lombard suggested they return home, you killed him with a kettlebell.'

'Do I look like the type of person who owns a kettlebell?' I snapped.

The DI's gaze flickered over my fawn blouse and tweed slacks, my sensible shoes and my generous midriff.

'Eloise is lying, I'm afraid,' I said. 'She's the one who hit him over the head with a kettlebell in the flat they shared. She thought she'd killed him and turned up here with him in the boot of her car, pleading for my help. But he wasn't dead.'

He raised an eyebrow.

'It's true!' I cried. 'He was unconscious. I pretended to do as she asked out of some misplaced sense of duty. But I let him go. I even bought his bloody Eurostar ticket. Nearly sixty quid, it cost me. You can check my bank statement if you like. All this,' I said, nodding at his notebook, 'is Eloise trying to frame me.'

He frowned. 'Why would she do that?'

'She blames me for the death of her parents. She thinks I should've been able to save her father. Her mother killed herself when Eloise was a child. She never got over Danny's death. This is Eloise wreaking revenge. I've done nothing wrong.'

He pursed his lips. 'In that case, I assume you don't have any objections to us having a quick scout around the place?'

'What if I said I did?'

'Then I'd be back with a search warrant before you had time to boil the kettle,' he said smoothly.

I shrugged. 'Then I don't have any objections. Look all you like, but you won't find him.'

Within minutes of the DI striding from the room, police

officers with powerful torches were crawling over the garden like an army of ants. I watched from the kitchen window as they poked about in the long grass and peered into the wheelie bins. A gormless-looking PC stood guard by the door in case I made a bolt for it.

As the police officers looked for clues that weren't there, I replayed my final visit to Theo. Fighting my way through the undergrowth in the slacks and court shoes I'd worn to the inquest had taken longer than usual, and with every uncomfortable step I wondered if I was doing the right thing. But, as I reminded myself repeatedly, I didn't have a choice. I was merely doing what I should have done the day Eloise turned up on my doorstep with her lover in the boot of her car.

Better late than never.

As I slid open the bolts and ducked through the doorway of the pillbox for the last time, my heart was crashing in my chest. My hastily made plan could misfire spectacularly if I wasn't careful.

Theo's head had snapped up as my shadow fell over him and he'd frowned.

'Where is my food?'

'There is no food,' I'd said, thinking of the organic lemon curd yoghurt I'd stashed in a cold bag in the back of the Land Rover.

'But I am starving!'

'I'm letting you go.'

'Do not play games with me.'

'I'm not, I promise.' I'd patted my jacket pocket, feeling for the lozenge-shaped Swiss Army knife I'd taken from the toolbox I kept in the Land Rover. 'But you have to promise something, too.'

He narrowed his eyes. 'What?'

'That you'll go back to France and stay there. I've booked you a ticket for the Eurostar. It leaves at eight.'

'You have kept me locked up like an animal for days and you expect me to go quietly with my tail between my legs?' He laughed. 'You are as mad as Eloise.'

'I have to protect her. I'm all she has.'

'How many times do I have to tell you? She doesn't need protecting. She is the dangerous one.' He shook his head. 'Does she know you are letting me go?'

'She thinks you're dead. She asked me to bury your body.'

Theo laughed again, then twisted his face up to mine. 'But you spared me. Why?'

I was silent for a moment, then I took the knife from my pocket, knelt beside him and began sawing through the rope binding his wrists. 'Because I let someone die once before. I couldn't do it again.'

His hands jerked back, and I almost nicked his wrist.

'Careful!' I cried.

He was staring at me with a mixture of disgust and horror. 'You killed someone?'

'That's not what I said.' I reached for his hands again and continued cutting through the rope. 'I let him die when it was in my power to save him.'

'Why?'

'Because I hated him.' I shivered. 'And he tried to rape me.'

'Did you know him?'

'Yes.' I closed my eyes for a second. 'It was Eloise's father.'

Comprehension dawned on his face. 'So that is why you are helping her. You feel guilty.'

I nodded. 'And because I loved her mother.' The rope fell to the floor and Theo rubbed his wrists while I started sawing the rope binding his ankles.

'And now you are dancing to Eloise's tune.'

'I am not!'

He shook his head. 'You let me think I had been kidnapped.'

'I thought it would stop you trying to escape until I figured out what to do with you.'

'So, you were thinking about killing me?'

I sat back on my heels and met his gaze. 'Cards on the table. It was an option, yes.'

'Merde.' He drew his legs together and began massaging his ankles. 'But you didn't.'

'Perhaps you were right. Perhaps I am the fool.'

He raised an eyebrow, then said, 'Where is Eloise?'

'She's staying with me for the time being. Just until she sorts herself out.'

'And she thinks she killed me?'

I nodded. 'Why?'

'If she thinks I am dead, she won't try to find me. Finally, I will be safe.' He'd stared up at the roof of the pillbox for a moment, then he looked at me. 'If I report you to the police, she will know I am alive, and she will come for me.'

I nodded. 'Go back to France and start again. I'll drive you to your flat to pick up your passport and I'll drop you at the station. You can be in Paris before midnight.'

I held my breath as Theo struggled to his feet and staggered to the door. My future rested in his hands. If he had me arrested for kidnap and Eloise for attempted murder our lives would be over. But if he went back to France…

'Theo,' I said urgently. 'You said you wanted to be free. This is your chance.'

He turned to face me. 'All right,' he said finally. 'I will go home to France, where Eloise will never find me.'

'You won't report us to the police?' I checked.

'Eloise has wormed her way into your life now.' He gave a Gallic shrug. 'You'll end up paying for what you did to me. And when that happens, do not say I did not warn you.'

CHAPTER FORTY-NINE

Time was measured in cups of tea and I'd drunk four when a poker-faced DI Paul Barrett reappeared. He pulled up a chair.

'I've spoken to my counterparts in France and according to French border control, Theo Lombard did check onto the Paris-bound Eurostar earlier this evening.'

'I thought he was buried in my garden?'

He didn't rise. 'But I've asked the French police to speak directly with him at the Lombards' address in the morning. Our search teams have found no evidence of human remains, so I have to assume that the allegation made against you was false. Rest assured, we'll be speaking to Miss Cavendish and if we believe an offence of perverting the course of justice has been committed, we'll take matters further.'

'Good luck with that,' I said. 'Does that mean you're finished here?'

He steepled his fingers. The gold band on his ring

finger looked shop-new. 'We may need to speak to you again, so please don't plan any foreign holidays for the time being. But yes, the search teams are packing up and will soon be on their way.' He met my eye. 'You do understand that we have to take allegations such as this extremely seriously, whether they happened two weeks or two decades ago?'

His gaze was so penetrating I felt as though he was staring deep into my soul, but I didn't blink. He couldn't know what happened that day in John's flat.

'Of course,' I said. 'You wouldn't be doing your job otherwise.'

He gave a brief nod and thanked me for my co-operation. I watched from the window as he climbed into the unmarked car and followed the police van and the patrol car onto the lane and out of my life. I pictured his expression when he realised Eloise was on a British Airways flight to Punta Cana International Airport. She'd used my money to buy a first-class one-way ticket.

Suddenly I sensed her presence, and the sensation of her breath on the back of my neck was so real that beads of sweat broke out across my forehead. My eyes darted around the room, half expecting to see her standing behind me with a bloodied kitchen knife in her hand. But of course she wasn't there. My mind was playing tricks on me, that was all.

I was safe.

Once DI Barrett heard Theo's version of events, he would easily have enough evidence to charge Eloise with grievous bodily harm, maybe even attempted murder, let alone perverting the course of justice. She had everything to lose and nothing to gain by returning to the UK.

Except revenge.

It was like a twisted game of who blinks first.

Life slowly returned to normal and after a while the days Eloise spent with me took on an almost dreamlike quality, as if they'd taken place in an alternate universe. If it wasn't for the fact that Dinah's bed was empty and my bank account depleted, I might have wondered if they'd ever happened at all.

A week or so after Eloise left, I had a call from DI Barrett. He cut to the chase.

'My colleagues in Paris have spoken to Mr Lombard, and he has confirmed everything you told us about your goddaughter, Eloise Cavendish. We've issued a warrant for her arrest, but unfortunately it seems she's currently in the Dominican Republic and there's no formal extradition treaty between the two countries.'

'Which is precisely why she's there,' I said crisply. 'Is there anything else?'

'I've read the coroner's report into the death of Danny Reeves and it appears you did everything in your power to save him. And as Miss Cavendish's allegations have been thrown into serious doubt by her subsequent actions, I am satisfied there's no basis for reopening the case.'

'I'm glad you've seen sense,' I said, glad he couldn't

see the relief on my face. 'While I have you, is there any word on the criminal damage at Sisterline?'

'I understand we've charged a man with threatening behaviour and criminal damage.'

'Roy Matthews?'

I heard the muffled click of a keyboard. 'Yes,' the DI said after a moment. 'Looks like his prints were on the letter. Says here he's due before magistrates next week.'

'Excellent,' I said. 'Thank you.'

'You can return the favour by contacting me the moment Miss Cavendish gets in touch,' he said.

'Oh, rest assured I will. But don't hold your breath. I think that boat has sailed.'

He sighed. 'I fear you're probably right.'

CHAPTER FIFTY

Over the next few weeks, I threw myself into work, spending long hours at the office working on my proposals to drag Sisterline into the 21st century. Corporate partnerships, crowdfunding and collaborative opportunities - I explored them all. I planned to build our digital community and start chasing legacies. I wanted to set up proper structures and practices so the charity was as professional as it could be. I even looked into the viability of recruiting volunteers in New Zealand so we could answer people's calls around the clock. My vision was for Sisterline to be the first port of call for every woman needing support in the UK. Through the charity I could potentially save thousands of lives - more than I ever could have saved as a doctor.

To achieve my vision, I needed to be focussed and at the top of my game. So, I decided not to go back on the amitriptyline. I didn't want the rest of my life to be softened by a pharmaceutical panacea. Once the drug had worked its way out of my system, I felt alert and in control. A force to be reckoned with. And yes, I was in a better place when it came to winning battles at work, but I was also psyched up and ready to retaliate if Eloise ever turned up on my doorstep, hellbent on revenge.

And there were battles to be won. Eddie and Dorothy were open to new ideas, but the rest of the trustees were a cautious bunch who saw pitfalls in everything. I may have been chief executive, but I quickly discovered that they wanted me to justify every decision, no matter how trivial, and it took all my powers of persuasion to get the sign-off for my ambitious ten-year plan.

Every minor victory was an achievement, but victories were of little consequence when you had no one to share them with. Once I'd have told Dinah, and for a couple of weeks I'd had Eloise, too, but now the house was empty, and there was no one.

The trustees may have been a tricky bunch, but the real fly in the ointment was Rhona Richards, who voiced her disapproval at my every turn. I only had to mention the possibility of time sheets for volunteers or reducing the budget for the Christmas party and she'd be sniping behind my back and whipping up discontent among the ranks. Managing Rhona was a job in itself and I spent many sleepless nights wondering how to manoeuvre her out of the charity.

She reminded me of the limpets we used to see clinging to the rocks on family holidays to Dorset when I was a child. My father and I would spend hours crabbing at Kimmeridge Bay, scooping out the limpets' flesh with the blade on his Swiss Army knife to bait our crab lines. But there was an art to knocking the limpets off their rocks. Accidentally nudge them and they stuck fast as if they'd been superglued, and no amount of pushing or pulling would prise them off. You had to catch them unawares, striking hard and fast with a flat stone the size of your palm. But you only ever had one shot to get it right.

Things with Rhona reached a head the day I sent out a memo announcing my intention to hold monthly performance reviews for all staff and volunteers. I watched from my office as she read the email, her doughy face growing pink with righteous indignation. She closed her eyes for a moment, tapped urgently at her keyboard, then picked up her mobile and scuttled out of the room.

I grabbed my empty mug and was out of the office like a shot, marching over to her desk.

'Anyone for tea?' I asked, glancing at Rhona's screen and hoping she'd been in too much of a rush to lock it. I was in luck. I recognised the yellow and white Kent Online logo and quickly scanned the page. *Contact an editorial team…* and a list of newspapers, phone numbers and email addresses. I tensed. The interfering bitch was probably on the phone to the newsroom right now, bellyaching about my plans, casting a slur on the charity's name.

'Oo, that would be lovely, thanks. White, one sugar,' said a voice, and I turned in surprise to see one of the new volunteers holding a mug in her outstretched hand.

'Sorry, yes, of course,' I said. 'Anyone else?'

The murmurs of assent were more subdued than

normal, which led me to suspect my newly unveiled plans hadn't gone down as well as I'd hoped. Couldn't they see I was only trying to make Sisterline the best it could be? With a slight shake of my head, I took half a dozen mugs and headed for the kitchen, bumping into Irene on the way.

'Actually, could you make the tea, Irene?' I said, handing her the mugs. 'I've just remembered I have something I need to see to.' Without waiting for her response, I bolted back into my office and slammed the door shut.

I paced the room, anger mounting inside me. I'd sacrificed so much to get where I was. I wasn't about to let it slip through my fingers. As if in a trance, I crossed the room to the grey filing cabinet where everyone's personnel files were kept. I remembered that expensive counselling session with the wide-hipped therapist from Aberdeen. The leather-topped walnut desk and the black lever arch files. Now there was only one file on my imaginary desk. Rhona. I'd dealt with everything else.

What was it the therapist had said?

Acknowledge how important it is and file it away.

As Eloise would say: Fuck that.

I was going to deal with it.

Deal with her.

I tugged open the real filing cabinet drawer, my fingers a blur as I rifled through, searching for the Rs. And there it was: Rhona Richards' personnel file. I pulled it out and took it over to the desk, scouring for anything I might have missed. Anything I might use to prise this limpet off the rocks.

And then, buried between contact details for her next of kin and her previous employment record, I found what I was looking for.

Less than an hour later, there was a knock on the door.

'Come in,' I said warmly.

The door swung open, and Rhona squinted at me.

'You wanted to see me?'

'I did,' I said, jumping to my feet and pulling out the chair on the other side of my desk, full of bonhomie. 'Thank you so much for your time. I know how precious it is.'

She sat, clasped her hands in her lap, and regarded me with deep suspicion.

'What did you want?' she said.

'I feel we got off on the wrong foot when I took on my new role, and I thought it would be a good idea to talk it through to make sure we're both OK with everything.' I smiled to show there was no animosity on my side.

Rhona gaped at me as if I'd grown an extra head.

'Only I wouldn't want any resentment there might be between us to reflect badly on the charity,' I continued, still smiling. I tapped the file on my desk. 'I'd forgotten what a long-serving member of our volunteering family you are.'

She unclasped her hands and crossed her arms. 'You started a week after me.'

I gave a tinkle of laughter. 'So I did. But I never

achieved your dizzy heights. There are so many thank-you letters and emails on your file. Not to mention the recent tribute from the coroner. You're a real asset to Sisterline.'

She gave a slight nod.

I gazed around the room, as if seeking inspiration, then said, 'D'you know what my dearest friend, Juliet, once said to me?' I played with the corner of Rhona's personnel file, flicking it with my thumb, enjoying the satisfying slapping noise it made against the desk. 'She said, "Oh, Rose, don't ever change, will you?" And it was the nicest thing anyone has ever said to me, because it made me feel maybe it was all right to be me after all, you know?'

Rhona was silent.

'Because I have spent my life trying to be good,' I continued, my voice thick with emotion. 'Trying to help people, even if they didn't think they needed helping in the first place. Everything I have done, every decision I have made, has been for the greater good, do you see?'

She shifted in her chair, her currant eyes darting around the office as if she was looking for an escape route.

'Anyway,' I said, fixing her with my gaze. 'I didn't drag you in here to talk about me. I want to talk about you.' I rested my chin on my steepled fingers and cocked my head. 'Is there anything you would like to say to me? Any problems you've been having? Anything you want to get off your chest?'

This was her opportunity to come clean, to admit she'd contacted the local newspaper to whinge about the way I ran Sisterline. But she shook her head and said, 'Nothing I can think of, no.'

'Well, I don't mind telling you that's a relief,' I said. 'Because it wouldn't do to bad-mouth either me or the charity. It wouldn't do at all.'

A dull flush crept up Rhona's neck. 'I would never -'

'I'm sure you wouldn't,' I said smoothly.

'Is that all?' she asked, standing to leave.

'It is, thank you.' I picked up her personnel file and tapped it on the desk. 'Oh, there was one more thing,' I said, as she was halfway to the door. 'Just a silly thing, but it would be remiss of me not to mention it. Your welfare is my primary concern, after all.'

Rhona turned and frowned. 'What?'

'According to your records, you have asthma. I never knew.'

'That's because I manage it properly,' she said primly.

'It would be good to know what your triggers are, so we can make sure we keep you safe.'

'You don't need to worry. I'm allergic to the particles in bird feathers. They call it feather dust.'

'They do, do they?'

'They do. So, I'm hardly likely to come into contact with it here, am I?' Rhona said with a hint of scorn.

I thought of my mother's beloved collection of stuffed birds.

And I smiled.

'Hardly likely at all,' I said.

AFTERWORD

I hope you enjoyed *The Promise You Made*. It would be great if you could spare a couple of minutes to write a quick review on Amazon or Goodreads. I'd love your feedback. But please, no spoilers!

To join my readers' list to hear about my latest releases, promotions and giveaways, visit my website, www.ajmcdine.com.

ACKNOWLEDGMENTS

The Promise You Made is my fourth thriller, so you'd think by now that I knew what I was doing. Not so!

Much procrastinating, belly-aching, soul-searching and faffing about has gone into the making of this book. Not to mention a few crises of confidence along the way!

As usual it's due to my lack of planning. But, frustratingly, I'm a discovery writer, starting with the seed of an idea - and not much else! - and seeing where it takes me.

Which sounds fine on paper, but it can lead you down all sorts of rabbit holes and blind alleys.

My 'seed' for this book was the promise by a woman to her grieving goddaughter that she would help her if she was ever in trouble. And from that Rose and Eloise's story slowly revealed itself to me.

Too slowly at times!

But I got there in the end, thanks to the wonderful and much-appreciated support of my family and friends.

In particular, I would like to thank Dr Penny Davies for

her insights on all things medical, and to Natalie Spain, whose enthusiasm for the book gave me the lift I needed when my confidence was flagging.

To my friend and fellow thriller writer Carrie Magillen, whose excellent idea for a scene towards the end of the book really helped ratchet up the tension. Thank you, Carrie!

Thanks also to my trusty team of first readers: Sarah Hawes, Di Connors, Sue Williams, Sue McDine and Pauline Cowell. Your insights are always so helpful.

Last, but definitely not least, I would like to thank all you amazing readers, bloggers and reviewers for taking the time to read my books.

I love having you along for the ride!

ABOUT THE AUTHOR

A J McDine lives in Kent with her husband and fellow thriller writer A J Wills and their two teenage sons.

She worked as a journalist and police press officer before becoming a full-time author in 2019.

Endlessly fascinated by people and their fears and foibles, she loves to discover what makes them tick.

She writes dark, domestic thrillers about ordinary people in extraordinary situations.

When she's not writing, playing tennis or attempting to run a 5K, she can usually be found people-watching in her favourite café.

A J McDine is the author of four psychological thrillers:

When She Finds You

Should Have Known Better

No One I Knew

The Promise You Made

ALSO BY A J MCDINE

When She Finds You

Sophie Saunders has the perfect life.

Happily married to handsome Matt and expecting her first baby, she is the envy of her childhood friend, Lou.

Lou's family has splintered. Her husband is dead and her son has left home. She would give anything to turn back the clock.

But there's a secret buried deep in their past that the two friends can never forget.

And when Sophie's world starts spiralling out of control, it's her new friend Roz to whom she turns.

Trouble is, secrets have a habit of unravelling. And when they do, you can kiss your perfect life goodbye.

Sometimes, it's better when the truth stays hidden.

Should Have Known Better

The perfect boyfriend... or the perfect liar?

It's the moment single-mum Kate has been dreading.

With her only daughter, Chloe, about to leave home, she's terrified of being left on her own.

That is until she meets charming lawyer, Adam.

He could be the perfect catch – if only it wasn't for his clingy son.

Because Ben has a crush on Chloe. A crush that is fast becoming an obsession.

Flattered by the attention, Chloe is happy to string him along – for now at least.

But Kate can see the danger signs, even if her daughter is blind to them.

And when Chloe's life begins spiralling out of control, Kate must make a choice - trust her instincts or lose her daughter forever...

No One I Knew

Everyone has a secret to hide

When Cleo Cooper's daughter vanishes during a family barbecue, her perfect life begins to unravel.

Everyone thinks three-year-old Immy drowned in the river at the bottom of the garden.

Everyone except Cleo. Because all her instincts tell her someone took her daughter. Someone she knew.

With time running out, Cleo sets out to uncover the truth. But the deeper she probes, the more she realises everyone has a secret to hide. Especially her husband.

And as Cleo unpicks the lies, she discovers her carefully constructed life was just an illusion.

Printed in Great Britain
by Amazon

72366113R00218